For Emma, my constant, my rock.

And for Zac and Henry, my pebbles, for always.

To Michael,

Dream on.

D Thomas

Chapter 1

Michael dived into the surf before his brain had time to register the cold, plunging down beneath the waves for a few seconds before surfacing and stroking out into the calm open water. His shivers subsided as his body quickly acclimatised, the Californian sun warming his head and shoulders.

He swam solidly for ten minutes, heading straight out to sea. Glancing up at the sky from time to time he noticed a bank of clouds rolling in on the horizon, a storm perhaps, but too far away to be of real concern to the experienced swimmer.

A moment or so later and he felt a blast of unexpectedly cold air against the back of his head. The sea went dark at the same time, the colour of the water shifting from bright blue to slate grey. Looking up he saw the clouds had advanced impossibly fast to obscure the sun. As he watched, the mass of blacks and greys was ripped apart by seams of blinding white lightning.

'Shit.' He swore and turned back to land, increasing his speed to reach the shore before the storm could overtake him.

The change in weather brought with it increasingly large waves and a strong cross current, slowing his progress towards the safety of the beach, but when he felt his feet brush against the seabed, he knew that he was in the clear and without a drop of rain falling.

He began to wade up the slope leading to the beach, treading with care to avoid the larger rocks embedded in the ground whilst moving with as much speed as he could towards the pile of his clothes on the sand. He was mid-stride when a powerful wave hit him in the back, knocking him off balance and pulling him back from the safety of the shore.

He surfaced quickly, coughing and spluttering, trying to regain his balance and resume walking. Another wave broke over his head before he could take more than one gasping breath, leaving him no time to register his surroundings. This time he closed his mouth and eyes and allowed the water to push him down towards the bottom of the ocean.

The wave seemed to bear down with unnatural force and his feet did not touch the ground for what felt like an age. He bent his knees and pushed off from the seabed, striking for the surface. At the same time, he opened his eyes, ignoring the painful sting of the saltwater. He aimed for the light that heralded the sky.

Five strokes led to the surface and he gulped in air so quickly that his vision began to darken and blur. He forced himself to calm his breathing and his eyesight

cleared in an instant allowing him to appraise the situation once more.

The rain was now lashing down with so much force that at first he could not work out which way to swim to reach the shore. The wind had also picked up, causing the surface of the ocean to roll to such an extent that it formed a tunnel of water with the rain, a horizontal tornado.

Still squinting against the water pounding his face, he spotted a green brown blur that he figured must signify the shore. He struck out towards it in a powerful front crawl, unsure for the first time whether or not he would reach the beach.

A few minutes later a lessening in the rain's ferocity provided a clear view of land for the first time since he had been struck by the waves. The shore was still at least fifty metres away and he opened his mouth to cry out in anguish, the action interrupted as a wave crashed over his head forcing him to stop swimming to spit out the salty water.

He considered shouting for help or waving his arms around to attract attention but knew that the beach was not patrolled by lifeguards. Calling out would only waste what little energy he had left. All he could do was keep swimming. Then he saw a shape on the beach.

Someone *was* on the shore, a small figure, perhaps a child. Michael waved his hands, pumping his legs as he treaded water to avoid sinking.

'Hey' he shouted at the top of his lungs and the figure appeared to wave back. For a second Michael thought that he heard them calling out in response, but then their words were lost, drowned out by the wind. Then a wave, larger than any of the others, crashed down on top of the swimmer.

Again, Michael felt himself being driven downwards by the great weight of water, and this time he was not sure he would be able to fight his way back to the surface. He waited, trying to conserve what little reserves he had left, waited to hit the seabed again, but this time he just kept sinking.

He had been descending for half a minute when he began to feel the weight of the water compressing his body, squeezing the last of the air out of his tired lungs. He forced his eyes to open, prepared for the sharp sting of salt water, surprised when this did not come.

Instead he found he could see clearly, not that there was much to see. On all sides was a dingy, grey darkness, the colour of a shroud.

Panicking, he kicked out with his legs, moving his arms to try to propel himself, unsure which way he needed to travel. God alone knew how far he was under the water or how many metres he had now drifted from land, all he knew was that his lungs were burning, and that black was starting to creep into his vision.

Then he remembered the figure, perhaps a child, on the beach, and he prayed that they would have raised the alarm.

Then all at once he realised that he knew who the boy was.

Chapter 2

Michael opened his eyes, turned his head to the side and spat blood. He was lying on a smooth, hard surface in a pool of cold water stained pink by his blood. He lifted his head, awakening some sort of vindictive creature that began pounding on the inside of his skull like it was a drum, and looked around in a daze.

A strong scent of pine assaulted his nose and a mound of earth was visible out of the corner of his eye. He reached out and brushed his hand through the soil, bemused as the dirt fell from his fingers, expecting the golden sand of the beach. He turned with exaggerated care from his front to his back and squinted against the bright light of the sun, grateful that the storm had blown over as quickly as it had begun. He sat up, putting a hand out to support himself, grabbing the nearest thing he could in order to lever his battered body upright. The surface beneath his hand was cool and hard and he looked at it in confusion, imagining he was holding onto the hull of a boat.

His eyes alighted instead on a bath and he groaned in understanding. He was in a bathroom, specifically his bathroom in San Diego.

He turned his head from side to side, still bent almost double and holding on to the edge of the bath. He took in the scene in a detached dispassionate manner.

The bath was full; in fact, the taps were still running, and water had flowed over onto the floor. This was the source of the puddle in which he had regained consciousness. The shower curtain had been torn off its rail above the bath and lay crumpled beside the tub; towels had been ripped from a rail, knocking a pot plant off a shelf and spilling soil onto the floor. A small, ivory coloured object lay beside the bath.

Michael stooped down in a trancelike state, still in the throes of his dream. He knelt beside the bath, wincing against the pain in his head, and picked up the object. It was about the size of a pea, with a jagged edge and traces of drying blood. He gasped; he was holding one of his teeth.

The sight of the tooth seemed to break the spell that had been cast since he had awoken lying on the floor. In an instant his senses seemed heightened. For the first time he became aware that he was soaking wet, dripping water onto the already drenched floor. He could taste blood pooled in his swollen mouth, could even smell the coppery scent of it.

His vision cleared, becoming sharper and revealing a smear of blood on the edge of the bath. He figured he must have tripped and fallen getting out of the tub smacking his face onto the unyielding ceramic.

He glanced up at the mirror above the sink. His short black hair was soaking wet, plastered to his scalp, his dark blue eyes were bloodshot, staring back at him in shock and wonder.

Beyond the lost tooth, a few minor cuts and some throbbing aches, which would soon become Technicolor bruises, he was fine; at least physically. As to his mental condition he was beginning to have serious doubts.

'Well that was bloody stupid.' He cursed as he leaned forwards to turn off the taps and empty the bath, rebuking himself for falling asleep in a full bath, a misjudgement that could have proved fatal. As he pulled the plug however, he realised that what had happened was not an ill-advised doze interrupted by a nightmare in which he was drowning in the ocean. He had not been taking a bath, or at least he had not intended to take one.

Looking down at his body again he confirmed that he was wearing the t-shirt and shorts that served as his pyjamas and he vividly remembered going to bed. A glance at the bathroom clock revealed that it was 5am, Monday morning - about 7 hours on from when he had gone to bed on Sunday night.

Walking down the corridor to his bedroom as he towelled his hair, he recalled taking valerian tablets, a herbal remedy for insomnia that had become a regular habit. One look at his slept-in bed confirmed his memories of the night before.

It took only a few seconds to realise what must have happened, but much longer to accept the situation as he slumped down on the edge of his bed.

'Sleepwalking?' He whispered in awe to his silent apartment. 'Well that's new.'

Chapter 3

'Your father is dead.' The strident ringing of his mobile phone had interrupted Michael's contemplation of his near-drowning, and his mother had spoken without preamble or pleasantries.

Michael's answer was automatic, even as his mind wrestled with the concept behind his mother's words, his shoulders dropping under the weight of the sentence. 'What happened?' His voice sounded strange to his own ears, thick, swollen as his tongue kept returning to the gap between his teeth.

'How should I know? Probably crushed to death by his own wealth or simply too boring to remain alive.' His mother's voice was clipped and despite the earliness of the hour it already carried its customary slur.

Michael sat, phone pressed hard to his ear, waiting for the caller to continue.

'Anyway, contact Armstrong, he will arrange everything. Goodbye Michael.' The line went dead with a click that seemed to echo around the room.

Michael fell backwards on the bed, his head throbbing and his mind racing. Was he still asleep? Still caught in a nightmare that had moved with barely an intermission from drowning in the Pacific Ocean to the death of his father?

His breathing was ragged, his chest rising and falling in time with his pounding heart, and he screwed his eyes shut, willing his body to calm down.

He opened his eyes after a few moments, regarding his bedroom ceiling but imagining his mother's face. He still held his phone in his left hand, his fingertips tracing patterns over the screen as his thoughts played through the consequences of phoning her back. She would be standing, probably on the wraparound porch of her ranch house, short grey hair perfectly styled, green eyes fixed on the horizon with a steely gaze, mouth set in a thin line of disapproval. One hand would be holding her telephone, the other a glass of something cold. She would not even glance at the phone when it started ringing, would instead press the button to decline the call, before taking a long swallow of her drink and returning to her real life.

And yet he had to call her, had to find out what had happened to his father. Information must be something she could give him, simple cold hard facts, even if she could give him nothing else?

He dialled his mother's number with shaking hands, running his free hand through his still damp hair as he did so.

He was directed straight to a messaging service, as in his fantasy of a moment before, and he let the phone fall from his hand, watching with detached disinterest as it bounced once onto the bed and then dropped to the floor.

He was not surprised that his mother did not answer his call, but still he was struck by a wave of sadness, feeling as if he was an orphan – despite one parent still being alive. The thought brought his mind back to the present situation, that his father was dead.

The next thought that popped into his head was that orphan or not he was now very, very wealthy. As the main beneficiary of his father's will, he would be inheriting the family business along with property and other assets.

Michael shook his head, leaning forward with his hands on his knees, disgusted with himself for such an ignoble thought, but unable to stop visualising a life where he would not have to work, where he could afford to live wherever he wanted and where he could rescue Jess.

Simultaneously he wondered how he had come to be devoid of feelings of affection towards his parents. The strongest emotion that he felt towards his mother was anger, a bitter fury that had been cultivated over many years.

The phone rang, loud in the silent apartment and he scooped it off the floor, noting that the caller ID was withheld.

'Michael Manners here; who's calling?'

'Michael, my son, I am so sorry to hear about Ian's passing.' The unctuous voice dripped insincerity and Michael's lip curled as he recognised that the speaker was Robert Armstrong, his father's lawyer and long-time friend.

Chapter 4

'Good Morning Mr Armstrong, I've just spoken to my mother and was about to call you.' Michael closed his eyes and sighed, fervently wishing that he could fast forward beyond the current day.

'Good, I'm relieved I'm not breaking the news then. You must call me Robert though, and it's not morning here, as I'm sure you must realise. It's already late afternoon where I am calling from in sunny Scotland.' Armstrong spoke softly, gently reprimanding his late client's son. 'But no matter, I was just calling to let you know I've already started making arrangements for the funeral – as per Ian's instructions.'

Michael sighed again, a wave of relief washing over him as Armstrong went on to explain that a firm of funeral directors local to his father's home had already been contacted, and that they had begun following directions left by his father. These instructions included details about where the funeral service should be held, where his father was to be buried and that the wake was to take place at the family home. They even specified the colour and type of wood from which his father's coffin should be made.

His father had also drawn up a list of whom to contact in the event of his death, mostly business associates, and Armstrong had already worked his way through these telephone calls. Michael had very few decisions to make, though would have to speak to a number of people to confirm he was happy with arrangements and to provide a 'personal touch' as the lawyer put it.

Michael broke out in a cold sweat as soon as he hung up on Armstrong. He much preferred to conduct his social interactions by email rather than on the phone or face to face. Many people considered him to be a recluse, a view he was more than happy to cultivate.

'HEY BRO.' The message appeared on his phone as if it had been conjured up in response to his anxiety, but then he'd always known he shared some kind of psychic link with his 16-year-old half-sister Jessica.

'SORRY ABOUT YOUR DAD....'

'WANT ME TO COME OVER?'

'MUM'S A BITCH BTW'

He smiled as the stream of messages came through too fast to allow him to reply, waiting for a pause in the communication before sending back a brief message.

'THANKS. NO I'M OK. I KNOW. SPEAK LATER'

'OKEY DOKEY, RICHIE....'

'AS IN RICH.' Jessica fired back without pause.

'So, I'm not the only one whose first thought is about the money.' He mused to himself as he sent a final message.

'I GOT IT JESS, GOTTA MAKE SOME CALLS NOW. X'

Over the next hour Michael endured awkward conversations with Mr Henry Evans, the funeral director, and Father Macillroy – his father's local priest. He also dodged countless calls from his father's business contacts, housekeeper and others who had been given his number by Armstrong and who were calling to express their deepest sympathies.

Armstrong himself phoned again, though he was forced to leave a voicemail because Michael was on his call to Mr Evans at the same time. The lawyer sounded extremely disgruntled at not speaking directly to the man he had taken to calling 'son' and insisted on meeting Michael as soon as he arrived in Scotland. Armstrong went on to say how desperate he was to see him after all these years, offering to put Michael up in his own home, ending the message by saying how much he hoped they could be as close as he had been with Michael's father.

This was definitely not a hope that Michael shared, intending to have as little contact as possible with his late father's world.

By the time the UK had gone to sleep, hundreds of miles away and eight hours ahead of the western United States, Michael's head was spinning. He had learned a little about the circumstances of his father's death, second hand from Mr Evans, and knew that he had suffered a massive heart attack – seemingly collapsing and dying instantly, alone in his house. This, Michael considered, was better than a long, drawn out illness, but still, dying alone was an end that he would not wish on anyone. He sighed, overcome at last by sadness at the death of a parent.

His thoughts turned to memories of his early childhood, holidays and birthdays, meals and time spent together, the last times his family had been happy, whole and anything resembling normal.

His reminiscing was interrupted by a sudden pang of hunger, and he realised that he'd not moved from the bedroom for hours.

Fortified with coffee and doughnuts, he busied himself with arranging the earliest flight he could get to the UK and with throwing some clothes in a bag for the trip. His packing was hurried and erratic, five minutes that was sure to mean a visit to some shops to purchase essential items on arrival in Edinburgh.

Michael also made repeated attempts to contact his mother, determined that if he could not convince her to attend the funeral, he could at least be satisfied that he had tried. His efforts resulted in nothing more than a terse text to confirm that she would not be attending the funeral in five days' time.

He rolled his eyes at the brevity, used to his mother's lack of communication. Even when he had shared a house with his mother and stepfather, a situation that had changed only recently, days would pass without a word being exchanged between them as his mother drifted through the house like a ghost, bottle of vodka in hand. As for her refusal to attend the funeral, that was unsurprising, given the intensity of her dislike of Michael's father.

He also exchanged further hurried messages with Jessica, his closest friend. Jessica told him that their mother's reaction to her ex-husband's death had essentially consisted of a rant about how the useless man had left her with nothing, followed by her retiring to bed for the remainder of the day. Jessica offered again to come over to his home to support him, and had been on the verge of booking a seat on the same flight, or at least of flying to the UK for the funeral, until he had reassured her that he would be OK, that he would be back in the US within a week and that as soon as possible he'd buy a place with room for her to move in.

Chapter 5

Michael's head lolled against the airplane window and he jerked awake, glancing with unease towards the passenger beside him. The woman in the next seat was sound asleep; her chair reclined into a bed. She snored quietly and he smiled, relieved that he had not cried out or done anything more embarrassing or disturbing in the few minutes that he had nodded off. Despite this reassurance he was still anxious to stay awake and keep his nightmares at bay, pressing the button above his head to call over a flight attendant.

'Could I have another strong coffee please?' He spoke quietly, calmly but the attendant took one look at his bloodshot eyes before answering.

'How about a nice cup of herbal tea sir? It will help you to get some sleep. We won't be landing for another few hours yet.' She smiled nervously, knowing she had overstepped a line by querying a passenger's request.

'I appreciate your concern.' Michael's own smile was tight and without humour, 'but sleep is the furthest thing from my mind, so I'll take that coffee. Thank you.'

The young flight attendant bobbed her head in assent, returning quickly with the coffee.

Michael drank half the cup in one gulp, scalding his mouth in the process, and then looked out of the window. For most of the flight the view had been of the night sky and he had spent his time watching movies and television reruns on the screen set into the back of the seat in front of him, warding off sleep with endless cans of Coke and cups of coffee. Now however the sky beyond his window was growing lighter and a thin band of pink on the horizon announced the arrival of a new day, a day that seemed likely to be as difficult as the one before.

He sighed heavily and sipped the rest of his coffee as he recalled the events of the last 24 hours, a blur of activity that he had not had time to process and was reluctant to revisit. It was early August, the middle of a glorious summer even by Californian standards, with cloudless skies and high temperatures. Weather that was not suited to Michael's mood.

Several hours later at 9 am Michael was standing in the corner of a crowded board room, his fingers twitching nervously by his side, low on sleep and high on coffee. The collar of his new shirt was too tight, digging into his skin, reminding him why he never wore collars unless – as on this occasion – he felt that he simply could not avoid it. At least the shirt was not too bad a fit, considering that he'd bought it, the suit and tie less than an hour ago and without trying them on. He'd even made time to shave on the plane and bring his hair, badly in need of a cut, into some semblance of order. All in all he thought, glancing at his reflection in a window, I could pass for the chief executive of a company which exports traditional Scottish goods to America and Asia.

He fiddled with his collar again, waiting impatiently while the chairman of his father's, or rather his, company dealt with some boring minutiae. Michael was waiting for the moment when he would be introduced to the board of directors who oversaw the running of Global Scotland. He'd been surprised by the size of the business, both in terms of numbers of employees and volume of profits. He'd been well paid for writing programming for the online shop a few years previously, when he had needed all the work he could get so was happy to take the nepotistic handout, but even so, Global Scotland was much more successful than he had realised.

'Mr MacNair Junior, Michael.' Michael's head whipped up at the name, caught off guard by the chairman's apparently sudden introduction. The polite applause that followed from the twelve strong board gave him the opportunity to whisper a correction to

Douglas Foster, the chairman, 'It's Manners actually, not MacNair....but that's not really that important.'

Before Foster could respond, Michael strode from the corner of the room, standing at the head of the long conference table. He smiled, briefly acknowledging the applause before signalling his intention to speak.

'Gentlemen, ladies, thank you for agreeing to meet me at such short notice following the tragic passing of my father. I am sure he would have wanted me to thank you for your hard work to put this company where it is today.' Michael was sure of no such thing, not having spoken to his father about the business in years, but it felt like the right thing to say in the circumstances. He paused, mopping sweat from his brow with his left hand, wishing for the anonymity of the Internet, his regular office.

'As you can tell, I'm an American, been one for almost twenty years, but I imagine you also know that I was born here in Scotland, so I hope that'll stop you kicking me out, at least not just yet.

'What you probably don't know is that I'm a computer programmer, a geek, and I have absolutely no experience of commerce.' He paused again, treating the board to a sheepish grin while a few members shrugged and muttered that his lack of experience did not matter, and the rest glanced at each other as if they thought he was crazy.

Michael drew in a deep breath before continuing, 'And so, following discussions with Mr Foster and the company's legal team, I have agreed to sell Global Scotland to a consortium from Japan. With immediate effect.'

Michael turned, shook hands with Foster and left the room as it erupted into chaos.

Michael smiled to himself as he took a taxi into the city, where he was booked into a hotel for the next four nights until the funeral. His decision to sell the business that had been his father's life for nearly forty years, and his sole focus for the last two decades had not been a difficult one, relieving him of a massive responsibility and eliminating the need to ever work again. It also further eroded any connection to his father's life, and to Michael's own family in Scotland.

Michael finalised some further decisions on the way into the centre of Edinburgh. He had made a new plan to spend some time in the UK, reconnecting with close friends and considering what to do with his newfound wealth. To this end, he arranged to pick up the keys to his father's flat in Earley, on the east side of Reading – a little used residence required only for business meetings in the South of England. Michael would also be picking up the keys to the car his father had used when on those trips. This was a *rosso corsa*, racing red, Ferrari, identical to the car Michael owned in the US.

Robert Armstrong was waiting for Michael in the reception of the Caledonian hotel, confidently striding up to him the moment that he entered the lobby.

'Michael, son!' Armstrong spread his arms wide to hug him, an awkward embrace completely devoid of warmth. Michael took a step back, breaking the hug, looking down with a grimace as he regarded the short, stocky man in front of him. He had not seen Armstrong for twenty years, but instantly remembered his father's lawyer and felt his skin crawl as it always had done in the man's presence.

'I've been waiting here for hours.' Armstrong gently scolded the younger man – despite the fact that they had not made any arrangements to meet.
'But never mind that, how was your flight? You must be exhausted. Let me take your bag. I've cancelled your booking here; you must stay at your home, or with me.' Armstrong layered sentence upon sentence as he spoke rapidly, without pausing for Michael to respond, and was already turning to leave the hotel before Michael spoke.

'The flight was fine. I'll carry my bag thank you, and I'll be staying here, that house has not been my home for twenty years.' He spoke quietly, in a dangerously calm tone. 'Oh, and by the way, I have agreed with Foster to sell Global Scotland.'

Chapter 6

The time between arriving in Scotland and the funeral passed in a daze for Michael. He slept during the day, surrendering to jet lag out of a combination of convenience and a desire to spend as little time as possible around other people. His sleep was frequently broken, disturbed by the noise of guests and cleaners in the corridor outside his room, and by daylight seeping in around the cracks in his curtains. His sleep was also full of dreams, random and chaotic imaginings that often left him waking with a start, covered in a sheen of sweat and tangled in the bed clothes. He always awoke in his bed though, a situation that brought immense relief as it slowly dulled the edge of fear left over from his near drowning.

The experience of waking on his bathroom floor, soaking wet, battered and bruised had made him believe that his lifetime of disturbed sleep had taken a downward turn from insomnia, nightmares, and frequent awakenings to now incorporate sleepwalking – a much more dangerous activity. The fact that this somnambulistic excursion had not repeated, at least to his knowledge, was incredibly reassuring.

Michael got into the habit of having room service breakfast in the early evening and then walking around the city for a few hours, pacing up and down the Royal Mile and getting lost in the many alleyways that branched off it. He then spent a couple of hours doing laps in the hotel pool and the second half of the night in his room watching Netflix on his laptop.

He also exchanged messages with Jessica, at times a constant stream of texts. Ninety per cent of their conversations were inane banter, with the occasional serious enquiry into each other's lives. Most significantly, he shared with his sister that he had decided to spend a few weeks, possibly longer, in the UK, in order to visit with friends but more importantly to give himself space in which to decide what he wanted to do with the rest of his life – now that that life did not necessarily have to include work.

Jessica messaged back instantly with a series of furious emojis.

ARE YOU KIDDING ME?

YOU SAID YOUD BE BACK IN A WEEK

CANT BELIVE U R ABBANDONING ME!

The messages were the digital equivalent of a tantrum and Michael quickly called his sister over Facetime, half-expecting her to block the call.

She answered on the tenth ring, at first connecting only to audio and not video.

'Jess, I'm sorry. Look, I know this is sudden, but believe me I am not abandoning you.' He leant close to the screen, once her video was turned on. Jess refused to make eye contact however, pouting, the vision of a spoilt brat.

'I'm certainly not going to live here for the rest of my life, it's way too cold. And listen hun, you can visit whenever you want. Hell, you can come and live with me during the school holidays – if I'm still here.'

'You bet I can. But you better not stay that long!' Jessica's face was set in a scowl, but her eyes were now turned towards her brother, and he could see at once that she was no longer furious with him.

'I won't Jess, honestly, I miss the sunshine – and I miss you. But listen, I should try to get some sleep now, the funeral is tomorrow.'

'I know Mikey. I hope it goes OK, well, it's a funeral so it won't be "OK" …. but you know what I mean. Love ya, night!' She blew a kiss at the screen.

'Love ya too sweetie, night!' Michael disconnected the call and lay back on his bed. He yawned widely and closed his eyes, willing his mind to be still but fidgeting and twitching at the thought of the day to come.

The next day was grey and drizzly, wall to wall miserable weather that suited Michael's mood. The undertakers orchestrated everything at the church and graveside, ensuring the event went smoothly and with the efficiency customary to their profession.

Michael had abdicated all responsibility for the wake to Armstrong and to his father's former housekeeper, the indomitable Mrs Abigail Stewart. He spent the day feeling vaguely detached from the events, as people bustled around him sharing stories about his father, and enjoying the copious refreshments provided by the caterers. From time to time a hand would be thrust into his, condolences muttered and then he'd be left alone again.

Mostly he was able to observe from the side lines, subject to covert glances and only speaking more than a few words to two people all day.

Douglas Foster, his father's former chairman, seemed genuinely interested in Michael and his plans for the future, and gave him a succinct update on how the sale of Global Scotland was proceeding.

'So, you'll be glad to know that no one will lose their jobs among the workforce, and the majority of the board are more than happy with the settlement terms they are receiving. Two other members of the board are staying on with me to ensure the transition is a smooth one.' Foster spoke with the measured confidence of a business leader, patting Michael on the back as he finished speaking.

'Good, good.' Michael replied, nodding, thinking at the same time that he actually couldn't give a damn whether people were happy, sad or indifferent about his decision to sell the company.

'So, what are you going to do now? Back to the States?' Douglas smiled with polite curiosity.

'Not straight away.' Michael gestured out of the window at the rain. 'I want to enjoy the British summertime for a bit longer first.' He joked, coughing awkwardly as Foster just gazed at him blankly.

'Um, seriously though, I am going to head south to my father's flat for a while, I've got some close friends who live near London. Then I'll decide what I want to do long term.'

Foster nodded; the two almost strangers standing in awkward silence until the older man excused himself and crossed the room.

Michael's paternal uncle, 'Mac' was the only other person he spent any time speaking to during the day. The two had been close when Michael had been a child; his Uncle had always been much warmer than Michael's own parents, in tune with and sensitive to his nephew's moods. While they had not spoken a single word to each other since Michael's mother had uprooted the thirteen-year-old and settled in America, they had corresponded on email and quickly settled into an easy conversation. They spoke for fifteen minutes or so, catching up on recent events – beyond the death they were together to commemorate.

'Come and see me anytime Michael, I'd be happy to tell you more about our family. I'm glad to hear you've already offloaded the company; no one needs a millstone like that round their neck at your age. I hope that's the only thing you've inherited.' Mac had whispered his last words, almost as an apology and had then left the wake early, the two men embracing warmly before he'd squeezed through the crowd towards the entrance hall. Michael had no idea what to make of the statement, his uncle had never been one for cryptic comments, but assumed it was a reference to his father's heart condition and he put it out of his mind almost immediately.

Michael took his leave soon after his uncle. As he excused himself, he thanked a very displeased Armstrong for arranging everything, receiving a grunt of affirmation in response. Michael also reiterated that he was happy for the lawyer to make arrangements to sell everything, regardless of the fees Armstrong would charge and with the exception of the flat in Reading and the Ferrari, and then he dashed out into the rain to a waiting taxi.

Two hours later and Michael stood in the narrow aisle of his plane to London, squeezing his bag into the overhead locker.

'Hello! Would you mind putting my bag up there too?' He half turned towards the posh English voice. 'It's a bit of a stretch for me.' The young blond woman continued, holding out a small suitcase.

'Sure thing.' He smiled for the first time all day, pushing the case in beside his own. He moved to the side to let the woman through, realising that they'd be sitting next to each other for the short flight. Once they were both seated, he held out his hand in greeting. 'I'm Michael Manners.'

'Poppy Stevens. A pleasure to meet you Michael.' Poppy smiled as she shook his hand.

Chapter 7

Michael jolted awake; easing into a sitting position as he warily surveyed his bedroom. For a moment he was disoriented, unsure what had disturbed his sleep, and then he heard it again. A low, scratching sound, unlike any of the regular noises that filled the apartment during the night, the plink of cooling light bulbs, the hum of the refrigerator motor kicking in, the creaking as the building settled, materials contracting slightly in the cool of night. His disturbed sleep patterns meant that these were all noises to which he had quickly become habituated in the brief time since he'd moved into his late father's flat. The scratching however was a novel noise, but also one that was so soft, so quiet, that he began to wonder if he had imagined it. He sat in silence, for perhaps a minute or two.

Remaining very still, listening intently, he focused on hearing the different, the alien sound. His eyes began to adjust to the low light level in the bedroom as he waited, starting to feel foolish, beginning to wonder if he should just lie down and try to go back to sleep. When he'd woken the darkness had been relieved by just one light source, the blood red glow of the alarm clock on the bedside table. The clock had revealed the time to be 2.43am, a comforting sight showing Michael that he had at least slept for half the night.

Now the clock read 2.48 and the contents of his bedroom were revealed as outlines in varying shades of grey. Chest of drawers, chair, wardrobe, bedside table, all seemed normal. No bogeyman stood hunched at the foot of the bed.

Then the noise came again, slighter louder, and he finally recognised the source of the sound. The front door of the flat.

He slipped out of bed, and moved quickly towards his bedroom door, thankful that his eyes had adjusted to the gloom. He paused at the threshold, one hand on the door handle, the other pressed firmly against the centre of the door.

Gripped by indecision, he was torn between wrenching the door open to confront a would-be-burglar and holding the door closed, ensuring his own safety, and that of Poppy. Cocking his head, he strained to hear further evidence of the intruder. All he heard was his own heart, thudding loudly in the vicinity of his throat. There was no sound coming from the hallway.

Slowly he inched open the bedroom door and seconds later Michael thrust his head out into the short passageway. The corridor was a lighter shade of grey than the bedroom, illuminated by the moonlight which filtered through a light well in the ceiling. Turning to the left he saw his front door, dark wood outlined against the magnolia walls of the hall, the origin of the noises that had woken him up. He froze again, listening for any further sounds of an intruder, fearing that a burglar could similarly paused be in another part of the flat.

After what felt like an eternity, he once again began to feel foolish, standing in mid step, his head in the hall and his body in the bedroom. An image of the cartoon character, Elmer Phudd, sprang to mind, the diminutive hunter standing stock still in the forest before turning to camera and announcing 'Shhhh, I'm hunting wabbits!' Meanwhile Bugs Bunny would be standing behind him, waiting to ask, 'What's up, Doc?' Michael resisted the urge to look behind him and instead moved forwards and to the left, towards the front door.

A cursory examination of the door revealed that it was locked, bolted and with the chain on, exactly as it had been left after he had let Poppy in the previous evening. Convinced now that he must have imagined the earlier noises, or at the very least they had been the product of an opportunistic thief trying the door, he began walking back towards his bedroom, passing a door on his left which led to the lounge and kitchen and a door on the right to the spare bedroom, both doors were closed.

In front and to the right the door to the master bedroom lay slightly ajar, as he had left it moments before. Directly ahead lay the bathroom, a yawning mouth of perfect darkness, its door completely open. Michael stopped in mid stride, temporarily unnerved by the open doorway. He was directly opposite the door to his bedroom and could hear Poppy's indistinct breathing, a quiet snore with which he had become intimately familiar over the preceding weeks since their chance meeting on the plane from Edinburgh.

They had chatted to each other for the whole flight, the young woman providing a bright counterpoint to the gloom in which he had been living for the previous week. They'd ended up sharing a taxi from Heathrow airport to Reading and he had surprised himself by accepting her offer to come in for a drink when they had arrived at her flat near the university. He supposed that the out of character spontaneity was a reaction to the death of his father. He'd spent most nights with Poppy since they'd met.

Standing in the hallway he smiled to himself, picturing the twenty-two-year-old curled up in his bed; body concertinaed as if she was more accustomed to sleeping in cardboard boxes than in regular sized beds. He could visualise the fresh-faced law student, her blond hair fanned out over the pillow, sleeping the contented sleep of the innocent.

He could also imagine her waking in the night and going to the toilet, returning to the bedroom and leaving the bathroom door wide open. Michael always left doors closed, a habit he'd learned as a young boy growing up in a draughty house in Scotland, and the reason why he had been startled to see the bathroom door open. But this was not a habit shared by Poppy and so he relaxed, walking on towards the bathroom out of necessity rather than through fear of confronting an intruder.

Two steps from the bathroom, hand absent-mindedly scratching his two-day old stubble, and another sound punctuated the silence. Again, he struggled to place the noise, did it come from the bedroom, Poppy turning over in her sleep? Was the sound even inside the flat? He started to turn around, trying to get a bearing on the sound, and then it came again and this time the direction was obvious. The bathroom.

The noise had sounded like somebody shuffling from one foot to the other, changing their weight as they struggled to stay still, to stay silent. He became convinced that this was precisely what was happening and, suddenly emboldened, he took quick steps towards the open doorway.

Unlike the hallway, the bathroom was dimly lit, full of thick shadows and impenetrable corners. The room featured a large window, but this was covered with a dark venetian blind. Michael stood in the doorway for a moment, studying the room, allowing his eyes to readjust to the lower light level within, but also knowing that any would-be attacker had the advantage. Michael was clearly visible in the doorway, back lit by the moonlight streaming into the hall, a sitting duck.

His whole body tensed, every muscle tightened, poised to fight or retreat, ready for an attack. A minute passed, maybe two, and the expected assault did not come. Slowly, the contents of the room swam into view. Directly ahead was the window, a dark square surrounded by the pale glow of moonlight seeping in around the edges of the blind. To the right of this the sink, underneath a large mirrored cabinet. The mirror cast a vague reflection of the hallway, a pale view that seemed to move as if the surface of the mirror was not solid but rather liquid, like the surface of a pond. Further right and the toilet could just be discerned, an irregular shape, slightly lighter than the dark corner in which it was positioned. He was fairly confident that this half of the room did not harbour any burglars.

Instead he turned his attention to the left-hand side of the room, an area offering more opportunities to hide. His view to the immediate left was blocked by the solid wood of the door, and beyond that by the shower curtain hanging above the bathtub. The bath seemed to be the most obvious hiding place, if also the most clichéd and he took a step towards the tub, hands held up in readiness to defend against an attack.

The shower curtain, a dark red, but drained of all colour by the night, appeared to float above the pale grey bulk of the bath, suspended a foot from the ceiling by a rod and hooks that were all but invisible in the dingy half light. This vision gave birth to a supernatural chill throughout his body as he reached out a hand to tear back the curtain. He feared a bloody scene reminiscent of *Psycho* but expected an empty tub, or at worse a rat, however he never completed his intended action.

The shower curtain billowed out, even as Michael's hand reached forward to grip the thin, plastic material. The curtain moved like it was attracted to him, like a moth to a flame or a metal filing to a magnet. Or as if it had been pushed from the other side. Shocked, he stumbled backwards caught off guard by the movement. He had become convinced that the bathtub - and indeed the flat - contained nothing more than himself, his slumbering girlfriend and his wild imagination.

Before he could regain his balance, he felt and heard the impact of a blunt object with the top of his head. Through the instant flash of pain his mind nevertheless registered the fact that a second intruder must have been waiting in the shadows, possibly in one of the other rooms. He did not have time to consider the consequences of this fact, and whether Poppy was safe, before a movement caught his eye.

Someone, presumably whoever had attempted to reshape his skull, was moving towards him from the right side of the room. A darker shape, a moving shadow, and Michael instinctively ducked, bringing his right fist up to connect with his assailant's body. Pain exploded through his right hand and up into his arm, as if he had connected with a brick wall rather than a human body. He fell backwards, colliding first with the wall before crashing to the ceramic tiles of the floor.

On the verge of passing out, he sensed more than felt somebody moving past him down the hall and then he heard the sound of the front door. And then he surrendered to the darkness.

Chapter 8

'Michael? Michael, where are you? What's going...oh my god!' The Home Counties accent cut through the thick confusion in Michael's head.

Opening his eyes, he was temporarily blinded by the bright overhead light and by the pain in his skull. He closed his eyes again.

'Burglars.' He spoke through gritted teeth, 'Check. Door.'

He lapsed into silence letting his head flop back onto the floor as Poppy dashed off down the hall.

He stirred again a few minutes later, aware that she had returned and was talking rapidly to him, but unable to comprehend her words. Of more pressing concern were his surroundings. Ceramic 'trees', the scent of pine leaves, a coppery taste, it was all too familiar.

'Michael, can you hear me?' Poppy's words came fast, breathlessly. 'I said the door was unlocked, slightly ajar, but no one's here. I think I heard something, but I'm not sure what. Then I heard you cry out and came running. What happened?' She paused, gazing down at him with wide eyes.

Michael groaned, a response he knew to be inadequate but, in the current circumstances, all he could manage.

'Never mind that, I'm getting you to casualty.' Normally a young 22, she was all business now, every trace of fear gone from her voice.

'Police first.' Michael's words were slurred as he struggled to stand. Then he saw the mirror.

A huge gaping hole was all that remained of the glass above the sink. Shards of the mirror littered the basin and floor, only a few splinters bristled around the edges of the cabinet door. He lowered his gaze to his right hand, bloody, throbbing, and covered in silvery fragments of the mirror. Raising his left hand to the back of his head, he confirmed that he had suffered a blunt trauma, but now he doubted how he had received it.

'No.' He spoke softly, his voice shaking in disbelief. 'You're right. If noone's here and nothing's missing, hospital first. Police later.'

Three hours later, the couple sat in the waiting area of the Emergency Department of Reading's Royal Berkshire Hospital. Michael's right hand and lower arm were bandaged - two broken fingers, sprained wrist and multiple lacerations, one on the arm deep enough to require stitches. His head was badly bruised but not cracked, and he was enjoying a medicinal recuperation.

Poppy explained her theory about the night's drama. 'I did not hear much, could not say someone broke in, and you never got a clear look at anyone. So maybe you sleepwalked again, you know, like you told me you did back home? And maybe you tripped? Not sure about the door being open though, maybe you opened it in your sleep?'

'You're right I did it.' Michael spoke slowly, methodically, without emotion.

'I dreamed there was a burglar. I fought myself in the mirror; I cracked my head into the wall. I must have opened the front door too. I must be losing my mind.'

'No, I'm sure you're not.... and, well, at least we were not robbed.' Poppy smiled, keen to see the bright side as she squeezed his left arm.

'It's not the first time. When I told you I'd walked in my sleep the other day I didn't mention I almost drowned myself.' Michael continued with his voice still devoid of feeling.

'What if I had left the flat and attacked someone. What if I hurt you?' He turned towards his girlfriend, 5 foot 6, slender and about as streetwise as a newborn puppy.

'What if I killed you?'

Poppy did not reply, but he felt a shudder travel through her where their bodies touched.

Chapter 9

The skies opened the minute that Michael pushed open the heavy wooden door of the pub. Looking back towards the car park it was already almost impossible to distinguish the Ferrari from the other cars filling the small courtyard; the storm had robbed the vehicles of their colours, reducing them to amorphous blobs.

'Maybe my luck's changing?' he muttered sarcastically, cradling his bandaged hand as he turned his attention to the busy pub.

Low ceilinged, atmospherically lit and with a rich smell of hops, The Flowing Spring was a quintessential English pub. While comforting in its familiarity this did mean that it was inevitably crowded, regularly with groups of tourists searching for the 'Real Thing'. He scanned the people sitting at the bar and was about to wander off to search the rest of the pub when a hand clapped him heavily on the shoulder.

'Hello Mikey.'

He spun round, instantly recognising the soft Scottish lilt in the greeting. For the first time all day, he found himself smiling as he saw his oldest friend.

'Christ Russ, I swear you look more like Paul Bettany every time I see you! While I just get hairier, shorter and, frankly, more like a hobbit every day.'

Russell McCloud shrugged, running a hand through his white blond hair. 'You said it, not me. Come on Mr Frodo Sir, let's get a drink'

Russell sat quietly, nursing a pint of old-fashioned English ale while his friend outlined his recent nocturnal activity. 'Is this a new thing, or has it happened before?'

Michael paused, his own pint half raised to his mouth. 'You know it happened before, the nightmares, the sleeplessness, when Ben....' He looked away, taking a gulp of his beer before continuing. 'When Ben died. It's happened on and off since, normally when I've been, you know, stressed. But never like this, I've never sleepwalked.'

Russell leaned forwards, 'Do you think it's related to your Dad's death? Bringing up memories of Ben?'

Pain blossomed in Michael's eyes and he looked away, down at the table, his head bowed as if in prayer. 'I don't know what it is; mostly I think I'm going crazy. And I'm worried that I'll hurt someone.'

Russell regarded his friend with a frown, his eyes bright with concern. If he had been surprised by the intensity of Michael's response, he didn't show it.

'I don't think you're loopy mate, just under a lot of strain. You know, with your Dad, moving back here for a while and all that. Maybe you should talk to someone?' He suggested tentatively.

'Like who? Doctors? No, absolutely no way. I've had enough of that prodding, poking and drugs to last me a lifetime.' A flash of anger as Michael glanced around at the room, his body language sending clear signals to his friend. Drop the conversation.

The pub had become more crowded around the two men. People were loitering close to their table, ready to claim it the second Russell and Michael showed signs of leaving. Many of the newcomers were American tourists, bedecked in garish windbreakers and baseball caps, and wandering around looking for someone to tell them what to do, as if they were at a conference or in Disneyland. They were also leaving puddles on the floor, soaked to the skin from the continuing storm.

Michael couldn't help smiling at the sight. 'Do you think they're looking for a guide or waiting for the show to start?'

Russell grinned back, pleased that his companion's mood had lightened, but unwilling to let the previous conversation end unresolved. 'So, do you fancy coming over for dinner tonight? We could chat about this sleeping stuff, brainstorm a bit. Maybe talking about the problems could relieve the stress?' Russell spoke casually easing back into the topic before delivering the line that he thought would clinch the deal.

'I'm sure Rosie would be pleased to see you.'

Russell glanced up in time to see the smile cross Michael's face at the mention of his wife's name. The smile vanished as soon as it appeared however, replaced by a deep frown.

'I, not tonight Russ, I'm not feeling too sociable. Say hi to Rosie for me though.' Michael reached into his pocket as he spoke, drawing out his wallet to settle up for the drinks.

'Alright, I'll let you off tonight, don't be a stranger though. OK? The offer still stands, you know, dinner whenever you want. We'd all love to see you more.' Russell stood, angling his body so that a young red headed woman could be the first to claim their table, blocking it off from the group of noisy Americans who'd been banging his elbows for the last ten minutes.

'OK, I'll sleep on it. Or at least I'll try to.' Michael replied over his shoulder, pushing through the crowd to the bar.

Outside, Michael was about to start his car when his phone rang. Glancing at the caller ID he answered straight away.

'Hi Poppy, how are you?' He relaxed, feeling the defences that he had built up during his conservation with Russell begin to fall.

'I'm OK.' She paused; she didn't sound OK, which Michael considered was not surprising given the events of the previous night.

'But, I just, um, have lots of work to do. You know, studying? So, I'm not going to come over tonight.' Poppy continued before abruptly finishing speaking, leaving an awkward silence.

Michael sighed, disappointed at the prospect of being alone, despite rejecting Russell's offer of dinner. 'Would you like company? I promise to be quiet, and to not interrupt you…. too much!' He laughed - a noise more like a bark that sounded false and hollow to his own ears.

She responded quickly, obviously flustered. 'No, it's OK; I really do need to knuckle down. I'll see you soon though, OK?' Her voice shook slightly on her last word, an unmistakable note of fear in her voice.

'Sure. Bye.' He hung up, agitated and also feeling a sense of betrayal that he could not immediately place. 'It is not like she has another man round, but I'm surprised she'd choose a textbook over me.' He drew in a deep breath, attempting to calm himself.

'But if she is scared of me, she's definitely got every right to be.'

He turned the key in the ignition, the powerful engine at once roaring into life. Hand on the gearstick he noticed a message flash up on his phone.

I THINK U SHOULD TALK TO SOMEONE.

I'LL SEND U FRIENDS CONTACT.

PLEASE CALL HER.

POPPY X

A ping announced the arrival of another message, this time an electronic business card for a Doctor E Byfield. Michael sighed, turning the phone over, and raced out into the stormy evening.

Chapter 10

Michael sprang awake, his body soaked in sweat, his mind full of images from the night his brother had died. He got up out of bed and ran his hand through his damp hair, glancing at the clock. The display read 00.00, midnight, less than an hour since he'd turned off the light, barely ten minutes since he'd last checked the time. He presumed his body had briefly succumbed to sleep.

He walked to the kitchen, poured himself a glass of water and then returned to the bedroom. As he passed the mirror above the chest of drawers he froze, certain he had seen a second figure reflected in the glass.

He fumbled for the light switch beside the door, almost dropping his glass of water. He turned slowly to face the mirror in a state of dreadful fascination. He recoiled from the image that met his eyes. In the mirror he saw himself, behind him his bedroom but to his left there was a second figure, the young boy from his dream of drowning. At first the figure's features were in shadow, the identity of the boy hidden, until he stepped forwards towards the mirror, towards Michael.

As the boy stepped into the light Michael suppressed a shudder. He was looking at himself as a teenager, a teenage self wearing the smart black jeans and button-down white shirt he had worn the night his brother had been killed. He spun round to face the room, searching for the boy from the mirror. The room was empty and offered nowhere that the boy could have hidden.

'I am losing my shit again.' He almost choked on his words, his body sagging as if he had run a marathon. He turned slowly to face the mirror once more. 'It's a dream' he murmured, upon confirming his suspicion that this time the mirror held only his own face.

'It's a dream.' He spoke the words more loudly and with conviction. 'I'm still asleep in bed and this is all a dream.' He set down his glass and rested his hands on the chest in front of him, bowing his head in exhaustion; then he noticed Poppy's lipstick resting on the wooden surface. He picked it up, an idea forming in his head as he removed the lid and twisted the bottom in order to reveal the scarlet make up.

Facing the mirror once more he used the lipstick to write on the glass. After a minute he stood back to consider his work. He had filled the centre of the mirror with neat block capitals: THIS IS A DREAM. He turned back to his bed. 'So, I've been asleep the whole time and in the morning the mirror will be clean.' He spoke softly to himself, a soothing tone, daring to believe his own words.

Twenty minutes later and the flat was silent. Michael's sleep was deep and uneventful for the rest of the night. In the lounge the telephone rang, an urgent signal that was muffled by two doors meaning he slept on. After five rings the answerphone clicked in and a woman's voice spoke into the darkness.

'Michael, are you there? Please make the effort to call when you get this message. It is urgent, it's about Jessica.' The answerphone clicked off.

Michael awoke at 7am to the sound of his alarm clock, an insistent buzz that seemed to drill through his skull and that interrupted his dreamless sleep. He rose quickly, pleased to find he was waking in the same place where he'd gone to sleep, and with no recollection or evidence of further nocturnal activities. He headed to the bathroom. Passing the mirror, he had a strange sensation that something important had happened in the night, but he didn't glance at his reflection.

He spent the next half hour going about his usual daily rituals, getting washed, grinding beans and then brewing coffee in his French press, pouring some fresh orange juice and heating a Krispy Kreme doughnut in the microwave. As he went through these motions, he continued to have a feeling, like an itch at the back of his brain, that he was forgetting something vital. It was not until he finished getting dressed, pulling a black sweater over a white t-shirt and fastening the belt on his jeans that he finally glanced up at the mirror above the chest of drawers. It came to him then.

Studying the reflective surface carefully, he could find no trace of the message 'THIS IS A DREAM'. There was not even a smear of lipstick marring his reflection and, when he searched the top of the chest of drawers, the lipstick itself was nowhere to be found. He sat down heavily on the end of his bed, amazed and relieved to discover that the night had passed without incident. He crossed his arms, hugging himself in shock as he spoke in tones of wonder. 'So, it really was just a dream.' And then he noticed his arm.

A dull, throbbing pain, mild but persistent was coming from his right forearm. It was the arm he had injured fending off an imaginary burglar, and he assumed he must have caught the wound when he'd clasped himself in shock.

Pushing up his sleeve he saw he was bleeding again, patches of bright red blossoming on the white surface of the bandage. He began to take off the bandage, hoping that he'd only reopened one of the small lacerations, rather than bursting the stitches that were holding the larger cut closed. The wounds were certainly not bleeding heavily, and the pain was still not much more than an irritation. He remained confident that he would be spared a return visit to the hospital. He slowly unrolled the last piece of bandage, pulling off the dressing beneath, careful not to drag the fabric against the cuts, and then he froze.

He gazed, unmoving, at his arm. All the old injuries were clean, knitting together, healing, but now a new wound marked the underside of his forearm. A criss cross of thin, shallow cuts, stretched all the way from his wrist to his elbow, blood seeping slowly from the wounds. He shuddered, not from the pain but from what the cuts represented. In direct opposition to the message he had recorded on the mirror in his dream, another pronouncement now marked his arm: THIS IS REAL.

The letters were small and crudely carved into the flesh, but they were legible, even through the thin streams of blood. He hurried to the bathroom and threw up, the acid taste of his barely digested breakfast burning his throat. Once he could trust himself to stand, he washed his face, his hands and the wounds in shaky disbelief. For a moment he watched the water, pink from his blood, as it ran down the smooth sides of the sink before vanishing into the plughole. He felt like he was watching his life force draining away and he fell back to his knees, his body suddenly boneless, as the last rivulet of blood disappeared.

It took his last reserves of energy to drag himself from the bathroom to the lounge, his skin sheathed in sweat. In desperation he called the number that Poppy had forwarded to him the night before. The simple act threatened to overwhelm him. He was not surprised when his call was diverted to a voicemail service, the clock in the kitchen read ten to eight, and he left a short message and his mobile phone number. Replacing the handset on its base unit, he sat back heavily onto his sofa, his body shaking and his vision blurring. He was oblivious to the flashing message light on his answerphone.

Chapter 11

Elizabeth Byfield stood with her back to her office, staring out of the window at the dreary August day. Most of the view was obscured by the crowd of concrete blocks that formed the hospital. Beyond the buildings was a road choked with traffic and, in the distance a thin strip of green denoting an urban park. She shivered.

The sky was low, full of dark grey clouds that looked like sacks of coal bursting at the seams.

Her gaze was not on the window, she looked further, beyond the buildings, the cars, the grey. In her mind's eye she saw rolling green fields, punctuated by low stone walls and terminating at the sea. Blue sky, unmarked by clouds completed the view, a happy memory of the summer she had spent travelling in New Zealand after her doctoral graduation.

'What's up Lizzy?'

She stiffened, closing her eyes momentarily before slowly turning away from the window to regard the man who'd entered the office. Dr James Booker, tall, dark and handsome in an obvious way was leaning on his desk, smiling faintly. It was a smile that said 'Hi, I'm here, your life is complete', a smile that she had quickly grown to dislike in the brief time during which they had shared an office.

Elizabeth smoothed down her skirt, glancing at her desk. 'Nothing is up. And I would really appreciate it if you would refrain from calling me by that name.'

The edge in the woman's voice took James by surprise, but he attempted to rally straight away, turning on his charm as he quipped.

'Sorry, forgot, I hate Jimbo, is it a family nickname then?'

Her face froze at the word 'family', remembering her parents, the only people who had called her Lizzy. They had even set her name to a song whenever she was sad 'Lizzy, Lizzy, in a tizzy. Don't cry baby, let's get busy'.

'Yes. My mother called me it, so please, don't.'

James quickly moved on, keen to change the conversation. 'Did you know you had a message on our phone?' He gestured to his colleague's cluttered desk.

'Of course, I knew.' The woman lied as she took a step forward and pressed 'play' on the telephone's answerphone, grateful for the change of subject. 'I was just catching a breath before listening to it.'

They both listened in silence as an unfamiliar voice filled the office.

'Good Morning Dr Byfield. My name is Michael. My number is 07213 682561. Please call me back as soon as you can.'

The message was brief and business-like, but the voice brought her up short as she grabbed a pen to note down the caller's telephone number. An uncomfortable mix of fear, excitement, anger, desperation and resignation, the short message was a rollercoaster of emotions.

'Wacko, or a malingerer' James delivered his diagnosis with a lack of consideration, smiling as he did so and causing her to add another reason to her long mental list of why she'd never date him despite his obvious interest in her.

'Well, you know doctor, we'll see. I heard some wild new theory that you shouldn't always trust first impressions, something about books, covers and judgements?' She paused, staring at her colleague for an uncomfortably long time before continuing. 'Then again, sometimes one look is all you need.'

Chapter 12

'Michael Manners, and I know, it sounds like I should be a spy, superhero or something, believe me I've heard it all.'

'Elizabeth Byfield, but I grew up as Betty Byfield so believe me I've heard my fair share too!' Elizabeth gave a short throaty laugh as she shook Michael's hand.

Michael smiled, relaxing as he followed the woman into her consulting room. He was caught off guard by her friendly tone, a far cry from his previous experiences with the mental health profession. Her age, a long way under 50, and her gender were also at odds with the middle-aged bearded men he had encountered in his childhood. He had been surprised and relieved to receive a call from the psychologist less than an hour after leaving his message. The offer of an initial appointment later the same day had led to a silent prayer of gratitude.

For her part Elizabeth had been somewhat relieved that he had been available for an assessment so quickly, sparing her from an awkward afternoon of office small talk with Dr Booker.

Glancing over at her new research subject she considered his appearance and body language carefully. He was dressed casually in jeans, t-shirt and, despite the wet yet warm weather, a thick hoodie. His dark hair looked clean, but was untidy, and his face was covered with short stubble, by design or neglect Elizabeth could not be certain. What was clear however was that the thirty-three-year-old was not sleeping peacefully, if he was sleeping at all.

His face, momentarily brightened by her welcome, was deeply lined and his eyes seemed dulled, their dark blue virtually hidden by his furrowed brows.

'So, where should I start?' Michael spoke quietly, crossing his arms over his chest in an unconscious gesture of defensiveness.

Elizabeth's eyes were drawn to the bandages on his right hand as he moved, and she almost asked what had happened. 'Let me tell you a little bit about the study first.

'Essentially, I am looking at the reasons behind somnambulism, sleepwalking. By identifying events that have preceded changes in sleep patterns and behaviours, and then by working through the events, over a number of sessions, there is very good evidence that sleep will become less disrupted, and more settled.' She paused and looked up, checking that he was following her words.

'So, there are two aspects to the study. The first involves you telling me about the current events that have been troubling you, disturbing your sleep. At the same time, we will conduct tests, and observations of your sleep.

The second part of the study involves a course of therapy where you and I will meet on a regular basis to understand what might be causing you to sleepwalk.

'There are also two people involved in the study, myself and my colleague, Dr James Booker. Dr Booker is testing some experimental medical equipment and will be....'

She paused again as Michael put a hand up to stop her. 'Look, doc, I really don't care what you do to me. I just want to go back to sleeping in my own bed and waking up there too.'

Elizabeth nodded, pushing a lock of her long brown hair back behind her ear, an unconscious movement, done more often when she was nervous. She felt slightly disgruntled by his interruption. 'I understand, OK. Before we go on though, I just have to ask you a few questions about risk.' She glanced at the bandages before continuing. 'Sorry if these sound blunt, they are, but I need to ask them. Have you ever had thoughts of hurting yourself?'

Michael rubbed his bandaged arm, shaking his head. 'No, this was an accident.'

'OK, good; well, not good that you're hurt of course.

'Secondly, finally in fact, have you had any thoughts of ending your life?'

'No, definitely not. Not sleeping is properly stressing me out to say the least. I'm tired and worried, but I'm definitely not planning to kill myself. OK?' He considered his previous answer a half-truth. He had sliced up his own arm, essentially hurting himself, but not intentionally, so was that still an accident? Michael was taken aback by the questions, and didn't want to complicate things by explaining further, keen instead to move past them.

'As I say, I'm sorry to have to ask, but it would be remiss, unethical of me not to check in with you in this way.' Elizabeth smiled reassuringly as she continued. 'So, why don't you start by telling me why you got in touch? What brings you here today?'

Chapter 13

'What brings me here today? Well, I guess that would be our mutual friend. Ms Stevens.'

Elizabeth smiled back. 'Ah yes, you said Poppy gave you my details. She's actually the younger sister of one of my friends from University, so I don't actually know her very well.' She had been surprised by this rash action from her friend's sister but had not got in touch to find out more, vowing instead to only contact Poppy about the case if she was concerned for the woman's safety.

'Yes, I said she's my girlfriend, right?'

Elizabeth nodded. 'Yes, and she has mentioned you, one or two times when we've both been with her sister.' She raised an eyebrow.

'Well, that's awkward.' Michael glanced away embarrassed before continuing. 'So, the actual reason I'm here is that I've been having nightmares, and associated activities.'

He spent the next five minutes recounting the events that had plagued him over the course of several weeks. He described the near drowning and would-be-burglar in detail, but felt too ashamed to describe the previous night's self-harm, instead just referring to 'other incidents'.

Elizabeth made a few notes as she listened, choosing for the time being to set aside the fact that there were episodes that he skipped over, deciding instead to return to these in a later session. 'And what's been happening in your life recently, any changes that might have triggered your sleepwalking?'

'Well, I moved back to the UK a few weeks ago, temporarily, probably. That's because my father died, so I suppose that could have triggered this.' Michael shrugged, increasingly uncomfortable to be talking about himself.

Elizabeth nodded. 'I am sorry to hear that Michael. Certainly, the loss of a parent is incredibly upsetting and unsettling, so it could well have precipitated your sleepwalking. Have you ever sleepwalked before, either as an adult or a child?'

Michael shook his head. 'I've had trouble sleeping in the past, insomnia and vivid dreams, and nightmares. Never sleepwalking though.'

'That's interesting, is your sleep regularly disturbed in that way, can you recall any specific incidents when it has been worse?'

Elizabeth watched as her client's face darkened, he pursed his lips, shaking his head. Again, she made a note to come back to this area of the assessment, but for now concentrated on finding out more about his personal and family history. 'OK, that's good. And what do you do, workwise; if you work?'

Michael's shoulders dropped from where they'd been drawn up by his ears and he leant back in the chair, eager to talk about something completely unrelated to his sleeping disorder, or to his family. 'I'm a computer geek, a programmer, you know? I worked for Google when I left university, spent ten years as a small cog in a very big machine, then left there a few years ago to set up a small business for myself. I design the backend of websites for individuals and corporate clients. It pays well and I love it, but it's not exactly exciting enough to stop anyone from sleeping. In fact, when I tell most people what I do it puts them to sleep.' He laughed, his eyes lighting up fleetingly.

'Now I'm taking some time away from work, my father left me more than comfortable. So, I'm going to take a while to figure out what to do with my inheritance I guess.' He shrugged.

Elizabeth smiled, pleased by how much he had relaxed, and seeing a way into her next question. 'Can you tell me a bit more about your family?'

'Well, I was born in 1989 and grew up in Scotland, just outside Edinburgh. I moved to America in 2002.' The answer was short, and Elizabeth detected that the mention of his family had struck some sort of a nerve, considering how freely he had been speaking a moment before.

Chapter 14

For the next five minutes Elizabeth probed, asking questions about his history that were met with a mixture of one-syllable answers and stony silences. It was the longest five minutes of her life. She did learn that Michael had one brother, Benjamin, who was a couple of years older than him and that his parents were divorced. He had moved to Reading recently, after his father died, having been living in America since he was 13.

Of his brother, he would say very little and she perceived that a big part of his current problems likely centred round his sibling. She also suspected that a significant and traumatic event had taken place within Michael's family when he was 13, causing it to splinter. His parents had separated, and he had been moved to America, presumably with his mother as his father had been living in the UK prior to his death.

The event that had originally triggered Michael's sleeping disorder could simply have been the separation of his parents; certainly, she knew that similar events had caused problems of this type in younger children. Elizabeth voiced her theory.

'Quite often the trauma of a divorce wreaks havoc on children's sleeping habits, especially when the family has not undergone counselling to smooth the rocky ride of the separation or if the children have not even been told the reasons why their parents are no longer living together. Did your family have any counselling around the time of the separation Michael?'

He did not answer, did not even meet her eyes as she continued.

'It is all too easy for a child to imagine they are the reason for the family breaking up. In fact, often one or both of the parents are happy to agree with this view, anything but admit the reason for a break up lies with them. A child's feeling of responsibility, often not communicated, can easily manifest itself as nightmares, enuresis – bed wetting – and other symptoms of disturbed sleep.'

Michael shrugged, this time meeting her eyes. 'That is not what happened to us, to me.' His face was set in a pose of grim determination, glaring at Elizabeth, daring her to break the stony silence that followed his brief declaration.

Elizabeth let the silence draw out as she considered the timeline. It was actually unlikely that the separation of Michael's parents had been the sole cause of his current troubles, seeing as he was a teenager when the event took place and would have been able to communicate his feelings in ways that a younger child could not. It was also unlikely that he would have been blamed or would have blamed himself for the deterioration in his parents' relationship – unless of course it was his fault. It was certainly unlikely that the sleeping disorder would have persisted for so long after the divorce. She did want to know more about the circumstances surrounding the separation, deciding to probe her taciturn patient a little further.

'So, I know it's difficult to talk about; but what did happen? Why did your parents separate?' She watched carefully for his reaction to the question, looking for body language that would doubtless carry more significance than his words.

'I guess that they just stopped loving each other. That's normally it right?' He answered quickly and with a lack of emotion in his voice. He had his eyes down, looking at his hands fidgeting in his lap, once again avoiding meeting Elizabeth's eyes as he spoke. It was a conscious attempt to avoid betraying his true feelings; however, she had noticed the look of pain in his eyes as she asked her question and she also saw that his shoulders were shaking slightly as he answered.

She continued, tentatively. 'Well, generally I suppose people do separate when they stop loving each other, or more usually when they admit that they have stopped loving each other. But,' She paused, feeling that she was on dangerous ground by persisting with the subject and resigned to receiving a short answer, or no answer at all. 'Do you know why they stopped loving each other?'

'No. And seeing as it was 20 years ago it doesn't much matter does it?'

His answer was abrupt and final. Well, she thought, I guess I asked for that. Elizabeth paused, running a hand though her hair, gathering her thoughts and attempting to calm the growing frustration that she was feeling. She decided to return to the subject of Benjamin, Michael's brother.

'And what about your brother, where is he now?'

'I don't know.' He looked at her, eyes blazing. His feelings were clear. I am angry, stop asking me about my family.

OK, she thought, how about a change of tack: Sort of.

'Tell me more about your sleeping problems, do you know if either of your parents suffers, or suffered from anything similar? How about Benjamin?'

Michael's face was full of fury at the fresh reference to his brother. The reaction added fuel to Elizabeth's theory that whatever had triggered his sleeping disorders, his sibling was a core component of the problem. Michael stood abruptly, heading to the door.

'I have to go.... I don't have time for this.... I can't take part in your study. I just need to get some medication.'

Elizabeth stood, opening her mouth to call her client back.

'Wait, Mr Manners; Michael, we don't have to talk about your family at the minute, we can...' She tailed off as the door to the consulting room slammed shut.

'Well, that went well!' She pinched the bridge of her nose, closing her eyes. She cursed herself for rushing her client. Her focus had been on her research, rather than his mental health, an error of judgement that she could not explain.

Chapter 15

A young woman was slumped on the floor outside his flat when Michael returned home from the hospital. She was slight, 5 feet 5, had long bleach blond hair and was wearing designer jeans and a *Prada* T-shirt. She was also sitting on a suitcase.

'Jess, oh my god!' Michael rushed forwards, beaming as he gave his half-sister a hug. In the instant of their fierce embrace he felt more at peace than at any point since he had awoken on his bathroom floor to the news of his father's sudden death. He drew away abruptly.

'What the hell are you doing here?' Did something happen to mum?'

Jessica took a step back, wiping at fresh tears with shaking hands.
'Well it's good to see you too big brother.... I thought mum had spoken to you?'

'No, not since before the funeral. I figured she was ignoring me, why would she have called?' Michael frowned, totally confused before he remembered having a message from his mother asking him to call about Jessica. He had not called back but now guessed that the 16-year-old had had another row with her 'mom' and had come running to him. It had happened before......just not since he'd moved to the other side of the world.

With everything else going on Michael felt like he needed to babysit like he needed a hole in the head. 'Does she know you're here? I guess she must because you couldn't have got a flight by yourself. I'll give her a call, smooth things over for you. I'm sorry sweetie it's not a good time, I'm really busy. You can't stay.'

He glanced at his sister's face, saw her chin wobble as disappointment and betrayal entered her eyes. She sniffed before answering.

'That's cool; I figured you must be busy, that that was why you were ignoring my messages. I'll just get a cab back to the airport and get the next flight.'

'Permanently' Michael said.

'What?' She drew in a breath puzzled.

'I was going to say that I don't think you can stay permanently.... not unless you find somewhere to study here. But you can definitely stay for a while until things blow over with mom. I would love the company.' He rearranged his features into a smile, holding the door open as his sister wrapped her arms around him, relief transforming her face from jaded young woman to elated teen.

Michael showed her the spare room and then left his sister to unpack while he took a shower. He turned the temperature up high, needing the scalding water to relax his muscles and clear his head.

Returning to the kitchen 20 minutes later his skull was still pounding.

'Hey Michael, I'm literally starving here.'

'Hello again to you too Jess. And yes, you're welcome for dropping in from the other side of the world to stay with me; or to simply grab a snack it seems.' He crossed to the kitchen counter, regarding his sister with irritation.

Jessica leaned back, surprised by her brother's tone, and crossed her arms protectively over her chest. Her voice bristled. 'Whatever. I'm wasting away here like a poster girl for famine or Africa or something and you just keep droning on about how I turned up on your doorstep. Like, get over it already.'

Smiling despite himself, he sat down on one of the bar stools lined up beside the counter, preparing himself for another foray into the world of teenagers. 'Why didn't you make yourself something to eat? I mean they do still make their own meals in the US, don't they? It's not got to the stage has it when genetic modification or advanced technology means dishes prepare and serve themselves?'

'Your fridge is full of crap.' Jessica pouted to punctuate her succinct response.

'What are you talking about? I know there is loads of food in the fridge, I only shopped a day or so ago.' Right before I shadowboxed with a mirror, Michael thought darkly as he continued. 'There's plenty of stuff, cheese, meat, there's bread right there on the side. You could have made yourself a mean sandwich, could have made me one too and set it here on the counter for the minute I came out of my shower.' He steepled his fingers as he regarded the empty counter and sighed dramatically. 'But I can see you didn't.'

Jessica opened her mouth to interrupt, but Michael carried on.

'There are ready to eat meals in the freezer. I've got tinned food enough to either sink the *Titanic* or survive the end of shopping civilisation as we know it. There's crisps, popcorn and chocolate, coke, diet coke, juice, beer and wine - not that I expect you to drink either of those last two of course, on account of you being 16 and all.' He paused and smiled at the teenager still leaning against the wall, anticipating a lengthy monologue in reply to his own.

Jessica stared back with a bored expression, yawning expansively. She spent a moment silently regarding her brother, not trusting that his verbal diarrhoea truly had run its course, before announcing simply. 'Your fridge is full of crap.'

'You really are a woman of few words aren't you Jess? But I guess what you mean is that my ample supply of food and drink is not adequate to your culinary needs.' He peered at her suspiciously 'Is this because you're from California?' Finally, the girl's carefully blank face revealed a flicker of a smile. As an older brother Michael was conditioned to spot such a sign of weakness in a younger sibling and homed in on it straight away. 'It is isn't it? Of course, I should have realised. You guys are all health nuts, aren't you? Juicing every foodstuff into finely blended submission, jogging a gazillion miles before and after eating - and possibly also during meals.

'Well, there's some wholemeal bread outside on the bird table, it's a bit stale but I daresay it would be alright in a smoothie with some banana skin and a couple of vitamin C tablets from the bathroom cabinet. What d'ya think?' He grinned at the girl and was rewarded with a full strength smile this time.

'I think you're an arse! Give me some cash and I'll go to the grocery store myself.'

'No, I know you; you'd be straight down to Macdonald's for a quarter-pounder.' Jessica responded with an involuntary shudder before her brother continued.

'Seriously though, I think there's some low-fat cheese style spread in the fridge and a packet of Ryvita. If you've not tried them, you'll soon discover they're like crackers made out of funny tasting cardboard; they're in the cupboard over the sink. My girlfriend leaves them here for when she's on a healthy eating binge. Help yourself, I'm sure she won't mind'

'I didn't know you had a girlfriend, Oh....' Jessica tailed off, looking down at her feet.

'Why 'oh'?' Michael braced himself against the counter.

'Well, someone super posh called while you were in the shower and said they wanted to speak to you, so I asked who they were and they were like 'well I'm Poppy, who are you?' and they sounded kind of confused and angry so I said 'Poppy?' meaning for them to give me a little more detail before I revealed your whereabouts.' Jessica glanced up, instinctively knowing she was in trouble. Michael's face was inscrutable. She shrugged nervously, 'So, well I know I sound a bit paranoid, but you know they could have been debt collectors or, you know, gangsters...'

'You really must stop watching TV.' Michael sighed, 'but go on, what happened?'

'Well, this lady goes 'Poppy, his girlfriend', and I think she was gritting her teeth. And now I was really confused 'coz I didn't think you had a girlfriend.

'You never mentioned one.' She added, glaring at him with a wounded look.

Michael rubbed his face and blew out a long breath. 'We don't share everything, it's not like we're joined at the hip.' he muttered, knowing that they usually were that close, exchanging the minutiae of each other's days. 'Besides' he added 'it's new. We've not been seeing each other for long and I wasn't sure how serious it was going to be, I'm still not sure.'

'Serious enough for her to leave food here it seems.' Jessica shot back, doing an uncanny impression of their mother.

Michael's face grew hot as he blushed. 'I've um...' He paused, flustered. 'We met after the funeral, and, well, it is kind of out of character, so...'

She interrupted. 'You're embarrassed? Cute – but actually I don't care who you're seeing, so long as you're happy.

'Anyway, I said to this Poppy character that she must have a wrong number because you didn't have a girlfriend, and I would know because I was your sister. Then the line went dead, or at least it went quiet for like a minute and I was about to put the phone down when she said 'Well, please tell Michael that I called to arrange to come over tonight but, seeing as I am not his girlfriend, I won't bother.' She said this really cold like and then she hung up.' Jessica took a step towards her brother hands raised in apology and then seemed to think better of it and shrank back against the wall. 'Sorry Mikey, maybe you should give her a call?'

'You think?' He sighed, closing his eyes for a few seconds and biting his bottom lip while another weapons-grade headache exploded in his already frazzled mind. 'It's not your fault Jess, though a bit of guesswork and vagueness on the phone wouldn't have gone a miss.

'In fact, maybe next time the phone rings and I'm not here you should let the answer phone deal with it. It seems to be less interrogatory in my experience.'

He sighed again before continuing. 'Anyway, it seems you may as well eat the food Poppy left.'

Jessica glanced up, abashed, 'I'm sure she'll forgive you in a while.

'And that reminds me, before I had a chance to speak on the phone, before she realised that she wasn't speaking to you, she blurted out something like 'No need to worry about the other night, it was weird, but no worries.' She gave a tentative smile, anxious to avoid annoying her brother further.

'What's that about? She sounded scared.

'And what's with the lack of mirror in the bathroom?'

Michael groaned inwardly as he considered whether or not to tell his sister what had been happening. After a moment he decided that it was best for her to know the full story, best for someone to hear it all. Besides, the longer she stayed at the flat the more likely it was that his nocturnal activities would become obvious. 'It's a long story' he said slowly, 'you may want to have something to eat while you hear it.'

'More secrets?' Jessica shot back, arching an eye brow 'Who are you? And what have you done with my brother?'

Chapter 16

'You are so screwed.' This was Jessica's considered opinion an hour later when her brother had filled her in on the events of the last few days and provided a sketchy description of the history of his sleeping problems.

They were sitting on the sofa in the lounge area of the small flat, bodies angled towards each other and both balancing food on their laps. Jessica had taken advantage of the crackers and soft cheese left by Poppy and had announced grudgingly that they were 'healthy enough'. Michael had a bowl of buttery popcorn, declared to be a rare treat - after Jessica had pursed her lips and slowly shaken her head on reading the nutritional information disclosed by the packet. He had barely touched the snack however and it was now cold, the butter congealed and leaving a greasy sheen on the surface of the bowl.

Michael set the popcorn aside with exaggerated care and turned back to his sister. 'Thank you Jess for those few kind and no doubt carefully chosen words. I feel as if, as ever, you have cut through my complex life and identified the nub of the problem. Perhaps I should stop bothering with professional healthcare and turn my tortured psyche over to you?'

Jessica grinned, rolling her eyes, 'Nah, you couldn't afford my fees, I am American don't forget!'

'How could I ever forget? The accent and attitude alone are all too obvious. Look, maybe we should both sleep on the matter - or in my case not sleep - and return to the issue of just how screwed I am tomorrow morning.'

Jessica nodded, standing to put her plate in the kitchen sink before giving her brother a hug and heading to the spare room.

Chapter 17

Michael had no intention of going to sleep and waking up to some fresh horror. The last two nights had seen an escalation in his activities, with imagined intruders and an unconscious case of self-harm. God alone knew what he would do next. Instead he spent the night in his bedroom in front of his computer, sustained by strong coffee and cold popcorn, scouring the Internet for information about sleeping disorders, or parasomnias. He began with scientific websites, skimming countless articles about normal and abnormal sleeping patterns, the physiological background to sleep, and studies about sleep deprivation.

Knowing the basics of why sleepwalking, technically known as somnambulism happened, Michael was not starting from scratch. He understood from research carried out over the previous fortnight that the disorder was a result of the brain trying to exit from deep sleep straight to being awake rather than through stages one or two of non-Rem or REM sleep. This apparently left the brain 'stuck' between a sleep and wake state. He also understood that stress, depression and a lack of sleep made it more likely to happen. All conditions he knew he had in spades.

What *had* been new information was learning that sleepwalkers had open eyes, and that they retained their motor skills, despite the myth that somnambulists often stumbled and fell. Michael read that sleepwalkers could not recognise faces, so that any people they 'saw' in their sleep were considered to be strangers. At this revelation he determined that he would not share a bed with Poppy until he had a handle on his condition, for fear of attacking her without realising who his victim was.

He moved on to newspaper archives, searching for stories about somnambulists. The first few reports that he came across were light hearted tales of people carrying out mundane tasks in their sleep, getting dressed, making a cup of tea, doing the washing up. Their harmless activities had often become a source of amusement for their families, leading partners or children to take photographs or record video of the family member who had been sleepwalking, pictures and movies that they then sent to their local newspapers or to television stations for a laugh and a quick buck. Had Michael not been suffering from an extreme version of sleepwalking himself he was sure he would have found these reports humorous. A tale about an old woman who had taken her dog for a walk in the middle of the night and woken up to find herself standing in a duck pond at the local park had in fact made him laugh out loud. And the pages on sexsomnia caused him to raise an eyebrow.

But digging deeper he soon found reports that turned his blood to ice.

Stories about tragic accidents befalling sleepwalkers were worrying, tales of people falling downstairs in the middle of the night and breaking an arm, a leg, or worse a neck, but these reports were far from being the most disturbing accounts that he unearthed while trawling the internet.

Seeming to confirm his fears, he found accounts of injuries and even deaths caused by sleepwalkers. In fact, there was a whole host of information about homicidal somnambulism, also known as sleepwalking murder.

The earliest recorded case he came across was from 1846, the so called 'Boston Tragedy'. Michael read how a socialite, Albert Tirrell murdered a prostitute, Maria Bickford, but was acquitted because of the defence of 'sleepwalking'.

Moving forward to accounts from the 20th and 21st centuries, one of the most brutal cases he reviewed was from 1987, the case of Kenneth James Parks. Parks was a married 23-year-old Canadian man with a 5-month-old daughter. He had a very close relationship to his in-laws, with his mother-in-law, Barbara Ann Woods, referring to him as "her gentle giant." The summer before the sleepwalking events, Parks had developed a gambling problem and fallen into deep financial problems - covering his losses with money from his own savings and then from his employers. In March 1987, his embezzling was discovered, and he lost his job. On May 20 of the same year, he went to his first Gamblers Anonymous meeting and made plans to tell his grandmother and in-laws about his gambling and financial difficulties. Early on the morning of May 24, Parks drove 14 miles to the house of his in-laws. He entered their house with a key they had previously given him and used a tire iron to bludgeon his mother-in-law to death. He then turned on his father-in-law, attempting to choke him to death, an attack the man managed to survive. Parks got back in his car and, covered with blood, drove straight to a nearby police station and confessed, turning himself in, stating, "I think I have just killed two people."

Parks' defence was that he was asleep during the entire incident and was not aware of what he was doing. This defence was disputed, even by sleep specialists, however, careful investigation revealed no other explanation. Parks' EEG readings were highly irregular, even for a parasomniac. This scientific evidence, alongside the facts that there was no motive, that he was incredibly consistent each time he gave an account of what he remembered, that the timing of the events fitted perfectly with the story, and that there is no way to falsify EEG results, led to a jury acquitting Parks of the murder of his mother-in-law and the attempted murder of his father-in-law. The Supreme Court of Canada upheld the acquittal in 1992, and the case was the inspiration for the movie 'The Sleepwalking Killing' with Hillary Swank.

Michael also read about the more recent case of Brian Thomas who in 2008 had strangled his 57-year-old wife to death while on holiday in a camper van. Thomas had suffered from sleepwalking since childhood and on a recording of a call to the emergency services was heard saying 'What have I done? I've been trying to wake her. I think I've killed my wife. Oh my God. I thought someone had broken in. I was fighting with those boys, but it was Christine. I must have been dreaming or something. What have I done?' The Thomas' had moved on from a campsite earlier in the day, due to the noise from a group of boys. Brian Thomas was freed in 2009 by a judge who found him not guilty of murder.

Michael ran his hands through his hair, making it stand up in uneven spikes as he contemplated the possible harm that he could cause without being aware of it. His palms were slick with sweat, even though he felt frozen to his core. What scared him the most was that he might have already committed crimes in his sleep, unknowingly and without premeditation. He sought comfort from the fact that he would surely have been caught either at the scene of the crime or at least afterwards, trapped by evidence unwittingly left behind. Unless of course his crimes had remained undiscovered.

Chapter 18

Even as the credits began to roll, the young man was up and out of his seat, leaning down to his date to tell her he would dash out to beat the crowds, hail a cab and then wait for her outside the theatre. The blond woman blushed, caught off guard by the man's gallant nature. She knew she'd have been lucky if her last boyfriend had taken her on a proper date at all, let alone picked her up, paid for everything and got her a taxi to take her home. Stan had only really been interested in one thing and had inevitably gone out to a bar by himself whether he got what he wanted or not. She scowled at the memory and then stood quickly, shuffling along the aisle after her date. The woman had to push past a couple of people who were half out of their seats, eyes glued to the massive screen as the seemingly endless list of best boys, key grips and the like continued scrolling past. Getting their money's worth, the woman thought, not unkindly. It was an activity she herself usually indulged in, prolonging the escapism of a trip to the cinema for as long as possible. On this occasion her recollections of Stan had soured the atmosphere quicker than a one-eyed witch can sour milk, as her mother used to say, and now all the woman wanted was to be wrapped in the warm and protective embrace of her new - and much improved - beau.

Hurrying on, she flung open the doors to the lobby area, almost bowling over a young usher holding a broom. 'Steady on miss, where's the fire?' Blushing for the second time in five minutes, the young woman muttered an apology and then pushed on into the busy entrance hall. 'If it's a rush you're in, best take the side door to your left. Beat the hordes that way miss.' The woman turned to thank the usher, but he'd already gone, swallowed up by the still dark interior of the auditorium.

A short corridor and a heavy fire door led the woman out into an alley, presumably running the length of the old brick building that housed the Empire Theatre, unless she had lost her bearings in her haste to leave her memories behind her in screen 2. 'Which should mean, I need to turn left' the blond spoke softly to herself, popping a piece of popcorn in her mouth as she considered her surroundings. The alley was dimly lit and lined with large dumpsters. Puddles, scraps of rubbish and god-knew what else covered most of the ground, presenting the woman with a treacherous and unsanitary obstacle course between her and the well-lit main road. She couldn't even see the end of the alley because of a large iron fire escape about ten metres to her right. 'This is such a bad idea' she whispered to herself, turning back to re-enter the theatre, and facing the door through which she had exited moments before.

The woman pushed futilely against the metal, even as she visualised herself pushing the door open from inside and remembered that it was a fire exit, and therefore unlikely to be able to be opened from outside. A quick examination of the featureless surface of the door confirmed her fears. Leaving just one option.

The woman turned back to face the alley. The narrow passageway looked as uninviting as before, dark, rubbish strewn and smelling faintly of urine, but, the woman tried to convince herself, it was just an alley, not the bullet strewn fields of a warzone. Still she paused, taking a deep breath, letting it out slowly, quietly, gathering her nerve for the short walk that lay before her. Looking left and right she was unable to see any movement in the alleyway, straining her ears all she could hear was the sound of her own breathing. She began walking to the left.

The blond had walked a little more than five metres before a scream broke through the silence at her back. Spinning towards the sound she almost lost her footing, her heel twisting in a grate in the ground. And then she saw the source of the sound.

A cat, blacker than the night, but glimpsed briefly in the pale-yellow light from the lamp above the doorway. Just a cat, slinking away having realised that the acoustics in the alley were not conducive to its virtuoso singing. The woman's body sagged as she let out a sigh of relief, but as she turned back to face the way she had been walking she immediately noticed that the scene had changed.

Fog had begun to fill the narrow alleyway. Silvery, white, almost luminescent, it was creeping towards her, moving slowly but with purpose, as if in a cheap horror movie from an earlier age. As the mist rolled forwards, the woman took a step back, a move dictated more by instinct than by common sense. She turned again to face the way from which she had come, knowing what she would see. The path she had trodden upon exiting the theatre was already shrouded in mist, even though it had been clear moments before, revealing the black cat that had almost scared her to death. The woman could no longer make out the solid, reassuring shape of the doorway, although a dirty yellow hue to the fog suggested its existence. Or at least the position of the lamp above the portal.

The woman turned a fourth time, taking two hurried steps towards the main road. Towards freedom. The fog continued to roll forwards, filling the alley and chilling the air. But it had not yet reached the woman. An area of perhaps five metres lay untouched, waiting for the tendrils of fog to find it, the woman hurried across this gap, towards the fog.

A brief pause and then she stepped forwards into the fog, determined to rush through it to the safety of the street. The young woman was surprised at the drop in temperature within the fog, amazed at how quickly her clothes became soaked but, shivering, she hurried on. Until a new sound filled the night.

Footsteps, heavy, unrushed, their sound undistorted despite the thick fog. There was one other feature that the woman noticed about the footsteps, they were coming closer. One thought entered the woman's mind 'He wears a trench coat'. And then she turned, running blindly through the fog, not stopping until she reached the doorway, hammering with her fists upon the cold hard metal, screaming for help even as her voice was swallowed up by the fog.

She heard the footsteps, immediately behind her, felt his breath on her hair. And as she turned, spellbound, unable to resist him the fog solidified, wrapping around her body like a shroud. And...

Jess dropped the book she was reading and let out a squeal of shock as she heard a sound in the hall outside her room. She had been tired when she'd gone to bed, snoozing for a few hours, but jet lag had foiled any attempt at sleeping through the night, so instead she'd been reading the trashy paperback that she had picked up in the airport in California. She sat stock still in bed for a few seconds before chastising herself. 'Of course, there are sounds.' She whispered. 'Michael's here.' She shook her head and got out of bed, padding across the carpet to the door, intending to go to the bathroom and then maybe grab a snack.

The sound of a door opening shocked Michael awake. It took him a second to realise that he was standing in the hallway of his flat, a step away from his spare room, where Jess was staying. He took a sideways step and slipped into the lounge, not wanting to scare his sister on her first night in a strange place. He froze just inside the doorway as Jess, seemingly half asleep and oblivious to his presence, shuffled past to the bathroom.

Letting out a sigh of relief he brought his right arm up to check the time, three am. As he slowly calmed down, he realised that he was holding something in his left hand, guess I'm still holding my pen he thought as he looked down. 'Oh shit.' He breathed almost silently, taking in the sight of a 10-inch carving knife held tight within his grip.

Chapter 19

Michael had not slept since waking in front of the door to his spare bedroom at 3am and had left the flat soon afterwards, keen to put some distance between himself and his sister. He'd left a note for Jessica explaining that something had come up and that he'd be out all day, a lame explanation for his absence but the only one he was willing to give.

He hoped to avoid telling Jessica about his latest somnambulistic activities. He did not want to scare her to death, but he did know that he needed to talk to somebody about what was happening – and fast. The increase in frequency – one a night for the last three nights – and escalation in intensity of the incidents was worrying, to put it mildly. The fact that he was no longer living alone, was now in danger of hurting someone else, made him even more determined to find a solution.

He had called Elizabeth at 8.30am, planning to leave a message on her phone but surprised when she had answered on the third ring. Without preamble he had asked, or rather begged, the psychologist to meet him to discuss his case further. Perhaps it was the desperation in his voice; possibly it was professional curiosity in his case, either way she agreed to meet him at short notice.

'So, is he hot? Is it a hot date you've got lined up huh?'

'What?' Elizabeth paused, her head in a filing cabinet drawer as she replayed James's sudden question in her mind 'I mean, what?'

'You're blowing off the chance of joining me for cardboard sandwiches and weak swill masquerading as coffee in the hospital canteen. Tell me it's for a hot date and not just to do some work?' James was waving a Post-it in the air in front of her face.

'Oh,' Elizabeth looked from the note to James's face, checking if he was annoyed or just teasing her. She had left the note on his desk a few minutes before he came in to the room, in case she had not seen him before they were due to meet for lunch.

'I mean, I struggled to read the note at first – you have such a doctor's scrawl – and then I spent a minute or two trying to comprehend what it meant. But I *think* what you are doing is blowing me off, am I right?' He was wiggling his eyebrows and grinning as he spoke, determined to make his colleague squirm a little and making it hard for her to get a word in.

She plucked the note off his finger, suddenly uncertain as to whether her note had included any ambiguity. The small square of fluorescent yellow paper contained just eight printed words:

SORRY GOT TO CANCEL LUNCH, WILL REARRANGE. ELIZABETH.

'Would a picture have helped you Dr Booker?' She reached past him to her desk, picked up her pad of Post-its and drew a quick sketch of a sandwich and a drink. Next, she put a cross through the picture and drew an unhappy face next to it. Finally, she pulled off the note and slapped it down on James' desk. 'Better?'

He smiled, feeling relaxed as he sat on the edge of Elizabeth's desk. He was enjoying their banter, which was starting to feel a little like flirting as he sensed he was getting closer to becoming friends with his colleague. A move that he assumed would be a prelude to a date. 'That's much better. You learn fast partner. Still, shame about lunch, what's up?'

'Well, you know Wednesday mornings are always manic? Trying to recruit new subjects, encourage old ones to stay in the study and actually give us some data to research, yadda yadda.'

'Yes, so you *are* brushing our date off to do more work. Shame on you Dr Byfield!' James was starting to look slightly annoyed.

'Well, yes I am.' She blushed, finding references to their lunch date as being a 'date date' very uncomfortable. While James was clearly attracted to her she absolutely did not feel the same way. In fact, the

100

rushed phone call from Michael Manners asking for another meeting had been a relief, if a little unorthodox, offering as it did an opportunity to cancel lunch.

'But it *is* because I am following up on a potential subject whose case appears to be really interesting, and who clearly needs help.' She saw James's mouth open and for the first time managed to interrupt him before he could speak. 'And yes, he'll definitely give us some useful data for the Portable EEG machine as well.'

'Well that's something at least.' James grumbled as he pouted, reminding her of a petulant child. 'And it's 'Peggy'. You know all inventions need a cool name?' Elizabeth frowned, genuinely unsure how he had managed to qualify as a doctor. 'OK, sure Peggy.... that's.... cool.'

Chapter 20

'Have you eaten anything today?' Elizabeth sat opposite Michael, sipping a latte and watching with a look of concern as he drained his large take away coffee cup.

'No, I don't think I have to be completely honest.' He smiled sheepishly, his stomach gurgling as if to confirm his answer.

She smiled back uncertainly 'and I know it makes me sound like your mum, but how many coffees have you had today?'

'Three, maybe four cups. And believe me, you do not sound like my mum.'

Elizabeth nodded slightly, storing away his last comment for a future line of inquiry. 'And I'm sure you know that caffeine stimulates the brain and prevents people from getting to sleep?'

Michael's head bobbed rapidly, 'Yes, yes I know. But I didn't sleep well last night, so I need the coffee today.' He shrugged, staring across the table, daring her to pass judgement on his habit.

She frowned, biting the inside of her lip as she considered his attitude. There was something about him, some edge, which made her feel more than a little uncomfortable. Perhaps it was the knowledge that he was dating someone she knew, not that Poppy was a close friend. They had not spoken since Poppy had passed on Elizabeth's details to Michael; nevertheless, the fact that the two women had a personal relationship had blurred the usual patient-therapist boundaries. Elizabeth considered the feeling that Michael was engendering in her a little further. It wasn't that she felt threatened or endangered around him, but she did sense that he could be a danger to himself, despite his adamant response when she had asked him that very question the previous day. His body was slumping, and his eyes were wild as waves of desperation emanated from him.

She had been surprised when he'd called to make a second appointment. The fact that he had stormed out of their first session had seemed to send a clear message. This was not someone who was likely to engage in therapy. She had been saddened by this because he so obviously needed help, at least assuming the reasons given for his injuries were to be believed.

'OK, so you like your coffee, but you know it disturbs your sleep.

'I'm going to go out on a limb here and say that you don't want help to try and sleep.' She smiled, hoping to reassure him that her questioning would not be as searching as in their previous session.

'Actually, I would love to be able to sleep, sleep would be awesome, but where I really need help is to stop me dreaming.' He learned back in his chair, breaking eye contact as if embarrassed by this admission.

'So anyway, tell me more about your research. I cut you off yesterday. Is the aim to get people to relax, drink hot milk before going to bed, that sort of stuff? So that they can sleep more easily?'

Elizabeth smile stiffened as she forced herself to answer politely despite the sarcastic tone that Michael had used, and the fact that she had tried to give him an overview of the study the previous day. 'Sleep hygiene? Yes, that is part of it. Sometimes I just get people to keep a diary of their sleeping habits and then I make suggestions about how they could do things differently in order to sleep more easily.

'As I said yesterday, we also video participants' nocturnal activities at the hospital, monitoring brain waves and other vital signs in order to help us – the medical profession – learn more about the process of sleeping. That is information that can then help subjects to sleep better.'

'So, do you want to watch me sleep?' He regretted the words the moment they left his lips and also the slightly creepy tone with which he had spoken. 'God, I'm sorry, I am just so stressed out by this nightmare situation, pun absolutely intended. Seriously I have not slept properly for days.'

Elizabeth was torn between a desire to treat Michael and discomfort at the way he had spoken to her. Her natural instinct to help, to heal, won through. 'Yes, bluntly we do want to watch you sleep. But I also need to know more about the history of your sleeping problems, what might be triggering them. We started to talk about that yesterday, and that's a big part of what I do because it is not enough just to teach people better sleeping habits.

'Often habits are bad because of stress or trauma, either current or past. If those issues are not discussed and resolved – if they can be resolved or perhaps simply acknowledged if they cannot be resolved - if those issues are not at least investigated, then it is impossible to break the sleeping habits that are causing problems. At least not in the long term.' Elizabeth paused; she felt as if she was rambling and looked at Michael, checking if he was still listening.

'So, let's talk a little more about the problem itself. You mentioned a desire to sleep, but not to dream?'

'Ah doctor, very Shakespearian. But yes, I've always had very vivid dreams, even as a child. My parents used to think I was afraid of the dark because of how often I used to call out in the night.' Michael took a breath, feeling vulnerable as he talked about his childhood. He smiled shyly at Elizabeth.

'But it's not that I am scared of the dark, not at all. Now I lie awake at night becoming increasingly anxious that I will dream again: and that that might lead to another dreamwalk. It's not something that has happened constantly of course, and I think that sometimes sleeping tablets do help. So, the prescription for Restoril, or whatever you guys call it over here, that I hope you will give me could form a line of defence – as could any pills to combat anxiety of course. But I don't want to be on drugs for the rest of my life.' He shook his head to emphasise his point, before picking up his cup, putting it straight back down when he realised it was empty. 'Do you know what I mean?'

Wow, you really are strung out, Elizabeth kept this thought to herself as she nodded her agreement, 'No, of course you don't want to have to take medication for life if you can avoid it, and I would consider myself a pretty poor psychologist if a drug-induced stupor was the best I could offer.

'There are certainly medications that can help sleep, perhaps something less likely to cause dependency than temazepam, or Restoril as you know it. And of course, I'll discuss these with your GP; however, as a psychologist as opposed to a psychiatrist, I cannot actually prescribe medications myself.' Michael sighed, exasperated, and she continued swiftly.

'But a prescription via your GP will be easy to arrange. In the meantime, what do you mean by 'dreamwalk'?'

Michael shrugged, running his hand through his unruly hair before answering. 'Well, as I understand it sleepwalkers don't generally realise they are moving about, whereas I feel like I am awake. I am aware that I am moving around. It's like I'm acting out my dreams, except instead of dreaming about swimming and actually going to the sea I do the closest, easiest equivalent and jump in the bath'.

'Or fight intruders, like you said yesterday?' She interjected. 'OK, dreamwalking seems like as good a name as any for what you're experiencing. So, what happens when you start to feel anxious that you're going to have another incident?' She looked directly at her patient as she spoke, pleased to note that he was now making good eye contact, albeit with eyes made jittery by the quantity of caffeine that he had consumed.

Now he did glance away, gathering his thoughts as he stared out of the window at a view of cars lined up in tight rows across the car park. He turned back to her, revealing a face etched with pain and anguish. He cleared his throat and ran his hand through his hair again, before responding to the question. 'Well, once I start to get anxious, I become wide awake, so I have been trying to distract myself by reading, or watching television, or anything really. Trouble is what I am reading and watching inevitably turns to sleeping disorders – of which there is a lot of material on the web.... I bet that's a real bane for you guys isn't it? Armchair psychologists? So yeah, I try to analyse the situation, in the hope that I can find the cause, but I just end up more tightly wound up and anxious, thinking I'm going crazy.'

He broke off again, slumping back in his chair and closing his eyes. Elizabeth quickly fired another question at him, sensing that he needed encouragement to tell his distressing and, she imagined, embarrassing story. 'But if you do manage to distract yourself rather than get more wound up, does that work? And yes, self-diagnosis by Google is not the most useful thing the web has brought us!' She finished with a wry smile.

'If I can distract myself, often with dross on the television, of which there is also a tonne available, then I do become sleepy.' He acknowledged, leaning forwards again and gripping the edge of the table between them. 'But as soon as I turn off the light and lie down the anxiety hits again, only by then I'm too far gone to come fully awake.' His speech, still soft but full of tremors, came faster as he continued. 'And then sleep begins to creep into my mind, it's like a physical presence, a black cloud moving across my vision and as my eyes begin to close, I try to fight it. I don't want to sleep, I'm scared to sleep, to dream, but my body always betrays me and eventually the darkness wins.' He crumpled back in the chair, covering his face with shaking hands.

Chapter 21

Wow, where did that strung-out but soulful monologue come from? Elizabeth glanced at the coffee cup, explanation all by itself for the 'strung-out'. She waited a few minutes, sitting in silence so he could compose himself before continuing. She considered how remarkably brave he was, admitting his problem so quickly and openly. But she also thought how vulnerable and desperate he seemed, and her heart went out to him.

'Have you ever talked to anyone else about your sleeping problems?'

'Recently? No. Well, I have spoken to Poppy about it, couldn't avoid that after she saw the aftermath of the 'burglary'; and I've talked to Russell, my best friend, because I was so freaked out.

'I've also seen doctors in the past to get stronger sleeping tablets. I've never suffered such extreme or such continuous problems as are happening now, so one short prescription has been enough, and I guess they've not considered it necessary for me to be referred for talking therapy.'

He barely kept the scorn out of his voice as he said, 'talking therapy' and she was surprised he avoided placing air quotes around the words. Clearly, he would rather be taking the pharmacological route and she suspected that he genuinely believed that people who needed to see psychologists were – to use his own word – 'crazy'.

She noticed that he had also rounded his shoulders, slumping further into his chair as if he wanted to escape her questions, a defensive posture that might mean he thought that she was implying he was crazy and should have sought therapy years ago when the problems started. She chose her next words carefully, intending to clarify her question and to encourage him to lower his defences.

'Have you ever met with a 'talking therapy' specialist, a psychologist?' She did use air quotes as she repeated Michael's own words. 'Will you talk further to me?'

His face fell. He tried to mask it with a grin, but she could read disappointment in his eyes and the reason was obvious. He had been hoping for a miracle cure, and more importantly one that would be instantaneous, a magic bullet.

'Well, yes, I have had a course of talking therapy, when I was thirteen and we'd just moved to the U.S. This was with a psychiatrist, and was intense, to say the least. But yes, I will talk to you. What do you want to know? We talked about my background yesterday, so what else is there to say?' He shrugged, sitting forward.

'Psychiatry is a very different field to psychology in many ways, and certainly practices in America can be different to those here. So, what do you mean when you say it was intense?' Elizabeth leaned back, re-establishing the gap between them.

'Well, I saw this guy weekly for about six months, and he used a whole bunch of approaches with me. You know, like hypnosis, meditative breathing, ink blots, the works. In the end he just gave me some medicine, zopiclone that time – the medical equivalent of saying "meh" - and told my mother that I would grow out of it. Now that, that definitive conclusion, she was relieved to hear, given the cost of medical care in the U.S. 'And I did grow out of it, at least on and off, for two decades.' He grimaced, though at the mention of his mother or the psychiatrist she could not be sure.

'Ok, well that is intense. It also sounds like enough to put you off therapists for life.
'I am planning to use a more delicate, nuanced approach however.' Elizabeth smiled, again hoping to reassure and to encourage him to keep talking. At the same time, she was thinking that what he had described seemed a heavy-handed response to the impact of divorce, wondering if the disturbed sleep had been just one of the abnormal behaviours exhibited by the thirteen-year-old.

'So, at the same time as this your parents divorced, and you lived with your mother? What was that like? Are you close to her?'

Michael squirmed, fidgeting in his seat, still uncomfortable to be talking about his family and specifically about his mother. 'Well, I lived at home until about six months ago. I could afford to move out, but I needed to, um, help out.'

Which means what? Elizabeth thought; and also, that answer didn't actually tell me about your mother. She pursed her lips, considering a different approach.

'What about your father? I know you said that he passed away very recently, and that may have triggered the recent episodes of sleep, or rather dream, walking. What was your relationship with him like?'

'Dad was only 60 when he died, that's not old really is it? But I think he may have been relieved when he died; he wasn't happy, he was driven by work, but he wasn't alive, not really, since Benjamin.

'As for my relationship with him, well I haven't lived with him for twenty years and only saw him a handful of times during that period so I don't suppose that you would have called us close.

'But I guess you always have that invisible, unconditional bond to your parents. Right?'

Elizabeth considered her own parents, both dead by the time she was eight, and almost shook her head in disagreement. She chose her next question after some deliberation, forcing herself to avoid asking what he had meant by 'since Benjamin', knowing that he was reluctant to talk about his brother for some reason. 'How did your mother react to your father's death?'

Michael laughed, a hollow sound devoid of humour 'I think she saw it as a very minor inconvenience, she had to deal with passing the news on to me, but really it had no impact on her life. She's got Brett and Jessica.'

Elizabeth flicked through her notes confused, 'Who are Brett and Jessica?'

'Didn't I mention them?' Michael looked confused himself and frustrated to have to back track. He answered rapidly and without care.
'When mum uprooted me and we moved to the US she hooked up with some cowboy guy and they had a daughter, Jessica, she's 16.'

OK thought Elizabeth, formulating quickly as she sipped her coffee. So, parents get divorced for some reason and that triggers Michael's sleeping disorder, then his life is messed up for a few year's while mum carves out a new life with her cowboy, so that prolongs the disturbances, then Dad dies and that brings all the issues to the surface.... makes sense, sort of.

She was still surprised by the severity of his symptoms however, more extreme than mere nightmares or sleepwalking, and she wanted him to keep a sleep diary for a few weeks to enable her to monitor his condition more closely. She also wanted to know more about the circumstances surrounding his parents' divorce, understand more about his maternal relationship, and that with his sister, and to find out if his brother had been affected by the separation. She glanced at her watch, 1.40pm, damn she thought, I've got to wrap this up. She brushed her hair behind her ear, smiling at Michael.

'I'm sorry Michael, but we have to finish soon, I've got another client in 5 minutes. Listen, I want to talk to you more about your family next time we meet, especially your brother.' She paused, studying the reaction caused by the mere mention of his brother. A look of anger passed across his face.

'Can you meet me here again in a couple of days?' She consulted her diary. '4pm Friday?'

Michael nodded blankly, scratching his chin, already checking out of the conversation.

'In the meantime, I'd like you to start keeping a sleep diary.... just in case you lay off the caffeine long enough to let yourself sleep.' She paused, grinning, hoping he had taken the comment in good humour. He merely gave a curt nod of agreement.

'I also think that you should stay at a friend's house for a few days. Having a change of scenery may help you break the habit of your disorder, at least temporarily. More importantly it will give you security in case you hurt yourself in the night again.' She smiled, standing to signal the end of the session.

'Thanks doc, I'll maybe do that. I'm not living by myself at the minute though.'

'Ah, of course, Poppy.'

Michael blushed, for some reason embarrassed, and shook his head. 'No, actually we're…. on a break I guess you could say. It's actually my sister, Jessica, who is staying with me at the moment.'

He stood as well, considering what she had said and the fact that he could protect Jessica as well as himself by moving in with friends.

Chapter 22

'Good afternoon Elizabeth. How's your week going?' Professor Rosenthal asked politely.

Elizabeth smiled at the older woman. A psychologist for almost thirty years and one of the most respected and eminent professionals in her field, Maggie Rosenthal was unlike any supervisor she had ever had. For a start off Maggie was friendly, without being intrusive, and – more important – she actually valued Elizabeth's opinions and insights, rather than riding roughshod over them and telling the younger psychologist what to do.

Elizabeth answered with a laugh. 'It's been a busy week, and its only Wednesday! I do have one client I would like to talk to you about. He's new and his case is unusual.'

Her supervisor leant forward, immediately interested. 'OK, my curiosity is well and truly piqued, do we need to talk about anyone else today or can we spend the whole time on this one person?'

Elizabeth smiled, certain that she was about to spend a very profitable hour discussing Michael Manners.

Returning to her office an hour and a half later Elizabeth was relieved that she had the rest of the afternoon free in order to process the lengthy discussion that she had just had with Professor Rosenthal. Having listened to a summary of Elizabeth's two sessions with Michael, Maggie had then suggested some theories and provided information about her own cases. This had led to a closer examination of his history, searching for clues as to which, if any, of the theories fitted his case. Both women agreed that there was likely to be some event, either the cause of, or in the immediate aftermath of Michael's parents separating that lay at the heart of his current problems. Possibly something had happened to the teenager that had triggered a specific behaviour, a pattern that repeated periodically and that had resurfaced as a result of the death of his father. One thing was certain, Elizabeth was going to have to pry further into areas of his life that Michael did not want to discuss.

Chapter 23

'So, here we are' Michael smiled weakly at his sister, stopping short of clasping her hand. The gesture would have been tender, supportive and probably one that Jessica would have appreciated. He figured that she must be nervous about meeting complete strangers having been told only that they had to move out of the apartment for a day or so. The only problem with the gesture was that it would have been for him, not for his little sister.

It was just before six o'clock when they arrived at Russell and Rosie's picturesque cottage in Sonning, a few miles from Michael's flat in Reading but with an abundance of green space that meant it felt like it was a world away from the urban sprawl. Michael stood for a few minutes gazing at the house, breathing in the heady aroma from the roses that lined the path leading to the late 19th century building.

The flowers were enjoying a brief respite from the rain that had been falling almost continuously for the past twenty-four hours, taking the opportunity to show off their ruby red beauty in the early evening sunshine. Michael was stuck by the resilience of the flowers, which despite their delicate appearance had refused to be bowed by the heavy downpour that had flattened most of the other plants in the garden. Staring at them he wondered if he could take comfort from the roses' spirit or see it as a sign that he himself would ride out his personal storm with only a few bruises but with his soul intact. Shifting his gaze from the flowerbeds to the sky however he noticed dark clouds gathering on the horizon. He took this to be a more likely portent of things to come and gathered their bags and hurried up the path towards the cottage with Jessica in tow, as the first heavy drops of rain began to fall.

The thought of seeing Rosie for the first time in years should have been pleasurable, a source of happiness. Rosie, Michael and Russell had met on their first day in primary school, had played together in and out of classes, and Michael had had a crush on the spirited redhead by the time they had left for secondary school. The two had actually gone on a couple of dates, a trip to the park and another to the cinema in the intervening summer holidays. They had even kissed; a hurried action while waiting for their parents to pick them up after the cinema. They had both turned away in disgust after their lips had touched, collapsing in giggles and declaring that it felt like kissing a brother or sister. Rosie and Russell had started dating a few years later.

After Michael had moved to the U.S he had stayed in contact with his friends, at first just over the phone and through emails, and then via Skype and Facetime. He'd returned to Scotland a couple of times, including for his friends' wedding; and Russell and Rosie had been out to California on one occasion, meeting Michael in Disneyland. The three had remained as 'thick as thieves' as their class teacher had once described them, despite the geographical distance between them.

Now though he felt shame instead of pleasure at the thought of the reunion. He was embarrassed that Rosie would be seeing him in such a desperate state. He could hide his bandages, stifle his yawns and make nice, if meaningless, conversation, but he knew that she would see through his act in an instant. One look into his bloodshot, shadowed eyes and she would see he was hurting, she had after all seen it once before.

Michael hesitated, standing in the rain, hand poised to ring the doorbell. He suddenly wondered if his decision to call Russell and Rosie and ask if they could accommodate a couple of guests at short notice had been the right one. Perhaps, he thought, I should just leave Jess here for a few days so that she at least is safe. Michael knew he could stay in his own place, in self-imposed solitary confinement until either Elizabeth could find a solution to his disorder or.... His thoughts trailed off, unwilling to finish the sentence in his mind.

Jessica reached past him to ring the doorbell, seeming to sense his discomfort and taking his left hand in hers as she stepped back from the door. She squeezed tightly her fingers warm around his cold hand. 'It's the right decision.' She spoke, reassuring, 'I always wanted to meet these guys; you speak about them all the time.'

She smiled up at him, 'I want to hear all the gossip about you running naked and wild on the Scottish moors. But hey, don't cry about it.'

Michael wiped his bandaged hand roughly across his face, turning away slightly to hide the silent tears.

The door opened a few seconds later, revealing a woman only slightly taller than Jessica, casually dressed in jeans and a sweatshirt. She smiled broadly, a grin framed by twinkling green eyes and a mass of auburn curls, barely restrained in a ponytail. Rosie's face fell however when she saw the look on Michael's face, the haunted expression in his eyes, and she reached out a hand to him as if trying to save a drowning man. He brushed the hand aside, almost knocking his host down as he passed her with a mumbled greeting. Rosie opened her mouth to call out, almost turned to follow him before noticing Jessica. She smiled and beckoned to the girl. Jessica had shrunk back and was standing to one side of the door, arms wrapped around her body in a defensive pose that Rosie, daughter of an oppressive father and a timid mother, knew only too well. Rosie opened her arms to the girl, stepping forward to hug her. 'Jessica, it is so nice to finally meet you, come inside out of that rain.'

Chapter 24

Michael sat with his friends and told Rosie about his nocturnal swim in the bath in California, and then his fight with a bathroom cabinet. He rushed through the details of these events, knowing that Russell would have told his wife about the two men's conversation in the pub. He took more time to fill his friends in on what had been happening since, starting with a hurried account of the dream in which he'd carved up his own arm. He then lowered his voice to a whisper, checking that Jessica was not listening, as he recounted his last episode of dreamwalking, how he had woken outside his spare room, carving knife in hand, something he had not told anyone else.

Michael went on to describe his two appointments with Elizabeth Byfield. He originally intended to omit the fact that he had almost stormed out of their second session, a few short hours ago, having bailed on the psychologist the previous day. He was acutely embarrassed about his behaviour, however he found himself telling his friends everything about the encounter, including his childish reaction to Elizabeth's questions.

In part Michael was dismayed by his friends' ability to create an environment that elicited complete honesty; nevertheless, he felt the burden of his problems sit a little lighter on his shoulders once he had finished telling his unsettling tales. He was relieved that his two long standing friends knew so much about him, everything about his past, meaning he didn't need to provide answers to the questions that Elizabeth had asked and that he had refused to answer. Their shared childhood also meant he did not have to defend this refusal.

'So, do you have any theories about what's behind the sleepwalking?' Rosie spoke softly, reaching forward to take Michael's left hand across the table as if she wanted to anchor him to the difficult conservation.

'I did start a list actually, a bit Sherlock Holmes of me I know, but...' Michael took a folded sheet of A4 paper out of the back pocket of his jeans as he spoke, smoothing it open on the table.

Possible explanations
Imagination
Stress
Brain tumour
Psychotic breakdown
Aliens

'Let me get this straight' Russell paused to take a gulp of tea. 'These five ideas represent your entire thought process about why you have been sleepwalking and sleep self-harming? Less Holmes mate, more Inspector Clouseau. It's a good job you're pretty.'

'Yes, those are my theories.' Michael answered defiantly, his voice strong, almost aggressive in defence of his list. After a minute he started to shift uneasily in his seat as his friends stared at him in silence.

'OK.' Rosie leaned forwards as she spoke. 'Give me your hand...your right hand.'

Michael slowly held out his hand, watching with fascination, wondering if his friend was going to hold it in order to channel psychic forces to either divine an explanation for his current somnambulism, or to simply banish whatever evil spirits were causing his problems. He smiled at this ridiculous thought, berating himself for watching too much Living TV in the middle of the night.

Rosie gently took his hand and begun to unwrap the bandages covering his lower arm, meaning to reveal the wounds he had inflicted on himself two nights ago. She only got as far as unpicking the tape holding the fabric in place before Michael pulled back his arm.

'What, don't you believe me?' Michael looked hurt as he considered his friend opposite him.

'Quite the contrary my love. Don't *you* believe you?' Rosie tilted her head to the side.

'Of course I believe me. I have the scars and pain to prove it.'

'Well, then I – we – believe you' Rosie gestured towards Russell as she continued speaking.
'So, you can cross "imagination" off your list. What's next?'

Michael leaned back smiling, grateful for the no-nonsense approach of his one-time girlfriend. He read aloud the next item on the list. 'Stress.'

'So, what's stressing you anyway? Besides your nocturnal activities that is.' Russell leant forward, as he re-joined the conversation, studying his friend intensely.

'Um, let me see.... stressful things typically include the death of a family member or close friend, moving house, changing circumstances at work, or the addition of a new family member......so I guess I've got the set!' Michael glanced at Jessica as he finished speaking, relieved to see that she was still preoccupied with a magazine and apparently ignoring the discussion.

'True.' Russell paused, knowing his next words would hurt his friend and could cause him to either storm away from the table or clam up. 'And we all know that you've been through some of that before, and we know how that turned out.' Russell's eyes were suddenly filled with tears, mirrors reflecting the pain that Michael fought to hide, unable as he was to tolerate the thoughts and feelings conjured by the nightmare incident to which Russell was referring. 'So, I guess we should underline stress on your list?'

'Guess so.' Michael's voice had a cold, hard edge to it, making it clear that he would not discuss the subject any further. His body had stiffened as soon as Russell had made reference to the past, and now it was with apparent difficulty that he picked the list up off the table and read the next item. 'Brain Tumour.'

Russell and Rosie were both well aware of the meaning behind the tone and body language that Michael was using and had never heard the words *Brain Tumour* spoken with more relief. Nevertheless, Russell was determined to avoid changing the subject quite yet. 'So, perhaps the cause of your broken sleep, and knackered hand, is stress, but not just current stress? Maybe you should keep talking to Dr Byfield?'

'I thought we moved on to tumours? And besides, I am going to keep talking to her.' Michael whined, feeling betrayed and hounded.

'Firstly, you moved on to tumours, not me, I was still on stress. Secondly, the good doctor could probably arrange a brain scan to check for a tumour; and tell you if you are psychotic at the same time as talking about your stress. You could kill three birds with one stone and half your list in one session. So, what's she like this psychologist? Is she pretty?'

Michael sat in silence for a few minutes, mulling over his friend's words. 'It always pains me to say it, but I think you might have a point. I've already been trying sleeping tablets and that hasn't helped, so other medication would probably be a waste of time. Plus, Elizabeth is studying sleeping disorders, specifically sleepwalking, so is somewhat of an expert.

'And I do like the idea of dealing with three theories at once; it appeals to the multi-tasker in me. And in answer to your last question, I've not been paying attention to her appearance.'

'Elizabeth is it? Not Dr Byfield? Tell us more about what you've not noticed about her?' Russell smirked, before his wife interrupted.

'So, what does that leave on your list?' Rosie looked between the two men as she spoke, by turns amused and exasperated at their banter.

'Aliens, as in little green men hooking into my brain and making me do things.... hmm, guess that's a little harder to tackle without Mulder and Scully.' Michael sighed, crumpling the sheet of paper.

Chapter 25

Jessica sat in the corner of the room, curled up in an armchair flicking through a fashion magazine she'd found on a coffee table in the cosy nook she'd settled into while Michael and his friends had sat at the table. She glanced up from time to time, checking on her brother to make sure that he was holding it together – letting him know that she was there for him. After a few hours there was a cry from upstairs and Jessica nearly jumped out of her skin, dropping the magazine and remaining in her seat only through sheer willpower. No-one else reacted to the noise, looking over at her as if they thought she'd gone crazy. The noise came again, high-pitched but quiet, and this time Rosie stood and went upstairs, returning a moment later with a baby wrapped in a soft, yellow blanket.

'Jessica, meet Donny.' Rosie approached the girl and lowered the baby so that she could see his face.

'Oh, hi Donny,' Jessica whispered, glaring at her brother. 'I didn't know you'd been born.'

Russell chuckled, 'Michael, what are you like? Clearly a lot on your mind recently!'

Michael shrugged sheepishly, 'Sorry Jess, he's only a few weeks old and, um I guess with everything going on I forgot to mention him. No more secret babies though.'

The appearance of Donny broke up the sombre mood and while Rosie nursed the baby Russell announced that he was going to sort dinner, disappearing into the kitchen. Michael looked over at Jessica, hoping to repair the damage he'd caused. His sister's face was back in a magazine, studiously ignoring him but clearly not reading as she just flicked through the pages.

'Look, Jess,' Michael began in a conciliatory tone as he joined his sister in the nook, 'You knew Rosie was pregnant, and you know I'm crap with sharing news and that we haven't seen each other since I moved out and well....' He lowered his voice 'to be honest I'd forgotten about the baby too until it cried.'

Jessica couldn't help herself, bursting out laughing 'Well, you'd better not be his godfather, that's all I say.'

Michael put his face in his hands, moaning softly.

'Oh, Michael really, come on big brother!'

The conversation was kept light over dinner by unspoken agreement, as Jessica chatted to Michael's friends about their lives and told them about herself. Russell had whipped up a Chinese meal from scratch, with sweet and sour chicken, beef with cashew nuts and prawns with mushrooms, all served with a huge pile of egg fried rice. Rosie had baked a chocolate cake earlier, gooey, rich and served with plenty of fresh cream.

Clearing the dishes after they'd all declared that one more mouthful would kill them, Michael walked in on his friends having a hushed conversation in the kitchen, a conversation that they terminated with a guilty silence as soon as they noticed him.

'Look guys, do you want me to leave? I would feel uncomfortable about me sleeping here if I was you.' Michael imagined that his friends were anxious about the idea of him sleepwalking around their house all night. He also did not blame them if this was how they felt, particularly with Donny in the house. In fact, he considered that he would have found it bizarre and a little offensive if they had been unconcerned about the seriousness of his problems.

'No, no, it's fine.' Rosie and Russell spoke at the same time as each other, smiling broadly at their friend.

'Come on.' Rosie stepped forward with her arms outstretched. 'Hand over those plates.'

Russell gave his wife a quick squeeze on the shoulder before walking past Michael towards the door. 'Come on Mikey, let's set up the bedrooms.'

Once upstairs in the spare bedroom Michael voiced his fears again. 'Look, Russ, if you are worried – and like I say I would be – we can rig up some early warning system to let you know I am out of bed.'

Russell nodded slowly. 'Alright mate, if that helps you feel better, let's do that.'

The two worked swiftly to set up a rudimentary alarm system. These measures consisted of stretching fishing line across the guest bedroom doorway as a trip wire and attaching it to Russell's heavy tool box balanced on a stool. The tools would fall to the floor in the event of Michael pushing on the line. The success of the early warning system hinged on the assumption that Michael would walk over the fishing line if he was awake but through it if he was sleepwalking. There was of course the risk that he would trip the wire accidentally whilst going to the bathroom in the middle of the night but there was a general agreement that being woken unnecessarily was a better prospect than waking to find that the house, or indeed Michael himself, had been trashed.

Russell and Rosie had moved Donny's cot into their room, putting Jessica in the baby's room on a blow-up mattress, and they had also conceded to Michael's request that they lock themselves in their bedroom overnight. As a final precaution Jessica's room had been secured by the old school technique of wedging a chair firmly under the door handle.

Michael spent the first fifteen minutes after he had gone to bed tossing and turning in an attempt to find a comfortable sleeping position on a mattress that felt as if it was packed full of potatoes. His wakefulness, however, was only partly due to his friends' torturous guest bed.

His mind was in overdrive as he tried to figure out the cause of and most importantly the solution to, his sleeping problems. He was also finding it far too easy to imagine the damage that he could cause if he had another episode of sleepwalking. It was one thing to put himself at risk by daring to go to sleep and exposing himself to his subconscious mind. It was quite a different matter to put his sister, two best friends and their baby in danger of meeting his Hyde-side in the dead of night. In fact, he was beginning to regret taking Elizabeth's advice of moving in with friends.

Lying in their guest bed thinking about the trip wire and locked doors and more specifically the problems that necessitated them made it very hard to put into practice the relaxation techniques prescribed by his therapist. Turning off the bedside lamp at 10.30pm Michael thought it incredibly unlikely that he would be asleep before midnight. He doubted he would sleep at all.

One aspect of his current situation was calming however, Elizabeth. In spite of the fact that Michael was still holding back a lot of information from her, and that their last meeting had ended abruptly, he found himself thinking about the psychologist with increasing frequency. She was, or at least appeared to be, a kind and an intelligent woman, someone that he thought could be a good friend. In different circumstances. Despite insisting to Russell that he had no idea whether she was pretty, that he hadn't even registered her face, he conjured up her image with ease: She was a striking woman; tall, athletic, brunette and with an attractive 'pixie' face. Her professional manner, and his own reticence, made anything other than a therapeutic relationship highly unlikely; however, the doctor's looks and personality were certainly a large incentive for him to give 'talking therapy' a chance and to continue to engage with her research study.

He found that the more he imagined meeting her again the less anxious he became. Soon he was on the verge of sleep, his body exhausted from the gruelling ordeal of the last few nights and his mind distracted by the thought of his next session with Elizabeth. His eyes closed for a few minutes, then a muscle spasm jerked him awake, confused and disorientated, to realise that time had slipped past.

By midnight he could barely keep his eyes open and it felt like weights had been placed on his eyelids. He could hardly remember where, or even who, he was, and then the darkness closed in behind his eyes. And then he slept.

Chapter 26

Russell woke to a loud crash. He had been deeply asleep, his arm wrapped protectively around Rosie, the way they had slept together for more than a decade. Donny was snoring in his cot in the corner of the room, a soft snuffle to which his parents had quickly become habituated.

Russell's first thought on waking was that he was having a nightmare. Sitting bolt upright in the dark he heard a second noise and, realising that he had not woken from a bad dream, he jumped out of bed and crossed to the door.

'What's wrong?' Rosie murmured softly, waking quickly, accustomed to sleepless nights since Donny was born.

Russell did not reply at first, looking at the locked door in confusion, forgetting for an instant why it had been locked and almost turning the key. He remembered at the last second how adamant Michael had been that his friends stay in their bedroom in case he decided to go for a midnight excursion. Turning back to his bed, Russell also remembered how compelling was the fear that had been etched on his old friend's face. A fear of the nightmares that were currently plaguing him, and of what their consequences could be for the others.

'It's nothing my love, just Mikey going for a midnight stroll.' Russell's resolve to ignore the sounds was short lived.

The thought that occurred to him as he climbed into bed next to his slumbering wife was clear and refused to be ignored.

'What if he's hurt? We know what's been going on, he could easily have hurt himself. I should go check. I know he told us to lock ourselves away and ignore any noises, but really, what's he going to do to me?' Russell chuckled, knowing he was much bigger and physically stronger than his friend.

'You can take him, tiger.' Rosie mumbled. 'But do it quietly and don't break anything.'

Looking at the dark ceiling, debating his next move, Russell heard a voice from the hallway downstairs unmistakably Michael's and unmistakably gripped by pain.

'Shit, argh hell. Russell, Rosie, help. I think I've broken my leg!'

Russell leapt back out of bed, unlocked the door and padded onto the landing before his brain caught up with what he was doing. The guestroom was directly opposite him and in the moonlight, he could see that the door was open, a yawning black mouth of darkness. The stool lay on its side, the tool box upturned nearby.

Glancing towards the stairs, Russell presumed that the alarm had done its job, waking a sleepwalking Michael before he had got very far. Hearing moans from the hall, he hurried down the stairs in search of his injured friend. I guess he was only half-awake Russell thought to himself as he moved, and probably disoriented so ended up falling down the stairs in his confusion.

Russell reached the ground floor, turned away from the stairwell and searched the darkness for Michael.

The hallway was narrow and full of shadows, its contours barely revealed in the scant light from the moon. At first Russell saw nothing out of place, no sign of life, and he reached out for the light switch next to the front door.

The next thing he knew he was lying flat on his back in the hall, wooden floorboards hard against his back. He felt like he had been cracked on the back of the head by a blunt weapon but looking up he saw that his assailant was now in front of him.

The only explanation of which his ringing head was capable was that the dark figure looming over him must be an accomplice of whoever had struck him round the head, and that they must have been standing in the shadows beside the front door. This conviction evaporated when the figure knelt over Russell's prone form and his features were revealed.

Michael's strong hands encircled Russell's neck and began to squeeze inwards. Pinned down and concussed, the taller man could put up little resistance to his friend's death grip. He knew however that he had to resist and his instincts to protect his life kicked in.

For what seemed like minutes or even hours, Russell struggled to breathe through his severely restricted windpipe whilst at the same time attempting to kick out at Michael. The larger man bucked his body like a rodeo horse but was unable to throw his friend off. Slowly Russell's struggles subsided, becoming less fierce, and his movements were punctuated with longer and longer periods of inactivity.

The unlit hallway began to lose what little colour it had had, and then went out of focus as Russell's breath was forced out of him. The only thing that he could see was the amorphous blob that had been Michael's face and that was now only recognisable by the gleaming white teeth, standing out like a ghostly grin in the darkness.

Eventually the struggles, now little more than muscular spasms, stopped all together. Russell lay still, his eyes closed, praying that Michael would decide he was dead, and release his grip. He was aware of only two sensations: he could feel the hands around his throat, slick with sweat but vice-like nonetheless, tightening still more as if his attacker was having a second wind; he could also smell a sharp metallic scent, unrecognisable at first and not unpleasant in itself, although a little harsh.

Suddenly the grip on his neck slackened, vanishing as instantly as it had begun, and Russell allowed himself to believe his ordeal was over.

An instant later and the remaining air in his lungs, what precious little breath he had been able to suck in while he was being strangled, was expelled as Michael's body smashed into Russell's chest.

Teetering on the edge of consciousness he finally realised what the metallic smell was that had been assaulting his nostrils for the last eternity: Blood. Then the world went black.

Chapter 27

'Jesus Michael, I thought I'd killed you!' Rosie's face filled Michael's vision as he forced his eyes open and tried to remember where he was.

He recalled being in the torturously uncomfortable guest bed in Rosie and Russell's cottage and, judging by his aching body and the fact that his friend was with him, he decided that that was where he still was. Though what Rosie was doing in the spare bedroom made a lot less sense, unless it was morning, and she was waking him up.

Within moments Michael realised that something was seriously wrong. He replayed the sentence to which he had woken and looking at Rosie saw that her face was a battlefield of emotions. Her words had suggested concern; the hard set of her face suggested the opposite.

'I thought you'd killed Russell!' It took a heartbeat before Rosie's words matched the anger revealed on her face and as she leaned in closer, her breath hot and sour from sleep, she snarled rather than spoke her next words 'You'd better pray to God that you haven't killed him.'

Michael recoiled when he heard the rage in her words, his stomach turning as he recognised the implication of the sentence. He sat up with a jolt, unleashing a fireball of pain within his skull, and automatically reached for the back of his head. As he gingerly fingered his scalp, he realised that his head was bleeding freely. His hair was sticky and matted and his fingers were painted bright red when he bought his hand back, staring at it in confusion.

'What the hell happened?' He raised himself up into a sitting position, realising as he did so that he was not in his friends' guest bed after all, but was sprawled in their hallway. This was a realisation that only added to his confusion and left him assuming that he had fallen down the stairs. At the same time as this question flitted through his woozy head, he was beginning to have a nagging sense of de ja vu. He tried to look past Rosie to the light coming from the lounge, but his friend was not about to let him do so and blocked his view, pushing him firmly back to the floor.

'What do you mean, what happened? Don't you dare try and tell me you don't know what you did.' Her face was contorted in rage, and tears were starting to course down her cheeks as she regarded Michael.

'Christ Rosie, honestly, I don't remember anything after I went to sleep, I guess...' He was ashamed of the whining in his own voice and of the conclusion that he was about to suggest, however his words were cut down mid sentence.

'You guess what? You guess you were sleepwalking? You guess you skipped down the stairs, lured Russell out of bed to half-kill him? You guess you didn't have any control over what you did, over any of it? How very convenient. Is that going to be your excuse for everything from now on?' Rosie was keeping her voice down, her words given more power by the fact that she was whispering them rather than shouting. In an even quieter voice, she added 'You bastard.' Before she stood up and turned to move away.

'Stop Rosie, please tell me what I've done. I swear to you I don't remember.' Whether it was the plea in his tone or memories of almost thirty years of friendship, but she did turn back, bending down to bring her face within inches of his ear.

'What you've done' she hissed 'is almost strangle my husband, your so-called best friend, to death, leaving him unconscious and I imagine with severe concussion. It looks like you have given him several cracked ribs, a punctured lung, and a broken wrist. I'm guessing there are more serious internal injuries that will only be clear when he can be examined at the hospital.' Rosie's lips curled up into a grotesque smile and she seemed to take pleasure from the pained expression that greeted her words before she continued. 'The police are here by the way, they were contacted by the paramedics when I phoned for an ambulance and described what sounded like a fight. I strongly suggest you play dead for a little longer, while you sort out your far-fetched sleep story.'

Michael watched, his eyes blurry with tears, as Rosie stalked away from him and into the lounge. Out of the corner of his eye he saw a tall figure leaning against the wall, a uniformed police officer who kept glancing towards Michael.

With an effort Michael managed to shuffle his body backwards towards the nearest wall, slumping against the hard surface a few seconds later. He rested a minute before using the wall to lever himself up from the floor, setting off a new explosion of pain as he did so.

'Go steady sir, we don't want you collapsing again.' The policeman spoke in an unexpectedly soft, quiet voice, a voice that seemed at odds with his size.

Michael's breathing was coming in ragged bursts, the respiration of an old man who'd been smoking for 80 years. All he wanted to do was find a bed, lie down and go to sleep until his nightmares were over.

But he had to see Russell, had to know what was happening and had to somehow reassure himself that it was not his fault. Stumbling along the hallway, one shaky step at a time, Michael heard voices coming from the lounge in front of him. Multiple people, at least two or three, were speaking softly but in quick, urgent tones. As he looked into the room, he saw several uniformed paramedics clustered around a stretcher. Snatches of the conversation drifted out into the hallway.

'I'm sorry madam....'

'That's all we can tell you for now....'

'We'll know more at the hospital'

'He's stable, we'll move him now'

Michael could not see past the medics to the figure on the stretcher, all he could see between the green coats were IV bags, tubes, straps, and that the prone figure – Russell – was not moving.

Rosie was standing close to the stretcher, eyes full of tears, shaking hands covering her mouth as the medics began to turn the stretcher, meaning to move it into the hallway. She glanced up at Michael, her eyes transformed from the bubbling sea green that he knew, and loved, to a cold, hard emerald. She began to speak, her voice clear above the soft, busy voices of the paramedics. 'No, you do not watch. You do not see what you've done. Stay back.' She spoke as if she were a priest casting out a demon from a possessed man and as she took a step towards the hall Michael shrank back, seeking refuge in the dining room behind him.

'Perhaps I am possessed' he whispered under his breath.

Chapter 28

'What was that sir?' A quiet voice spoke from behind him.

Michael turned in shock. He'd thought the dining room would be empty, that everyone was in the lounge with Russell. He recognised the police officer from the corridor, seeing now that he was broad as well as tall, with a rugged face and short blond hair. He looked to be a similar age to Michael and, judging by the bags under his eyes was having almost as much trouble sleeping. The officer yawned as he stood considering Michael in silence. Michael swallowed, aware that he'd just been asked a question. Struggling to remember what he had been asked, and indeed what he himself had said prior to the question, he stalled for time by turning back towards the hallway as the stretcher went past.

A paramedic was at each end of the rolling stretcher and Michael's view of his friend was again mostly blocked. This time however he was able to see Russell's face, and immediately wished he had been spared the vision.

Russell's neck was immobilised by a white brace and his face appeared to be swollen to twice its normal size, but it was the colour of his skin that made Michael shudder. Russell's normally pale face was a purplish-red, like a beetroot and his eyes were swollen shut. He looked like he was dead.

'Oh Jesus....' Michael breathed.

'Why don't you sit down sir?' A hand landed lightly on his shoulder and Michael flinched as he turned again to see that the policeman had approached him. Looking into the man's eyes he expected to see compassion to match the voice, or perhaps anger and disgust, emotions he felt the officer should be experiencing in the presence of the likeliest suspect in the house. Instead the brown eyes that regarded him were blank, expressionless, like the rest of the policeman's face. Michael sat down, relieved to not have to stand anymore, absent mindedly rubbing his head. He was shocked when his hand came away bloody having forgotten the injury, and he asked himself again: What happened?

'I'll get someone to look at that sir, and then perhaps you and I could have a chat?' The policeman spoke with authority and followed the stretcher towards the front door, pausing as he passed the lounge in order to mutter a command to an unseen figure. Moments later a second uniformed policeman entered the hallway and stood, watching Michael with an intensity that was anything but casual.

'What's happening?' Michael spoke softly, recognising fear in his voice. 'Is my friend going to be OK?'

'Your friend?' the policeman, a younger man with thick black hair above a narrow face, asked ironically, 'You mean the half-dead guy on the stretcher?'

Michael nodded, shame spreading up his face, presuming that the policeman thought he, Michael, had put Russell on that stretcher.

'I can't say sir, not being a medical professional myself, but it doesn't look good.' The man turned away with a sneer.

The first policeman returned a few minutes later and sat down across from Michael holding out an ice pack. One of the medics, a young woman with a streak of garish pink running through her hair took a quick look at Michael's head wound and announced that it was a fairly significant scalp lac that meant he would have to be taken to the hospital for stitches. The policeman nodded but told the ambulance crew to go ahead with the more critical patient, saying that he would follow shortly with Russell's wife and Michael. Michael could not see the paramedic's reaction because she was standing behind him, holding a dressing loosely over the wound, but he saw the meaningful look on the policeman's face, a look that said *just do what I say.*

Michael took the proffered ice pack as the paramedic left the house. 'Where's Rosie?' He asked, wincing as he held the cold pack gently against his scalp. 'Is she going to the hospital with Russell?'

'She's just gone upstairs to get her baby and pack a bag for him, she couldn't leave him alone here even to rush off to her husband's bedside. Understandably. Her mother is on the way to look after the baby for the time being. The man spoke slowly, choosing his words with care, watching Michael's face for reactions but never betraying his own emotions.

'I could watch him, for a while at least until her mum arrives, so Rosie can head on to the hospital. I am his godfather.' Michael paused, gingerly touching the ice pack back against his head, 'I mean it doesn't seem like I'm in danger of bleeding out.'

'That's an idea Mr Manners....why don't you suggest that when Mrs McCloud comes downstairs?
'But for now, I'd just like to ask you a few questions about what happened here tonight. Oh, my name's Police Constable Johnson, I forgot to say earlier, you know with all the drama.'

Michael blanched. He was sure now that he must have attacked Russell in his sleep, for some reason he must have slept through the 'alarm' going off when he'd left the guestroom. He shivered involuntarily, it was

151

his worst nightmare coming true, harming another person – especially a friend – due to his bizarre sleeping sickness. He had caused the 'drama' as Johnson had called it, a description that seemed both an understatement and an insult. Michael supposed that the only reason that he had not ended up murdering his friend was because Rosie had intervened, hitting him across the back of the head with, judging by the amount of blood, something big, blunt and heavy. He swallowed, attempting to generate some saliva and to rid his mouth of the foul taste of his crime.

'I don't really remember what happened. Am I being charged with something?'

Johnson looked confused, tilting his head to one side as he considered the man in front of him. 'Charged....why would you be being charged with anything? Mrs McCloud told me that you and her husband were up late talking, then on the way to bed you started playfighting, you know wrestling, and fell down the stairs, causing Mr McCloud's multiple critical injuries and your, how shall I put this, non-critical one. Is that not what happened?'

'I, um,' Michael stammered, at once grateful that Rosie was covering for him but at the same time frustrated that she had not let him know what she was going to say to the police. He also felt guilty for what he'd done to his friend, even if he was asleep, and unsure as to whether he should be spared from the consequences of those actions. 'Like I say constable, I don't really remember anything about how I got this injury.'

'Perhaps the knock on the head shook a few memories loose, eh Mr Manners?
'Well, regardless of what you can remember now, I would like to talk to you further, perhaps once your wound has been stitched and.....'

Johnson was interrupted by Rosie bursting into the dining room. She had dressed in the same jeans and sweatshirt that she'd been wearing the previous evening and held Donny in her arms. Her hair was in disarray, her eyes wide with fear.

'She's gone.'

Chapter 29

'Who's gone?' Michael spoke first, rising quickly from his chair, ignoring the pain in his head, rushing to his friend's side. Even as he spoke, he realised who she meant. 'Jess?'

Rosie nodded, biting her lip.

Johnson's face remained impassive, but he glanced towards the stairs. 'Who is Jess?'

'Jessica, my sister, she's only 16 years old. Where have you looked?' Michael's words came fast, pushing each other out of the way in their haste to be heard. He looked at Rosie; his friend seemed paralysed, rooted to the spot as if time had stood still for her. 'Where have you looked?' He repeated urgently, his eyes pleading with her, willing her to answer him, his hands clenching and unclenching.

'I, I looked everywhere Michael. She's not in the house.' Rosie's voice was no more than a whisper.

Michael sank back onto his chair as various scenarios filled his mind. Perhaps Rosie didn't look everywhere; perhaps Jess was hiding from the noise and chaos of what had happened; perhaps she ran away because it scared her; perhaps I hurt her? Perhaps I killed her? Head in hands, his breath was coming in ragged bursts again, his heart beating hard enough for him to feel the blood pulsing through the wound in the back of his head. All around him voices were calling out: he could hear Johnson giving orders for the house and garden to be searched, Rosie was trying to tell the two policemen what Jessica looked like, Donny was starting to cry in response to the noise and heightened emotions. Then the scene around him went grey and Michael passed out.

'Oh god, Michael?' Rosie's voice reached him as if from a great distance. Johnson knelt at Michael's side and turned his head to ensure his airway was clear. Michael had fallen from his chair and collapsed on the dining room floor briefly losing consciousness as a result of a combination of blood loss, shock and exhaustion.

'Sir, stay where you are for a moment.' Johnson spoke with firm authority as he placed a hand on Michael's chest to stop him from trying to stand. 'We will go door to door and try to find your sister'.

Michael nodded; his mind numb as he slowly twisted into a sitting position.

The next two hours were a frenzy of activity as Johnson and the other policeman searched the house and nearby street, canvassing neighbours in an ultimately futile attempt to track down Jessica. Most of the people that they spoke to had been in bed when the police knocked on their doors. Nobody had seen a teenage girl in the street.

Michael and Rosie sat in silence until her mother arrived to watch Donny allowing Rosie to go to the hospital. Both were completely preoccupied as the time dragged past, Rosie anxiously looking at the clock on the wall, desperate to leave to see her husband, Michael gazing at a fixed point in front of him, but not seeing his surroundings. Instead his head was full of horrifying images of what might have happened, might be happening, to Jessica.

As she left, Rosie turned at the front door offering him a brief smile, attempting to provide some much-needed support, although most of her emotions were still raging against her husband's attacker. 'I'm sure they'll find her soon.' She spoke softly before leaving the house. Michael was far from convinced of this conclusion.

In his mind he pictured the young girl as he had last seen Russell, strapped to a stretcher and deathly still.

Eventually Johnson returned to the house with the news that Jessica had not been sighted but that all local police had been provided with her description and would be looking for the girl. Michael protested that more should be done, that the nation should be looking for his sister, but his words had been brushed aside by the policeman who asked Michael to trust him, he'd done it all before. Michael was not reassured.

Johnson and the other officer took him to the hospital for his wound to be cleaned and stitched and left him there, requesting that he not leave the country for the time being and that he contact them if he remembered anything about the evening.

Once he was discharged, Michael took a taxi back to his friends' cottage and picked up his car. He spent the rest of the night, and the next morning, driving around looking for Jessica, checking in from time to time with his telephone at the flat and with the police. There was no sign of Jessica, nor had the police heard any word about the girl, so with a heart full of dread Michael phoned his mother in California to break the news that her only daughter was missing. The phone rang out, and his mother's cell phone was turned off, so Michael was forced to leave a brief message – during which he tried to sound as normal as possible – asking her to call him when she could.

Around midday he returned to his flat exhausted, took the high dose of codeine that he had been prescribed at the hospital, and passed out for eighteen hours straight.

Chapter 30

Michael thumbed through a year-old *House and Garden* magazine, glancing at the glossy photographs of grand gardens and impossibly tidy homes. He was sitting in an old-fashioned arm chair with a high back and wings, surrounded by heavy dark wood furniture – chairs and occasional tables – in a dimly lit corridor. His head lolled slightly, eyes closing as he fought off sleep. The low lighting, the waiting – he'd arrived twenty minutes early for his session – and the mind-numbing content of the magazines that had been left for patients to read, were all conspiring to put Michael to sleep, despite the fact he had been unconscious for most of the previous day. He rose from his chair and paced up and down the corridor in a bid to stay awake.

His mind drifted without the distraction of the magazine and he recalled the activities of the previous 36 hours, the fact that Jessica was still missing and that he had not spoken to Rosie since she had left him at the cottage.

Michael's reverie was interrupted by the door opening across the hall from where he had been sitting. He glanced up as a young woman exited the room. For a second, he thought it was Jessica, and his breath caught in his throat. The woman had the same long, bleach blond hair and a slender build like his sister, but as she turned to leave the room Michael saw her face and realised that she was at least ten years older than Jessica. His heart dropped like a stone within his chest and he sat down heavily in the winged back chair like a boxer returning to his corner defeated.

Elizabeth noticed Michael as she was showing her previous client out and was shocked by how he looked. He was slumped in the chair, eyes glazed as if he had seen a ghost. The look of desperation when their eyes met suggested that he'd either had a further incident of sleepwalking, or that he had received a piece of devastating news. She smiled warmly, holding the door open.

'Hello Michael, come on inside.'

Elizabeth had been bursting with questions as she had prepared for her session with Michael: Questions that had been sparked by her discussion with her supervisor, Professor Rosenthal. She wanted to find out the details about his dreams and sleepwalking. She felt that he had been holding back so far and certainly he had not revealed much about the problems that he had suffered from when he was younger. She also wanted to find out more about his family. She knew next to nothing about his mother and sister, let alone his brother. However, Elizabeth knew that her agenda would have to wait, at least for a short time, while she found out what had happened to Michael in the last forty-eight hours.

'Hello doc, good to see you.' Michael smiled briefly as he walked past Elizabeth to take the seat which she indicated, and she was struck by how genuine his statement was. His eyes had literally brightened when he had spoken to her, a brief spark that caused Elizabeth to realise how pleased she was to see him.

She dismissed her feelings immediately as being due to nothing more than the fact that his was an interesting case, nevertheless as she settled into her chair opposite him, she found herself noticing how attractive he was – despite his tired eyes and stubbled chin.

'So,' she began, 'how are you feeling today?' She had noticed a patch of shaved hair, about the size of a little finger, on the back of his head. The area of pale skin was broken by an ugly line of black stitches. 'What happened to your head?'

'Another dream, but different in that I wasn't dreaming – or at least I don't remember dreaming. But I did sleepwalk myself out of my room and downstairs and...'He paused, his face distorting into a mask of pain and something else – guilt?

'And? What happened Michael?' She was beginning to guess before her patient continued, realising that he must have followed her advice and moved into a friend's house, because if she remembered correctly, he did not have any stairs at his place, a ground floor flat. From the look on his face she theorised that he had probably hurt somebody else this time, and his reluctance to continue lent weight to her theory. 'Have you been staying with friends Michael?'

'Yes, we moved in with local friends, following your advice.' He spat out the words, an accusation, in a whining tone.

'We?' She was momentarily confused, before remembering that Michael's sister was staying with him.

'Yes, we. My sister, Jessica is staying with me. Don't you remember?' He rushed on before Elizabeth had an opportunity to reply. 'And I ended up hurting one of my friends – or at least that's what must have happened. His name is Russell and he's here in the hospital. He's my best friend, and I…. I put him in a coma.' Michael buried his face in his hands, his shoulders shaking.

Michael had found it almost impossible to obtain any information about how Russell was doing, whether he'd even regained consciousness, because Rosie refused to answer her phone or respond to Michael's messages. He had arrived at the hospital early for his appointment with Elizabeth in order to visit his friend. The staff member at the main reception desk had directed him to the Trueta Ward on the third floor of the hospital, after Michael had explained that his friend had been brought in following a trauma event.

On reaching the ward Michael had overhead a nurse being updated on Russell's condition by a colleague, stopping short of entering his friend's room when he saw that Rosie was by her husband's side. The nurse had remarked that Russell's condition was stable, but that he had not regained consciousness. Michael had interrupted and asked for more information, but had been referred him to a doctor, an older man who had been unwilling to share patient information with anyone who was not a member of Russell's immediate family.

Elizabeth could not hide her shock at his words, recoiling slightly and taking a moment to gather her thoughts before responding. She could not help feeling partially to blame for what had happened. It was after all her suggestion that Michael sleep in the company of others rather than being alone in his own flat, a recommendation that had ended up with somebody in hospital. Elizabeth shuddered despite the fact that the room was warm.

'I'm so sorry about your friend Michael; that is such an awful thing to happen. But you do realise that if you did injure him in your sleep you can't blame yourself?'

Michael shook his head slowly, 'It was still my hands that squeezed his throat, that half-strangled him. Whether I meant to do it or not doesn't change that. So please, tell me what to do to stop this. Make these nightmares go away.' He hid his face back in his hands, but not before she saw the tears running down his cheeks. She gave him a few minutes to compose himself before handing him a tissue.

'Help is what we're here to do.' The words sounded lame, trite. She leaned forward in her seat, 'Can you talk me through what happened? Was this last night? Try to remember everything you did in the hours prior to going to sleep and what happened after you woke up.'

Chapter 31

Michael spent ten minutes summarising the events that had unfolded at Russell and Rosie's house. First, he explained that it had been two nights ago. He went on to describe what he knew of the fight in the hallway and finished with the disappearance of Jessica, tearing up again when he mentioned his younger sister and how he'd put her in danger.

His reaction to the fact that his sister had gone missing less than two days ago, and with no sign of struggle, seemed to be out of proportion to the event. Sure, Elizabeth conceded, I don't know how I'd feel if a sibling disappeared, I don't have any siblings to disappear but still, his response – he appeared to be absolutely destroyed – was the most emotional she had seen him. He was certainly exhibiting more passion than he had shown when discussing his father's death.

Elizabeth wanted to dig deeper, to explore his connection to the girl and through that open up the topic of his brother, the phantom Benjamin who they had yet to discuss, but she sensed that that topic was still taboo, at least for the time being. She decided to return to the dreams themselves.

'When we met last time, you described two events of sleepwalking, during which you were dreaming, vividly, once that you were swimming and once that you were fighting a burglar. I'm interested in the fact that the first incident, which appears to have been sparked by the death of your father, involved....'

Michael shook his head as he interrupted. 'Actually, I was thinking after we spoke the first time that that dream happened the day my father died, but before I got the phone call from my mother callously breaking the news that he was dead. So, I guess that blows the idea that it was a trigger out of the water, unless of course I somehow subconsciously knew something had happened to him.... that sometimes happens right?'

Elizabeth frowned, annoyed that her neat and tidy idea of the death acting as a catalyst for the dreams was now reliant on a psychic link that seemed more at home at a séance than in her consulting room. She struggled to pick up her chain of thought. 'That is strange; but let's just talk about the dreams themselves for a minute. So, incident one, you wake up in your bathroom having fallen out of the bath, but you were dreaming that you were swimming in the sea.'

She looked to him for confirmation and he nodded, gesturing with his left hand for her to carry on.

'Sleepwalking incident number two, you wake up in your flat having been dreaming that you were in your flat, fighting off a burglar. Then in the next incident, two nights ago, you don't remember dreaming anything. Now, that of course may be due to concussion caused by being hit across the back of your head. In my experience, sleepwalkers are unaware of what they are doing when they are out of bed raiding the fridge, walking down the street, whatever. But that only fits with your last incident. 'The tendency for the majority of somnambulists is also to remember nothing about what they've being doing overnight when they wake the next day. But you seem to be dreaming at the same time, and those dreams seem to be tied specifically to what you are doing in your sleep. 'When you had vivid dreams in the past, prior to the last few weeks, did you sleepwalk as well?'

Michael shifted in his seat, clearly uncomfortable. 'No, I don't think I ever sleepwalked before this all started, I just had dreams about,' He paused, 'Stuff.'

Elizabeth sat straighter in her seat, and opened her mouth to speak, a question forming on her lips. Before she got her words out, he started to talk again, using his own voice as a wall against the unspoken question, *what stuff?*

'I have a confession to make, there have been two more incidents of sleepwalking, at least two more incidents that I know about.... but they are going to make me sound even crazier so please, please hold off on the strait-jacket.' He paused, knowing that he would rather appear crazy than talk about the content of his earlier dreams.

Elizabeth listened as Michael described dreaming that he had walked around his bedroom, leaving a message for himself 'This is a dream', and how the message had not been there when he woke up. This seemed to fit with her theory that his sleepwalking was becoming tied more closely to his waking hours. But the next admission, that he had discovered the message 'This is real' carved into his own arm chilled her to the marrow. It was hard to reconcile the person sat in front of her - a man who was obviously tired and deeply concerned about his friend and sister but who was speaking lucidly and was evidently capable of rational behaviour – with the person who was cutting themselves while, supposedly, asleep. However, Elizabeth was beginning to wonder whether he was going through some kind of psychotic breakdown or suffering from dissociated identity disorder – carrying out his night time activities while awake, but in a fugue or trance like state – rather than simply sleepwalking. She then remembered that he had mentioned there were *two* further incidents of sleepwalking.

'So' she asked, almost dreading his answer, 'What happened the other time you sleepwalked?'

'I don't remember dreaming, like the other night I guess, but I know that I was only asleep for a couple of minutes. I hadn't been planning to sleep. I was working on the computer and kept glancing at the time. Then I 'woke up' and I was standing in another part of the flat, with a knife in my hand....and that's when I knew I had to come and see you again, you know, when I called you the other day and we met?'

Elizabeth nodded slowly as she considered what he had told her. 'I'm wondering,' she began, careful to avoid unnerving her client, 'I'm wondering if you are actually sleepwalking. You see, in all the cases I've studied people are normally asleep for about twenty minutes before they sleepwalk....so when you found yourself with a knife in your hand a minute or so after you dropped off, that's much too fast for conventional sleepwalking.' She trailed off, unwilling to share her theories before speaking to her supervisor.

'What could it be then? You think I'm making this up? You think I'm crazy?' Michael rose in his chair, anger spreading across his face.

'No, I don't know what it is; there are lots of parasomnias, sleeping disorders. Your case doesn't seem to be like ordinary sleepwalking – which doesn't mean it isn't, and it certainly does not mean that I think you are making it up, or that you are 'crazy'.' Elizabeth spoke quickly, placating her client. The new information that he had given her strongly supported the idea that he was suffering from a recurring fugue state – losing time – rather than sleepwalking, and she was aware that the sooner she could bring him in for tests the better.

'Michael, I'd like to carry out some tests in our sleep lab. We can monitor you while you sleep and try and work out what's going on in your brain and elsewhere in your body. Can I telephone you later this afternoon to set up an appointment?' She glanced at her watch as she spoke, noticing that it was 12.40, so the lab would be closed for the next hour, and that she only had ten minutes left in the session.

'I'll try to get you into the lab over the weekend, hopefully tomorrow if that works for you?'

Michael nodded dully. Discussing his dreams or whatever they were had brought his situation into sharp focus and he felt utterly defeated. He stood to leave, presuming that his time with Elizabeth had run out.

'Wait Michael, we still have some time. Is there anything else you want to talk to me about?' On a hunch that he might be more willing to talk about other things now that he had opened up about his dreams she continued, 'How did your brother react to your father's death?'

Michael paused, not answering for almost a minute as his eyes dulled. 'My brother is dead.'

Chapter 32

Elizabeth sat back abruptly, unable to disguise her reaction to the news that Benjamin, Michael's brother, was dead. She suspected that this could have had a significant impact on his behaviour, could even be the trigger for all his problems. Her brain buzzed with questions: How did he die? Where did it happen? And when? Glancing at the clock on the wall behind her client she could see that the session was almost over, she knew that she should be wrapping up and sending Michael on his way, but she also knew that she had to find out more about the death of his brother – even if it meant committing the cardinal sin of running over on their appointment.

'What happened?' The question was hardly eloquent, subtle or sophisticated, but it was the only one that she could muster. Michael stared at her, his lips moving silently as if unable to give voice to his answer, his eyes empty, seemingly drained of all colour, of all life.

'There was a crash, we were out celebrating. This was, twenty years ago.' The words came slowly, quietly and without emotion, Elizabeth suspected that this was not because he was feeling nothing, but because he was feeling too much. She waited for him to continue, shocked by how long ago the event had taken place.

Straight away she guessed that the tragedy had been the reason behind his parents' divorce, and probably the trigger for all of his sleeping problems. She supposed that the event continued to haunt him after all this time and that perhaps the twenty-year anniversary – coupled with his father's death – had been the catalyst for the increase in severity of his disorder. She looked up from her notes as he carried on speaking.

'I was 13 and Ben was 18. He was a good kid – god I sound like my mother, or rather what I imagine a mother should sound like – but he was a bit wild, you know? And, well he'd just finished his first year at St Andrews – he was training to be a doctor....' Michael's voice trailed off as he gazed out of the window thinking about the countless lives that his brother would have saved.

'If you don't want to talk about this now, we can carry on next time.' Elizabeth offered gently, her voice soft. Michael was still looking out of the window, but his gaze was elsewhere, another time, and she recognised the behaviour from clients undergoing therapy for post-traumatic-stress-disorder. Michael was trapped, reliving the events of twenty years ago, and she decided to let his reminiscence run its course.

'Ben's reward for getting into University was a car, an Audi TT, flashy, really fast and new rather than second hand. He'd only had it a week because the family business hadn't done as well as Dad had forecast so they couldn't afford it at first. Pretty lame, but just like my parents, always promising and then not delivering. Anyway, Ben was going out to a party and I was really psyched coz he was taking me with him. I was tall and fairly mature for my age so he said I could come, as long as I could sneak out of the house. I did the whole 'pillows under the sheets' thing, though I could probably have just walked past my parents without them noticing me. The only thing Ben made me promise was that I 'be cool' around his mates.'

Michael was speaking fast now, and Elizabeth was struck by how his voice had changed as he had started to recount the tragedy. His Scots accent, barely noticeable after twenty years of living in America, was stronger, more pronounced and his words, particularly the colloquialisms, were those of a boy.

'Ben was a good driver, he was good at everything,' Michael was beginning to choke up, his mouth so full of emotion that he could barely get his words out, but there was no jealousy in his voice.

'Well, maybe not good at everything. He was driven by his mind rather than his heart, you know? So, put a book in front of him or a car and he could learn or do anything with it, the legend in our house was that at age two Ben taught Dad how to use the DVD Player. He wasn't just smart or a geek though; he was taller than me, strong and really athletic as well. Great at any sport, all sports, but particularly good at swimming – a regional champion in his early teens.' Michael smiled, lost in his memories, imagining a happier time.

'But he wasn't so good with feelings. He was popular, was great at acting the part of a sociable kid, but he never let anyone get too close.

'Controlled, that's probably the best word for it......he wanted to be a surgeon, I think he would have been a great one.'

Michael glanced up, his chain of thought derailed by a sound outside the room, and Elizabeth belatedly remembered that one of her colleagues always used the clinic room on Friday lunchtimes.

'I'm sorry Michael, we're going to have to carry this on in our next session.' She paused, somewhat flustered by the interruption, 'unless you have some more time now, we could carry on in a different room?'

The relief on his face was palpable and answer enough for Elizabeth. Now that he had begun to tell the story of his brother's death he could not bear to stop.

Chapter 33

Ten minutes later and Michael and Elizabeth were sitting on comfortable, high backed chairs inside a large bedroom. The walls were painted pale blue, the colour of a newborn sky, and a pair of thick navy-blue curtains covered a large window in one wall. A double bed dominated the room, neatly made with crisp linen sheets that matched the colour of the walls. *Hospital corners* Michael thought, with a wry smile. He glanced at his surroundings as he settled into the soft armchair.

'Just like home.... except the big window of course!'

Elizabeth smiled; she had explained the purpose of the window, actually a one-way mirror. It enabled researchers to study their subjects whilst ensconced in a small room connected by an interior door to the 'bedroom'. Elizabeth had shown Michael that both doors into that room were locked and reassured him that nobody would be eavesdropping on their conversation.

'So,' she began, considering her client, 'do you want to continue talking about your brother? About Ben?' Elizabeth was unsure whether he would feel able to pick up where he had left off, having had to break off from recounting the details of his brother's death in order to move to a different room.

It had obviously taken a lot of courage for him to broach the subject in the first place, and from experience she was painfully aware that such reserves of inner strength could run dry as quickly as they could well up. Her fears in this case were unfounded as he carried on speaking as if he had never stopped.

'The night he died it was dark, about half nine in the evening I guess, but the weather was good, and the roads were clear. Ben was a good driver, an excellent driver. Did I mention that already?
'We were on a fairly minor road, one that cut through the valley above our town, and we came to a fairly steep section with the valley floor to our right and an exposed cliff face to our left. And....well I guess you've already figured it out, haven't you?'

He raised his head and looked at her, his eyes once more full of tears. Elizabeth did not respond, recognising the distant look in her patient's eyes and knowing that his question did not require an answer.

'Ben had both hands on the steering wheel; he always did unless he was changing gears or something. He wasn't one of those people who drives one-handed while fiddling with the radio or using their phone. Then it happens.'

Elizabeth's body stiffened as his voice, in fact his whole body language, again became that of a teenager. The use of the present tense 'it happens' hung in the air between them like a spectre.

'The car speeds out of a corner, hugging the cliff, and shadows rear up and vanish, caught in the beam of the headlights.

'All of a sudden the vehicle slides, lurching to the right. It's happening slowly, the headlights light up the other side of the tarmac and then the rest of the car follows. Ben is battling with the steering wheel, wrenching it to the left in order to stay on the right side of the road.

'I can't hear anything, the engine is making no noise, the tyres are silent, even Ben's quiet – though I can see his lips moving as he utters what I imagine to be curses and prayers in equal measure. And then he drops his right hand down and turns the wheel towards the edge of the road driving into the skid. I smile at my brother, reaching out a hand to pat him on the shoulder for his quick thinking. Then we hit the barrier that marks the right-hand side of the road.

'I am deafened by a high-pitched screeching, a sound that begins the moment that we collide with the metal barrier. Now I can hear other sounds too: the roar of the engine; the fingers on chalkboard noise of the metal on metal collision with the barrier; and the irregular th-duh of a punctured tire contacting with the tarmac of the road. I am screaming but Ben is still silent.

'The narrow metal barrier breaks, and we barrel through into a patch of small trees and bushes. We carve a path through the rough ground and then we're flying.

'I have time to look at Ben – and he me – before we crash into the ground and everything goes black.' Michael spoke without a pause, his breathing rapid and shallow.

'I wake up to discover that I'm upside down. My head is touching the ceiling of the car; my left cheek is squashed against the passenger side window.

'I try to move my body and brace my arms against the sides of my seat. A low moan fills the car, an inhuman noise. I move my right hand forward along the side of my seat, stopping when I touch the edge of my seatbelt. I am scared to push the button, unsure where my body will end up. The moaning noise comes again, shorter this time but with a more desperate note. This is all the encouragement I need in order to press the button and release my seatbelt.

'I don't move at all, and I press the release button several more times, convinced that I mustn't have done it right the first time. After the fifth time I start to panic. Something is pinning my body to my seat. I move my hands again, forward over my legs, leaning as far as I can to reach my knees. Then I hear the groan for the third time, longer this time, a deep gravelly tone accompanied by a higher pitched creak, a new noise that is abruptly cut off by a sharp crack. The car is moving.

'I shift my upper body back against my seat, sliding downward slightly in my chair, trying to keep my centre of gravity as far back as possible while I stretch my arms out along my lower legs. They're trapped underneath the dashboard and I start to cry, convinced that I'm going to die.

'I stretch my left arm out towards the car door, intending to swing it open in order to grip on to the side of the car and pull myself out of my seat. The car lurches suddenly, tipping forward and I am so frightened that I move quickly, jerking my body to the side.' Michael jolted sideways in his chair, his body echoing his words, re-enacting his memory.

'Unbelievably, the car does not teeter over the cliff side as I force open my door and grapple for purchase on the undercarriage of the car. Within a matter of seconds, I'm out. The left side of my body, from head to toe is pulsing with pain from the contact with the ground. I taste dirt in my mouth and can feel grit scratching my eye. I can smell burning rubber and petrol.

'I struggle to my feet, moving slowly round the car to rescue Ben. The driver's door is wide open; its top edge has run a shallow furrow into the ground. Ben must have leapt out of the vehicle before we came to a stop, or he has done the same as me, crawling from the vehicle after it came to an abrupt stop here on this cliff edge. I glance around, taking in the destruction wrought by the out of control car, amazed that my vision has adapted to the extent that I can make out a lot of my surroundings. I don't see Ben however and this must be because he has crawled away from the car or was thrown out closer to the road. Then I realise he could be around the other side of the vehicle, looking for me even as I look for him.'

Elizabeth leant forward in her chair, absolutely gripped by her client's story, knowing the conclusion, Ben's death, but wishing fervently that there would be a miraculous happy ending.

'A soft groan, more a whimper, draws my attention back to the car. Gazing into the shadowy depths I can just make out a pale shape and a hand reaching out to me. I quickly cross the ground between us, leaning down, extending both my hands in order to free my brother from the car. We are stretching out towards each other, and then he is gone.
'One minute we are together, fingertips inches apart. And the next......'

Michael broke off, looking down into his lap. His body was shaking uncontrollably, but when he raised his head to face her, his eyes were dry, all tears shed.

'The car just seemed to vanish. It took him and it left, with nothing to prove it had ever been there except for a mark in the ground made by the driver's door. A scar on the surface of the earth like a grave marker.' He finally fell silent, leaving Elizabeth to fill the vacuum.

'I....I'm so sorry Michael. I....' I don't know what to say, I literally have no words to follow that, this was Elizabeth's first thought. A thousand different banal expressions of sympathy cascaded through the psychologist's mind, but none seemed adequate, or eloquent enough to suit the situation.

Elizabeth also felt frustrated with her patient for neglecting to mention a chapter of his life in which his current problems were clearly deeply rooted. She fought the urge to leap out of her chair and shake Michael by the shoulders while shouting: sleeping problems? Well duh, not surprising seeing as your brother died in a tragic accident in front of you and now your father just died.

At the same time the non-disclosure was unsurprising. Almost all of her patients had held back important parts of their family histories for the first few sessions. A need to build up a rapport with a therapist before baring their souls, shame about the events they were about to divulge and, with some, a desire to keep the physician interested lay behind this initial reticence.

Whatever the reason it did not stop her from wishing for full and complete disclosure each time she met a new client.

'I cannot imagine how hideous the loss of your brother must have been. Is that when you moved to America? When your parents separated, and your mother took you to see a psychiatrist?'

'Yes.' Michael's voice was little more than a croak. 'Well....mum and dad were torn up and torn apart, and I kind of faded into the background. My mother let her misery, her grief, run unchecked, essentially making sure that everyone felt the same – or worse – than she did.' Michael paused, swallowed before continuing. 'The first few nights I was given sleeping tablets, pretty strong ones I think and then the therapy, which....' A shrill tone cut through his chain of thought, Michael's mobile phone.

Elizabeth frowned at the interruption, leaning forward to ask her client not to answer the call.

'It could be Jess'. He pulled the phone from his pocket and swiped to accept the call before glancing at the caller ID.

Chapter 34

'Michael, what's so urgent?' the voice that issued from the phone was loud enough for Elizabeth to hear as he had pressed the speaker button in his haste to answer the phone. The tone was disinterested, the voice almost robotic and with an unusual accent that the doctor could not immediately place. A work colleague was Elizabeth's assumption, and she started to speak, 'Michael, please can you call back later if it is not Jessica?'

Michael ignored her, running his free hand through his hair before answering the caller in a voice full of defeat. 'Mum, it's Jess.'

If Elizabeth was surprised by the identity of the caller, she was completely floored by the manner in which Michael's mother responded.

'What's happened to my baby?' the voice, previously devoid of emotion was now in turmoil and the accent more recognisable as Scottish. 'What have you done this time Michael?'

Michael recoiled from the vitriolic nature of this outburst. 'Mum, I haven't done anything, please listen, Jess just ran away.'

'But why? Why would she run away? Where is she? Michael, where is Jessica? Is she on her way back here? Tell me!' the words came rapidly, without any space in which Michael could answer, the woman's voice rising in volume with each syllable.

As he replied Michael's hand gripped the phone more tightly, skin stretching across his knuckles, tension matched by his voice as he spoke: 'I don't know where she is Mum, she's been missing since yesterday, early morning. The police are looking for her.'

'Missing?' Michael's mother was shrieking now, 'My baby, oh God Michael, what have you done, it's Benjamin all over again'

Michael froze at the sound of his brother's name, all colour drained from his face. A split second later however and he seemed to come to his senses. He glanced around, appearing to take in his surroundings for the first time since his phone had rung.

'Doctor, I have to go' Michael's affect had completely altered, and he turned to leave the room, taking his phone off speaker and pressing the handset close to his ear before responding to his mother in an urgent whisper. 'No, it is not the same as Ben.'

Whatever else was said Elizabeth did not hear as the door to the laboratory shut with a quite hiss behind her patient.

'Dammit' she exhaled sharply, a breath she hadn't realised she'd been holding for some time. 'What else are you not telling me Michael?'

The door reopened before she could gather her thoughts, and without glancing up from her notepad she spoke 'Michael, I'm so relieved you came back, I am really concerned for you; please stay so we can finish our conversation.'

The response however came in a strong, home countries accent, not the American-Scottish lilt of her patient. 'Sorry Lizzy, but he is out of here, nearly knocked me flying. What did you say to him?' James sounded amused as he spoke.

Elizabeth bridled at his words, but also at the shortening of her name, a habit he seemed unable to break. 'He received an urgent phone call, so had to end our session.' She took a deep breath, attempting to calm her emotions before she continued, 'Was there something you wanted, something I can help you with doctor?' She finally looked up at the tall man, noting with some surprise that the usually composed Dr Booker was looking unsettled.

'I was actually looking for you, Penny mentioned you were seeing your new client in here, and frankly I was worried about you.' Penny, the administrator for the team, organised the booking system for the lab and so Elizabeth realised that she would have been aware that they were using the space.

Elizabeth arched an eyebrow, 'Concerned?'

James brushed his floppy hair back, a mannerism designed to attract attention to his luxuriant shoulder length locks. 'Well yes, I am extremely concerned. Do you know your patient was seen in A and E yesterday morning?'

'Yes,' Elizabeth answered with a curt tone. 'He told me.'

James continued, seemingly oblivious to her attitude. 'Sure, but did he also tell you he's been self-harming? That he's inflicted injuries on himself?'

'I know what self-harming is, thank you. And yes, I know about the injuries.' She stood, feeling uncomfortable with the way James was standing over her, telling her information about her patient as if she was an ignorant student. 'More to the point though, how do you know that?'

He shrugged, answering in a casual way that made Elizabeth's blood boil. 'Lucy told me over coffee.'

'And Lucy is?'

'The pretty blond nurse from A and E, she was telling me about this loon who came in in the middle of the night with various injuries: a cut on the back of his head, coupled with concussion, presumably from a pub fight, but also some broken bones in his hand from a few days ago. She checked the dressing on his wrist, and he'd carved up his arm.'

'Wow, loose lips......And, also there is so much wrong with that account. But, again, Mr Manners had told me all that.' Elizabeth was too angry to feel smug, turning her back on her colleague and beginning to gather up her papers.

'Well, I am glad to see that full disclosure is taking place.' James turned to leave the room, reaching for the door handle before speaking over his shoulder. 'The drug use is going to make for a challenging piece of work though. In fact, it probably excludes him from the study.'

Elizabeth froze in the act of placing her notes into her bag, 'Wait, what?'

James sneered, letting his feelings show. He turned around and strode back to his colleague. 'He's using. When Lucy was checking the dressing on his arm, she noticed a scratch in the crook of his elbow, higher up from the other wounds, she almost dismissed it as either another injury from the fight, or something else, but then she saw it was very precise; you know? Even? More of a puncture wound than a scratch.' He crouched down next to Elizabeth who was still bent over her bag. 'Now, Lucy's brother is a junkie, and she's seen similar marks on him, not to mention on all the people who OD and end up in A and E.'

Elizabeth glanced at James, unsurprised to note his expression was devoid of sympathy, rather he seemed thrilled to share the salacious gossip, excited to add this revelation, a look that said, 'what do you think of that missy?'

Her own face fell, clouded by sadness and by betrayal, her mind swirling as she considered what else Michael might be holding back.

Chapter 35

Michael slammed his car door and ran up the short flight of steps to the entrance of his building, nearly knocking over an elderly neighbour exiting the front door. He did not break his stride as he held his arm out behind him and pressed his key fob to lock the Ferrari. He burst through into the vestibule and unlocked the door to his flat, pausing briefly to notice the space where Jessica had sat waiting for him to come home, just a few short days ago. He closed his eyes, blinking slowly, hoping to conjure his sister back to the same spot, swearing under his breath when the hall remained stubbornly empty.

He dashed down the short hall into the bathroom and vomited what little food he'd consumed for breakfast, sinking to his knees in front of the toilet, his sides heaving long after his stomach was emptied.

He'd felt nauseous the moment he'd started talking to his mother and by the time he had ended the call with a promise to let her know as soon as he had any news he had barely managed to drive home before throwing up. Nausea was almost an automatic response to speaking with his mother and had been for years however this was the most extreme, most dramatic response he had ever had.

He knew that he was not responsible for his sister's disappearance; he had been talking with the detective when she had vanished. But of course, that meant nothing. She could have gone missing at any point during the night, and, given his recent nocturnal activities, missing time and attacks on himself and others he had to consider that he *may* have played a part in Jessica going missing.

But Ben, no, of course that was nothing to do with him, and it was not the first time that Michael had felt betrayed by his mother's accusation to the contrary. He had not been driving, he had not realised his brother was still in the car when it slid into the darkness. And yet, with everything else now happening, could he swear that he was without blame in the death of his older brother? Certainly, Michael could not prove it, after all no one else had been there on that night.

A sharp knock on the front door interrupted his morbid thought process, temporarily putting his self-loathing on hold. He ignored the noise, closing his eyes and slumping back against the bathroom wall. The knock came again, more insistent this time, and he was about to shout for whoever it was to go away when a raised voice called from the hall. 'Mr Manners? It's the police, the door is open. I'm coming in!'

'Hang on. I'm just in the bathroom'. Michael rose quickly from the floor, flushed the toilet and splashed water on his face before meeting the policeman in the corridor.

Michael saw at once that the man was wearing a suit, rather than a uniform and was relieved. Here, he thought, is a detective, so the disappearance of Jess is being taken seriously. The detective was an older black man, perhaps in his early forties, similar height to Michael but with a heavier build. He was balding, his hair cut short to minimise the impact of the hair loss, and his face was covered with day old stubble.

The policeman took in Michael's appearance, he had clearly not showered, or indeed changed clothes for some time. As he drew nearer and shook Michael's hand, he could not escape the smell of vomit on Michael's breath. He took a step backwards. 'Are you feeling OK Mr Manners?' He asked with genuine concern.

Michael responded quickly, well aware of his sour breath as he forced a smile on to his face, 'Sure, I'm fine.'

'I know I wouldn't be.' The detective continued, keeping his gaze on Michael, noting that the smile didn't reach the man's hooded eyes.

Michael shook his head slightly, as if trying to dislodge a thought. 'Wouldn't be what?'

'Fine, I was saying "I wouldn't be fine"'. The policeman now took a couple of steps towards Michael, a premonition that he was about to collapse crossing his mind.

'If my best friend was in hospital, and my sister was missing…. No, I would be far from fine.' The detective concluded; his grey eyes boring into Michael's.

Michael's body twitched at the mention of Russell, and of Jess, as if a jolt of electricity had surged through him, and he averted his gaze.

'What is it you said you wanted, and I don't believe you told me your name?' Michael turned before the man could answer and he began to walk back down the hall, heading left through the open doorway to the main living space.

'It's Detective Sergeant Steve West' West called after Michael, pausing for a second before closing the front door. A series of scratches on the door jamb, level with the lock, caught his eye, and he was leaning closer to investigate when a woman's voice came from the room that Michael had entered.

West turned sharply at the noise, his body automatically moving down the corridor. Thoughts sped across his mind: who is that? I thought Michael and I were here alone. Is that the sister, Jessica? Are they in danger? Twenty years of experience in the police force, ten as a detective, made him stop, edging slowly to the doorway rather than bursting into the room and interrupting the scene.

'Why haven't you been returning my calls? Why the fuck didn't you tell me your sister was visiting? If that snotty brat Jessica even is your sister?' The woman's voice was muffled by the thickness of the wall, distant as she was presumably speaking from the far end of the room, and yet West was able to make her words out, such was the volume at which she was talking. Anger, fear, curiosity, a mix of emotions could be heard in the woman's speech. But anger was foremost.

'The other night, it was all so strange, freaky. We never really spoke about it…Michael, I am worried about you.' The woman continued in a quieter voice and West had to edge closer to the doorway to hear the rest of the conversation. As she uttered her next words there was a clear note of compassion, 'Michael, call me.' And then a beep.

An answerphone message, of course, West almost laughed out loud, mentally berating himself for missing the beep at the start of the message. He didn't immediately proceed into the room, listening to make sure there were no more messages to hear, no further clues to glean.

The detective's instincts were rewarded when another message began. 'Michael, it's your mother. Jessica is….' Michael interrupted the message, pressing a button on the phone's base unit, evidently having already listened to the recording. A third voice, an automated female voice, filled the air 'Deleted'. At this West moved quickly into the room, speaking urgently as he entered 'Please don't delete any other messages sir.'

Michael jumped back in shock, as if he'd forgotten the policeman was in the flat. A look passed across his face, guilt? Before he spoke in a voice that was slightly higher than usual, as if forced, 'Why, am I being charged with something?' The younger man moved away from his answerphone, hands in the air in a pose that both indicated surrender and mocked the detective.

'Sir,' West stepped further into the room, again his voice full of concern 'Why would you be being charged?' This was the first time the men had met, but according to West's colleague, Constable Johnson it was not the first time that Michael had asked if he was being charged.

Michael didn't answer for a heartbeat, gazing around the room, looking anywhere but at his visitor. 'I guess I watch too many cop shows back in the US. The detective only turns up when someone's being arrested.' He shrugged.

'I see sir.' West responded, raising an eyebrow.

'Please, call me Michael, sir is, or rather was, my father.'

West made a mental note to find out about the man's father, presumably recently deceased. 'Well, Michael, no, I'm not here to arrest you. I'm here because the officers who responded to the call to,' West paused to check his notes 'Mr and Mrs McCloud's house in the early hours of yesterday morning filed a missing person's report and they also noted unusual evidence at the scene. 'So, I have been assigned to the case and I wanted to ask you some questions about your sister, unless she's turned up that is?' The detective paused, allowing Michael to answer.

'No, she's not here – clearly- and I've spoken to her mum, our mother, and she's not turned up back there, or been in touch.' Michael's body slumped. 'I'm not sure what else I can tell you.'

'Well sir, sorry, Michael, I understand that Constable Johnson didn't get chance to cover much ground yesterday, what with everything else going on. So, I'd like to find out more about Jessica, anything that could help us find her. You're evidently very close to each other. May I?' West indicated the sofa.

'Sure, have a seat. I'll make us a drink. Coffee?' Michael was already walking towards the kitchen as he spoke.

'Tea, please.' West sat and surveyed the room. In truth he couldn't stand tea, an English custom that his parents had embraced whole heartedly when they had arrived in London in the late 1940s on a ship from Jamaica. His mother had force-fed him milky tea from birth, a habit that had put him off the drink for life.

He generally drank water but knew that asking for a brew would give him a little longer to study his surroundings, and that the mundane task should serve to calm Michael's nerves.

The living space was open-plan and sparsely furnished with high quality, but generic pieces that suggested that they had been picked out by an interior designer and that they came with the flat. The large, black leather sofa divided the living space between lounge and kitchen and faced a wall on which a 60-inch plasma screen television was mounted, wires chased into the plaster, so it appeared to float halfway between floor and ceiling. The rest of the walls were blank. To the right of the television stood a bookcase, completely empty, and then the doorway leading to the hall. The left-hand side of the room featured a glass dining table surrounded by six black and chrome chairs. This was positioned in front of a large window, currently obscured behind white blinds. The only other furniture in this half of the room was a small coffee table, on which a remote control and the landline phone were placed.

That reminds me, thought West. 'Michael, would you like me to step outside so you can return your call?'

'Hmmm,' Michael paused, and West turned his body on the sofa, looking towards the kitchen. Michael was busy fixing the drinks and judging by the French press and other utensils on the counter was serious about his coffee. 'Oh Poppy, no, I'll call her later.' Michael spoke in a more relaxed tone, engrossed in the task of making drinks, as West had hoped he would be.

Five minutes later and Michael was sat opposite the sofa on one of the dining room chairs, a piece of furniture so angular as to appear devoid of comfort, a piece designed for form rather than function. He was cradling a large coffee cup, taking frequent sips. West's cooling tea was resting on a coaster on the coffee table, and there it would likely stay.

'OK. So, Jess is 16, a fully-fledged American citizen, and I gave your officers a full description and a photograph yesterday, right?' Michael's voice once again was filled with anxious tension, his body language closed, protective.

'That's right. But I understand that she's only recently moved to the UK?' West smiled, nodding at his host to say more.

'Yes, only a couple of days ago in fact. She's just visiting for a few days, she's not moved here. She had, has, these rows with our mother, they really don't get on and this time was the worst. She, our mother I mean, can be quite erratic, and is often "ill". Michael paused, leaving West to wonder what *ill* meant in this instance.

Michael continued, 'Her illness means that when Jess came along, I did a fair amount of parenting. I was already 17 when she was born. So, yes, we are close. In the past when they've argued Jess has done nothing more than storm off for an hour or so, to the mall with friends, you know? But this time when they rowed Jess booked a flight, hopped across the pond and pitched up on my doorstep.' Michael paused again acutely aware that he was babbling. He drew a deep breath before continuing. 'But detective, I really don't see how this is going to help you find her.'

West gave a thin smile, speculating why Michael was in such a hurry to get the conversation over. 'I understand your anxiety Michael, but remember your sister only disappeared yesterday morning, less than forty-eight hours ago. It is only because of the violent circumstances surrounding her disappearance that we are looking into this as a missing persons case. That and the fact that most of Ms Manners' personal property was left behind, which is fairly unusual in the case of runaways.' West leaned forwards, and opened his mouth to say more, but then let the silence draw out and fill the room.

Michael took another long drink before speaking, a note of resignation in his voice 'Look, I understand the process, protocols or whatever; but I've told your colleagues what happened to Russell was in no way related to Jess disappearing. I also told them that she wouldn't just run off like that – so that in itself should be causing you to treat this as suspicious. Jess is level-headed, she's certainly not impulsive or flighty.'

'Despite the fact that she left home and travelled to a different continent just a few days ago, and at short notice?' West allowed all his incredulity to show on his face.

'And besides, how do you know that your sister running away is not related to what happened to Mr McCloud, or to you?'

Michael rubbed his face with the hand not holding his cup, his bandaged right hand, making West wonder about that injury and how it had been sustained. 'Russell and I fell down the stairs, a horrific accident yes, but nothing sinister happened; so why would she run away?'

'You tell me sir. What do *you* think happened?'

Chapter 36

'Damn, are you a sight for sore eyes?'

Rosie started out of her half sleep, unfurling from the chair and rushing to the side of the bed. Russell's eyes were open, his head turned towards her, as far as the brace around his neck would allow. His voice was a rasping croak.

'Oh god Russ,' Rosie gasped 'I thought you'd left me.' She peppered his face with kisses and leaned her body gently against his. She had sat by his side almost continuously since arriving at the hospital thirty-six hours previously, even nursing Donny at the hospital when her mother brought him in.

Russell spoke again, in urgent tones. 'Are you OK? Donny? Oh God, Michael didn't…?'

'Attack us? No. We're both OK.' She answered hurriedly to reassure her husband.

'I know he told us, warned us; but God if you'd seen the look on his face Rose.' Russell's hand suddenly squeezed his wife's with a strength that was painful, a strength she should have been relieved to find that he still possessed. She leaned away from his body to look at his face.

'I can't believe that he wasn't in control.' Russell let go off her hand and slumped down on the bed, surrendering back into sleep, the little energy he had left completely depleted.

'Detective West?'

'Yes, this is Steve West. To whom am I speaking?'

'Rosie McCloud, Russell McCloud's wife. Your officer, Constable Johnson, he left your card when he visited the ward earlier today. He said to call to let you know when Russell regained consciousness. Well, he has – or at least had, briefly, he's sleeping again now.' Rosie stood sentry outside her husband's room, glancing back at the door as she spoke on her mobile phone to DS West.

'That is a tremendous relief, thank you for letting me know.' West sighed loudly, glad that this case was not a homicide.

'Yes, it is a relief, and that's an understatement.' She fumbled her words and wiped her eyes with her free hand as tears threatened to start falling.

'I presume you've not yet spoken about what happened?' West, sitting in his car, took out a notepad, grabbing a pen from his passenger seat.

Rosie took a deep breath, considering the lie she'd told immediately after the police had arrived; that Michael and Russell had been wrestling, a game, before they'd both fallen down the stairs. If she told the truth now, she'd be betraying her oldest friend, but if she didn't, if she perpetuated the lie, then what? Well first, if Russell was right and Michael was not asleep, if he was in fact in control when he'd attacked, then surely, she had a duty to tell the detective, in case Michael did something again? Even if he was asleep surely, she needed to tell the truth? Second, she knew that the police must already be suspicious of the injuries. The marks on Russell's throat were hardly evidence of anything but strangulation, the examining doctor had said as much when they'd arrived at the hospital in the early hours of Thursday. Mostly though, Rosie admitted to herself, mostly I want Michael to suffer, to be punished for what he did – regardless of whether or not it was a deliberate act.

'Mrs McCloud?' As the silence drew out West checked his phone to make sure the call was still connected.

'Yes, yes I'm still here. Sorry, I thought I heard Russell calling.' The lie, tiny compared to the one she was about to undo, lodged like a piece of glass in her throat. She swallowed.

'Detective, what happened, it wasn't what I told the other policeman. I'd gone to bed early, Donny – our son – often wakes in the night, so I was tired and knew the night was going to be a long one.

'What felt like moments later I woke to crashes and heard Michael's voice and I rushed downstairs. Michael was on top of Russell, his hands around his throat,' She swallowed again, forcing herself to continue.

'I thought they must be play fighting, like I said, but Russell was not moving, and Michael ignored me when I told him to stop, so I hit him with a door stop – you know, one of those metal ones that look like dogs?'

She paused and drew a breath.

'He, Michael, fell onto Russell, I pushed him off to check for a pulse, on Russell I mean, and then called 999 for an ambulance.' She had kept her eyes open, fixed on the door to her husband's room as she spoke, drawing strength from Russell. Now she closed her eyes and lent her head forward, resting it on the cool glass in the middle of the door.

'I see Mrs McCloud.' West paused, blowing out a breath of frustration. 'Now, if you knew Michael attacked your husband then why did you say that they had been play-fighting?'

'Well, I couldn't ask Russell what happened could I? Him being half dead and all, so I assumed they'd been fighting, why would I assume it was an attack?' She stopped, drew in another shaky breath and then continued.

'Christ, no, no that's not right. Sorry detective, let me start again.' Another breath, a whispered prayer for forgiveness.

'Michael…. Michael is sick, he's been having strange dreams, and sleepwalking, and he hurt himself. So, he and Jessica were sleeping at our house, for safety reasons' Rosie laughed, a bark that was devoid of humour.

'For the safety of whom Mrs McCloud?'

'Yes, it's ironic, I know. Michael got up in the night, Russell heard him and went to investigate, and then Michael attacked him, in his sleep – or so I thought. So, yes, I lied partly because I wanted to check with Russell what had happened, but mostly to protect Michael, he's my oldest friend you know….'

West interrupted, 'You say you *thought* he was asleep?'

'Oh, you're good detective, yes, I did say that.' She paused, replaying her words, *or so I thought.* They had been intentional, and as she spoke again, she massaged her left hand, recalling the way Russell had squeezed it so tightly when he'd spoken moments before.

'I'm not sure he was asleep, Russ said there was a very focussed look, a very *present* look on Michael's face as he squeezed the air out of his throat.'

West pursed his lips, considering. 'So, you think Mr Manners attacked your husband on purpose?'

'Yes, I do, I've no doubt it was intentional. And I am worried for Michael's safety, maybe even his sanity. Has Jessica, his sister turned up yet?' She shuddered as a new fear arose inside her.

Chapter 37

West massaged his neck, a wave of exhaustion washing over him as he considered his call with Rosie. He pushed open his car door and got out of the vehicle, stretching and yawning. The day was grey, a fine drizzle falling, weather that was clearly set in for the day 'or month' he muttered as he strode up the steps to the entrance to the police station. He had been driving to the station, having left Michael's flat and his untouched cup of tea, when Rosie had called and revealed that Michael had attacked his supposed friend, and that he had been suffering from sleep problems. That was something West had no difficulty in believing, having seen the bags under the man's eyes, and having noted his unfocussed and twitchy behaviour.

West had almost turned around and driven back to Michael's flat, especially when Rosie had suggested he might not have been asleep during the attack. It certainly seemed that Michael had more questions to answer, and West felt the time had come for that to happen in a more 'official' way.

What changed his mind however was one of the last things that Rosie had said. He had asked whether Michael had been violent before, and she had remarked that no, he had not, other than when he'd hurt himself recently, the event that had precipitated Michael and Jessica turning up at the cottage. But she had then mentioned a brother, Benjamin, and that Michael had been angry, that'd he changed after his brother had died, becoming withdrawn. She had ended the call soon after this revelation, saying she had to go check on her husband, but promising to call the detective if she thought of anything else or at least as soon as Russell was strong enough to answer questions.

'DS West, sir.' The constable at the front desk nodded to West as he strode into the station. 'It's a day to be grateful for riding a desk isn't it?' The petite brunette smiled, receiving a grunt and a perfunctory wave from the older man. God, she thought, he's like Inspector Morse and Luther rolled into one, but still, I wouldn't kick him out of bed.

West took the stairs up to his office and spent the next couple of hours at his desk. He checked with his team if there was an update on Jessica Manners and rapidly learned there was 'nothing to report sir.' Next, he looked for any records regarding Benjamin Manners, and finding nothing, spoke briefly with Rosie, discovering that Manners was not Michael's birth name, and that that had been MacNair. A new search generated one record, of an automobile accident from twenty years ago, during which Benjamin MacNair, the driver, had lost his life.

As he skimmed the report West noted that Michael had been in the car and had escaped with minor injuries, cuts and bruises. West surmised that there was likely to have been a significant psychological impact of an event of this nature, and he could well believe it would have altered the young man's personality. The car had not been found for several weeks, finally washing up on a beach, miles away from the crash site, and Benjamin's body, when that was eventually recovered a few hundred yards from the car, was identified only by dental records, due less to the crash than to the subsequent passage of time.

An addendum to the record included an updated address for Michael's mother, in the US, and that the boy's parents had divorced. There was no reference to a sister. West made a few notes, sketching out a timeline, and then turned to Google. A few minutes search enabled him to find out that Mrs MacNair had become Mrs Manners a short time, West mused that it was an indecently short time, after moving to the States. She and Mr Manners, a bona fide cattle rancher, were still married, had had one child together – Jessica – and were relatively wealthy, rich enough to appear in the news from time to time at galas and other events.

And Mr MacNair? Mused West. Further searching revealed that Michael's father had not remarried, pouring his energies into his business instead, and growing Global Scotland into a major brand - though West had never heard of it himself. Two further pieces of information leapt out from this line of research: First, Michael's father had died less than a month ago, certainly fleshing out the timeline. Second, Global Scotland had been sold, even more recently, to a Japanese conglomerate, presumably making Michael a very wealthy man. West, barked off a few commands to his team, focused on finding out more about the circumstances around Mr MacNair's death, and then headed back out into the rain to pay Michael another visit.

Chapter 38

Michael occupied himself with clearing up his mess as soon as West left. Starting in the bathroom he cleaned up his vomit, then moved to the kitchen to put on a clothes wash before returning to the bathroom to shower and dress. He paused in his activities every few minutes to call Rosie's mobile phone for news about Russell, each time being directed straight to voicemail. Twice he put his jacket on and got as far as his front door, intending either to drive around searching for Jessica or to head straight to the hospital to see his friends. A desperate hope that Jessica would turn up held him back from leaving the flat.

Keeping busy was a distraction from memories of recent trauma but also kept his mind from revisiting the car crash that had ended his brother's life. Michael knew he was also avoiding calling Poppy, unsure what he would say to her, but certain that he did not want to explain everything that was going on to yet another person. She'd clearly been afraid of him the last time that they had spoken and had been frustrated and angry on her most recent message – all completely understandable reactions in the circumstances. Yet he felt sure she would respond rationally, kindly, and offer to come around to the flat and keep him company if he did open up about the hell in which he was living. What he was equally sure of however was that he neither wanted, nor deserved her sympathy. Instead he intended to just ignore her last call, and any future calls, figuring that she would eventually get the message and give him up as a lost cause, just one more example of how crap most men were.

'What I really need to do' he muttered under his breath while towelling his hair, 'is eat; doctor's orders.' Michael smiled at the memory of Elizabeth that this conjured up, recalling her encouragement that he eat when they'd met two days ago. He made himself a panini with bacon and melted cheese, the mundane activities of this and of brewing coffee providing a further welcome distraction. When the food was ready, he felt certain he would not be able to face eating it. His guts were still churning and despite cleaning his bathroom, his clothes and himself, he still detected an odour of sickness. He forced himself to take a bite of the panini however, and once he had tasted the smoky bacon and sharp tang of cheese his stomach reminded his brain how hungry he was, and he polished off the meal in a matter of minutes.

West checked his emails on his phone before getting out of his car back outside of Michael's building. He reviewed the short report from Johnson. The constable had investigated Michael's father's death, caused by a massive heart attack, despite the man being just 60 and in very good health. Mr MacNair had been found in his study by his housekeeper, a cliché that brought a faint smile to West's lips. According to the autopsy this had been several hours after MacNair had died and there was no evidence of suspicious circumstances. The ever-vigilant Johnson had dug a little deeper, and on reviewing financial and legal records noted that Mr MacNair had been planning a large reinvestment and expansion of his company and was also reviewing his will with his lawyer. Johnson had speculated that with Michael the sole beneficiary of the current will, perhaps any changes would have been detrimental to his financial future. West supposed that could be enough motive for offing the old man before he could make any changes to his will and that perhaps Michael had made his father's murder look like it was a result of natural causes.

Michael was just draining the last drops of his coffee, feeling better, more human than he had felt in days, when an insistent hammering on his front door brought his situation back into sharp relief.

A few short hours ago, the last time West had seen Michael, the man had looked dishevelled, wearing two-day old clothes. Huge bags had lain under his eyes, he was jittering as if strung out on something stronger than coffee, not to mention he had reeked of vomit. The man who opened the door to the detective, while he still looked stressed, did however look more presentable. Michael had shaved and showered, changed his clothes, and seemed calmer and more composed.

'Detective, have you found Jess?' The words tumbled out of the younger man's mouth before the door was fully open, putting West on the back foot as his mind had been filled with questions about Manners' father.

'No, Michael, I'm afraid not.'

'Then what, you're here to search my flat?' Michael's frustration bubbled up 'Clearly she's not here, so wouldn't you be better served actually looking for her?' He drew a breath, working to calm himself, concerned that his response could be conceived as that of a guilty man.

'Actually, I wanted to ask about your father.'

'What's my dad got to do with anything, didn't I tell you he was dead?
Besides, he wasn't Jess' father, so why would she go to see him?'

DS West took a half-step back and considered the man in front of him further; clearly Michael was extremely on edge, anxious about his sister, and possibly worrying about his friend in hospital. OK sure, but what else was going on here? Was it simply the illness that Rosie had referred to? The sleepwalking, sleep attacking or whatever it was? Or was his reaction due to the fact that he was not actually ill, at least not in a conventional sense? Was his behaviour instead motivated by guilt and by fear that he might be caught for the attack on Mr McCloud, and perhaps other events including the disappearance of his sister? West deliberated again whether it was time to bring Michael into the station for questioning, but something caused him to hold back.

'In point of fact you didn't mention that your father was deceased, but in the course of our enquiries I found that piece of information myself.

I do however have some other questions, perhaps I could come in?' West had learned from experience that suspects tended to be more open in the comfort of their own homes. One look at Michael's sullen expression however made him doubt this would be the case on this occasion.

'What exactly did you want to ask about my father? And what other questions do you have?' Michael spoke in clipped tones, his face full of thunder. What he actually wanted to ask was for the detective to get out of his face and do his job.

Michael turned his back and strode away before West had a chance to respond, entering the lounge and moving out of sight. The detective followed, approaching the open doorway cautiously, not convinced that Michael was in his right mind. West had been jumped more than once in his career and had the scars to remind him to be wary. He took a step wide and past the door into the lounge, enabling him to locate Michael within the room before proceeding, noting that the man was sitting on a dining chair as he had been earlier in the day.

'So, can you tell me about your sleeping disorder?' West settled himself on to the sofa as he spoke, deliberately changing tact in order to keep the man off balance.

'My what? I thought you wanted to ask about my dad?' Michael jumped up from his chair, his temper flaring. 'And how the hell do you know about that? Did you speak to Elizabeth?'

'Please calm down sir, your friend mentioned you had been having problems sleeping recently.' West raised his hands in a placatory fashion.

'What friend?'

'Mrs McCloud. Who is Elizabeth?'

'Rosie, is Russell OK? Has something happened?' Michael ignored the question about Elizabeth, taking a step towards the detective.

West paused, considering for a moment how to respond, weighing up whether there was any benefit to be gained by withholding information. 'I can't tell you much, but Mr McCloud has woken up, or at least he briefly regained consciousness.'

Chapter 39

'Oh, thank god, I'll go and see him after we're done here.' Michael sat back down, closing his eyes and bowing his head as if in prayer at the news that Russell was going to be OK. He took several deep breaths before continuing. 'In fact, can we pick this up later? I'd really like to head straight to the hospital.' The relief in Michael's voice was palpable, and for a moment he seemed to have forgotten that his sister was still unaccounted for.

'I suggest you speak to Mrs McCloud before you head to the hospital Michael, I wouldn't want you to waste a trip if Mr McCloud isn't up to receiving visitors for the time being'.

I would speak to her if she'd answer my calls thought Michael, as he ran his hands through his hair and slumped in his chair, suddenly exhausted. 'What did she say about my sleep?'

'Well, she was explaining what had happened the other night.' West paused, watching Michael carefully. The man sat forwards in his chair, a look of something, perhaps fear on his face, but he didn't speak. 'As I understand it now, you attacked Mr McCloud in your sleep, causing his extensive injuries and leading to Mrs McCloud having to subdue you.' Again, West paused for a response, but there was further silence from Michael, just a slow breath out that suggested relief.

'I must admit that I was surprised that you both told a different story the other night, however in your case I presume that was due to your head injury...'

Michael rubbed the back of his head, gingerly feeling the stitches, taking comfort from the fact he had absolutely no memory of being struck on the back of the head, or of attacking Russell. This, he knew, was evidence that his friend's critical condition, his hospitalisation, had not been his fault, at least not intentionally, as he had been asleep at the time. 'What's odd, hell, more odd, is that I wasn't dreaming this time...' He muttered, almost to himself.

'Pardon sir?' West, leaned forward on the sofa, hands on his knees, 'This time?'

Michael closed his eyes and sighed loudly. He had not realised he'd spoken, but now felt a weight lift as he gave the detective a short summary of his recent episodes of sleepwalking and accompanying dreams, including waking to find himself outside his guest room with a knife in hand when Jess had been staying. It felt like a confession. 'I did not hurt her though detective, I swear. I have no other missing moments in my memory.'

West nodded, looking up from his scribbles, a raft of questions piling up in his mind. At the forefront was the thought that, seeing as he had no recollection or associated dream regarding Russell, how could Michael say with such certainty that he had not done something to his sister in the time after everyone had gone to bed, and before he attacked Russell. His story, bizarre though it was, did however sound plausible and West chose his words carefully before replying. 'I believe that you don't have any memory of something happening to your sister.

Michael's body tensed, bristling at the implication that he may have done something to Jessica.

'And prior to the recent incidents, how have you been sleeping?' West continued, ignoring the reaction.

'Fine most of the time; on and off I suffer from insomnia, vivid dreams and night wakening and I have been prescribed sleeping tablets in the past, but I never acted out a dream until the day my father died.' He was beyond feeling embarrassed about his nocturnal excursions, having told so many people over the past few days that they had begun to feel like fiction rather than fact, someone else's stories. He did however feel tension beginning to rise in his body, frustration that he was sitting have a chat with DS West when they should both be elsewhere. He was desperate to get to the hospital, to see for himself that Russell was alive, and the detective should be scouring the streets for Jessica.

'How did your father die Mr Manners?' West seized on Michael's reference to his dad in order to steer the conversation back to where they'd started.

'He had a heart attack. You must know that from your investigation?' Michael spoke bluntly, without emotion, staring at West as if to say *so what?*

'And you were visiting him at the time, staying at his house?' West recalled the report he'd received about Mr MacNair planning to change his will and preparing to invest huge sums of the family fortune back into his company. This coupled with the father's good health meant that the detective still felt something was 'off' about the sudden, fatal heart attack. West eyed Michael, again searching for some reaction, however small, that would betray the young man's genuine response.

'No, I was at home in America. Why do you ask?' Michael looked genuinely confused, but only for a second. 'Jesus, do you think I killed him in my sleep?' He laughed, a single derisive snort, as he realised what West was implying. 'You can easily confirm where I was or wasn't.'

West didn't bridle, wasn't angered by Michael's laughter, he just leaned back in his seat, considering his next question. In truth he was annoyed, but not at the suspect, witness, victim, or whatever category it was that

Michael fell into. West was frustrated with himself for not confirming the whereabouts of Michael at the time his father had died. For now, all he could do was take Michael's word for it that he had been on the other side of the world. He would check and have that verified, though he was willing to bet his house that the man was telling the truth and could not therefore have been directly involved in his father's death.

West rubbed his right hand down his cheek and across his chin, feeling the sandpaper rasp of stubble, a reminder that he had not been home to shave, and had barely slept since he'd been brought into the case. Lack of sleep, he reasoned, was an explanation for his lack of due diligence, and for his somewhat ham-fisted interview technique, however it was not an excuse.

'I was asking, Michael, because I wondered if you had discovered your father's body, if perhaps that had triggered the episodes of sleepwalking. West spoke slowly, choosing his words with care. 'But of course, the mere fact that your dad had passed away could have been catalyst enough.'

Michael nodded slightly, mollified. 'It could, you're right, but here's the damnedest thing, the first dream, when I nearly drowned, that happened before I knew he was dead.'

West pursed his lips, considering the man in front of him, and the facts at hand. So, here was someone recently bereaved. He rushes back to his native country to attend the funeral. At the same time, he is suffering from some sleep disorder, unrelated, but potentially exacerbated by the trauma of losing a parent. Sister turns up unannounced. More unsettling, more cause for disordered sleep. Move to friends' house for safety, but still more disturbance. Another episode of sleepwalking. Sister runs away in shock or fear, or both. It was all together possible that in these events he was innocent, that Michael was not hiding anything, but was simply suffering from an extreme sleep disorder. And yet West could not ignore the itch at the back of his skull, a sense that something did not add up. Particularly considering Rosie's assertion that Michael was not asleep when he had strangled his friend.

'Are you seeing anyone?'

Michael started in his seat, his mind had been looping back to his father, remembering the last time he'd seen him, at Benjamin's funeral. He had blamed his father for the death of his older brother, as a child it was simple cause and effect. If his dad hadn't bought Ben the car, he wouldn't have crashed it and died, case closed. Over the intervening years this sense of blame had not been dulled, but it had been refined into a more mature explanation, focused around his parents – particularly his father – being both absent and yet also demanding. Demanding that their sons 'make something of themselves' pushing them to engage in a wide variety of activities in and out of school, pushing them not just to be successful but to be the best. This, Michael believed, had bred a host of emotions in them both, but particularly in his brother as the eldest child. Some of these feelings were certainly negative, chiefly anger and discontentment. The praise that his narcissistic father had lavished on Ben when the young man proved he was successful, the constant assurances that Ben could do anything if he put his mind to it, this had caused him to be overconfident. This had caused Ben to crash.

Since moving to America Michael had spoken to his father only a handful of times, and only when his mother had refused to act as interpreter for them, or when he had carried out IT work for Global Scotland.

'Seeing someone?' West's question, totally unrelated to Michael's own internal dialogue, threw him at first.

'I, well I have been, but I don't see how that is relevant.' He felt a fresh pang of guilt about Poppy, and the fact he hadn't returned her calls.

West smiled, his eyes showing amusement at the obvious misunderstanding. 'I meant are you currently seeing a medical professional regarding your sleep?'

Michael grinned, shaking his head ruefully as he realised his mistake. 'Yes, I've only just started. That's who I mentioned before, Elisabeth. Dr Elizabeth Byfield is a psychologist at the Royal Berkshire Hospital, in the Clinical Psychology department, in case you need to verify that.

'I am hoping to find out what's causing me to act out in my sleep, and then fix it.' Michael paused for a second or two before continuing.

'Easier said than done though I guess.'

West nodded, pleased for the clearly troubled man, but also thinking that the problem could very well just be a result of stress and too much caffeine, in other words not rocket science. 'Good. I hope that will help, and fast.' West stood to leave, buttoning his rumpled suit jacket. 'Well, Michael, I won't take up any more of your time at the minute.'

Michael followed the detective out of the room, reaching past him in the hall in order to open the front door.

West turned to shake Michael's hand and to thank him for his time, and then remembered the other question with which he had arrived. 'Sorry sir, one more question if I may?'

Michael gave a tight-lipped nod, clearly frustrated.

'Mrs McCloud mentioned your brother, and that he'd died when you were young. That must have been horrific for your family. Did you suffer from sleepwalking back then too?'

'Ben died in a car crash. My parents got divorced and I got dragged to the other side of the world. So yes, it was horrific. But no, I didn't act out any dreams back then. Goodbye detective.'

He spoke in the same hurried, clipped tone West had heard before. A tone that was intended to shut down conversations before they could fully begin. West was barely able to say 'goodbye sir' before the door slammed in his face. He remained standing in front of the flat for a moment, sure he would be seeing Michael again soon, certain there was at least one piece missing from the puzzle of this case.

Chapter 40

Michael nearly threw up again as soon as he closed the door in the detective's face, his emotions left in turmoil by West's latest visit. Learning that Russell had regained consciousness was a huge relief, bringing Michael joy for the first time since Jessica had appeared on his doorstep. The feeling of elation was short lived however, a spark that died as soon as the detective started questioning him about his father, and then had moved on to asking about Ben. Michael could not understand the direction that the interrogation, which was what the 'chat' had started to feel like, had taken but as he had returned to his lounge, he had dismissed any worries that the detective suspected him in the deaths of his father and brother. His immediate concern returned to his friends.

He retrieved his mobile from where it was charging certain he would have missed at least one call from Rosie to let him know Russell was OK. He was also sure that the reason she had not answered his calls earlier in the day had been because her battery was dead, or she had been too busy dealing with Russell, or perhaps returning home to check on Donny.

Straight away he saw that he had not received any calls or messages since he had placed his phone on charge and he sat down on the edge of the sofa, the space West had been occupying just a few moments before, deflated and suddenly bone tired.

He dialled Rosie's number immediately, eyes closed as he willed her to answer, but again the call was directed straight to voicemail. This time he stayed on the line, listening to the message, savouring Rosie' voice and imagining her face and that she was speaking to him. Then he left a brief message. 'Hi Rosie, that detective told me about Russell. Thank God, please can you call me as soon as possible?'

It made no sense why Rosie was still not speaking to him, not now that Russell was conscious and, presumably, expected to make a full recovery. Michael did not understand why Rosie would ever have been blocking him out, even with her husband lying unconscious, that was why he had been imagining more palatable scenarios for the lack of calls. Michael and Rosie had known each other since they were toddlers, and while they had seen each other only intermittingly since Ben had died, they had a bond.

Michael had to acknowledge that Rosie could have blamed him for Russell's injuries, in the immediate aftermath of the attack and while he remained unconscious. She must have harboured some small fear that Russell would not survive. Now that he was awake though, and had presumably told her that Michael had attacked him in his sleep, surely now Rosie could have no reason to not speak to her friend? Unless of course she thought that he *was* in control of his actions, that he had not been operating in a trance-like dream state?

This thought made Michael furious, outraged that his friend could believe that of him. He paced his flat, moving from room to room as he considered whether he should head straight to the hospital and confront Rosie, or whether he should punish her – as she was clearly punishing him – by ignoring her.

'That's so childish' Michael muttered to his empty flat, sitting back down in the lounge. He breathed deeply, taking some calming breaths, and considered Rosie's reactions afresh.

She had woken in the night to sounds of fighting.

She had discovered Michael strangling her husband.

She had been unable to make him stop and so had struck him round the back of the head to knock him out.

Michael had no recollection of the attack, and Rosie knew full well that he had been sleepwalking and acting out his dreams recently.

Russell had been taken to hospital in a critical condition.

Russell had awoken, and presumably told Rosie what had happened.

So why was she still ignoring him? Her mobile rang each time he called, and then was sent to voicemail, which meant Rosie was monitoring the phone and choosing to reject Michael's calls. Was that because Russell had taken a turn for the worse? No, surely, she would be completely ignoring her phone if that was the case? It had to be because she did not believe Russell that Michael had been acting out a dream when he attacked. Michael jumped to his feet and resumed pacing around his flat.

Another thought suddenly occurred to him, perhaps that was not what Russell had told her. Perhaps he also believed Michael had been awake and in control of his actions when he had attacked. But if that was the case Rosie would presumably have pressed charges? Whatever the reason for his friend's silence Michael realised he would have to face his demons alone.

'I'm on my own now then' the words, so soft as to be almost inaudible, a breath in a silent room.

The words echoed in Michael's mind, stirring a memory, 'I'm on my own now', an older man's voice, with a thick Scottish accent. For a moment he could not place the voice, half convinced it was himself, and that he was having a premonition of his old age: a life where he was abandoned by Russell and Rosie, Jessica never found; his mother and stepfather disowning him. Then a face formed in his head, a round face, with ruddy cheeks and a bushy white beard. Uncle Mac.

His mind went back to his father's funeral and he remembered his uncle had been talking about himself and the fact that now Michael's father was dead he had no close family. Half-heartedly Michael had disagreed and pointed out that his uncle still had a nephew, Michael. 'Aye, that's true' the man had reluctantly agreed, 'but you'll be going back to America I presume?'

'Sure, I guess, once I sort out everything with the company.'

'And what will you do with Global Scotland?' Mac had spat the name out, clearly an underlying issue there Michael had mused, but had neither the time, nor inclination to press for an explanation.

'I'm selling it, I'm not a businessman'

'No, I suppose you're not. Well, good luck Michael' The old man had turned, shuffling to the door muttering something like 'Let's hope that is all you've inherited from your father'.

Michael had been about to call the man back, to ask what he meant by his cryptic statement, when he had been pounced on by his father's lawyer, Armstrong. When he had glanced back his uncle had already left the house.

Later that night, lying awake in Poppy's bed Michael had remembered the words and had decided that his uncle must have been referring to his father's heart, clearly an underlying health condition that no one had suspected, but potentially a weakness that had been passed on, inherited, by his younger son.

Sitting in his flat more than two weeks later and feeling hurt and betrayed by Rosie and Russell however, Michael began to wonder if his uncle had meant something else. Acting on an impulse, he scrolled through the contacts on his phone, found his Uncle's number and pressed 'call' before he could convince himself this was a waste of time.

'Hello Michael, how are you?' Uncle Mac answered as if he and Michael chatted every week, a friendly conversational tone that belied the fact they had barely spoken in twenty years. The voice was also at odds with the serious, almost fearful way his uncle had spoken at the funeral.

'Not great to be honest.' Michael sighed, thinking *what am I doing?*

'What's the matter?'

Ignoring the question, Michael hurried on 'What did you mean at the funeral, when you said you hoped the company was all I had inherited from dad?'

'Why do you ask?'

'Um, to be honest, I don't know, I think I am grasping at straws, but some weird stuff has been happening to me….'

The line went silent, a space of a minute before his uncle replied

'Come and see me, it will be easier than discussing on the phone.'

'I can't just head up to Edinburgh. Tell me what you mean?'

'In person Michael, trust me.'

The line went silent again, but this time when he had looked at the screen, he saw that his uncle had disconnected the call.

'Well that was bloody weird.' Michael stood up, looking around his lounge as if expecting a sign as to what he should do next.

Chapter 41

Trees, rivers, open fields, sheep, cows, horses, even a herd of deer. Countryside sped by the window, vanishing momentarily as the train hurtled through tunnels, fading into greys and blacks as dusk descended. Michael stared solemnly out of the window of his carriage, his eyes flitting between features of the landscape, but always refocusing on his own ghostly reflection in the glass, his mind still returning to the same question. *Why won't Rosie speak to me?*

He watched his own face reflected in the train window, a blurry outline growing more defined as night fell. *I must be insane* he considered as he sipped the long-cold coffee on the table in front of him.

Michael knocked on his uncle's front door around 11pm. He took a step back to look up at the well-kept façade of the large house. The taxi journey from Waverley station had taken ten minutes to bring him to Craigentinny, the suburb where Mac had lived on the outskirts of Edinburgh for the past thirty years. The older man opened the door after a few moments, a lifetime during which Michael had almost walked away, and would have done if he'd not seen his taxi already pull away into the night.

'Come on in then' Mac spoke gruffly, without preamble, almost pulling his nephew though the doorway.

Michael had barely taken a step over the threshold before he realised that the interior of his uncle's house was far from being as well looked after as the outside. The hallway was crowded with boxes, piled haphazardly against the walls from floor to ceiling, with only the occasional glimpse of peeling wallpaper visible here and there.

Mac noticed where his nephew's eyes were falling, shrugging 'Yes, it's a big place for one person to keep tidy. But I find I cannot tolerate living with anyone else, or even sharing most people's company for more than a few minutes. "Over sensitive" is how your grandparents often described it.' He turned and headed down the narrow passageway, clearly expecting Michael to follow.

Michael opened his mouth to speak, to ask his uncle to clarify his somewhat enigmatic statement, but held his tongue, not wishing to become one of the people that Mac could not tolerate so soon after he'd arrived. Instead he followed, moving cautiously, avoiding colliding with the boxes, for fear of setting off an avalanche of whatever the contents were.

'They are papers' his uncle called over his shoulder, as if reading Michael's mind, 'my research.'

'You're still researching the family history?' Michael asked carelessly. He planned to hear his uncle out and then to get back to Reading as soon as possible, however social niceties were too engrained for him to ignore the comment. He grimaced as his nose was assaulted by a pungent aroma coming from the kitchen, the door through which his uncle had vanished, but he pushed through regardless.

The kitchen was spotless, and decorated in a modern, minimalist way, in complete contrast to the hall. His uncle indicated a seat at the kitchen table and begun busily dishing out whatever was cooking on the stove into two large soup bowls. He waved away Michael's protestations that he was not hungry, placing a full bowl down in front of his nephew.

'Eat. And yes, I am still researching the family – *our* family. Someone has to do it.'

'Ok,' Michael managed, again wondering why his uncle was being so odd. He leaned forwards, his eyes boring into his uncle. 'My inheritance, beyond the company, what were you referring to?'

Mac shook his head, speaking round a mouthful of food, 'Eat now, then we can talk'.

Michael took in another breath of the strong aroma, looking down into the bowl. The contents appeared to be a broth, with pasta and chunks of – hopefully – meat. He took a small spoonful, blowing away some of the heat, before swallowing the contents. The taste was delicious.

'Minestrone' grunted his uncle. 'Now eat up'.

Wow, thought Michael, Uncle, you truly are an enigma.

Chapter 42

Half an hour, one bowl of soup and a slab of rich fruit cake later and Michael was sat uncomfortably close to his uncle, a steaming cup of fresh mint tea in his suddenly cold hands. They had 'retired' in his uncle's words to the first-floor study at the back of the house, a room of generous proportions that was crammed full of bookshelves, an enormous antique desk and a couple of wingback armchairs. The chairs were positioned very close to each other, probably for Mac to put his feet up on one - the one Michael was sat on judging by the wear marks. Mac was also sitting forwards, further closing the gap between them. He spoke with a voice gruff through lack of use.

'So, what's been happening to you?'

'Well, a shorter list would be what's not been happening to me. And I have to warn you, it's pretty far-fetched.' Michael hurriedly told his uncle about the events of the last few weeks, starting with the dream about drowning and ending with his 'sleep attack' on Russell, and the subsequent disappearance of Jessica.

Mac nodded slowly, calmly. 'Actually, that's not so far-fetched.'

Mac had neither recoiled in surprise nor exclaimed in horror at any point during Michael's account. He leaned back in his chair before speaking again, closing his eyes to gather his thoughts.

'Did you know that your father used to have dreams? Dreams like yours?'

Michael shook his head, numbly, his father had never told him this, and he had no memory of seeing or hearing his dad sleepwalking. He glanced up at his uncle, realised his eyes were still closed, and was about to vocalise his response when Mac continued.

'Ian, your da, used to wake me, at least once a week when we were little, four or five years old. He would be screaming blue murder and soaked in sweat, normally still in his bed, but sometimes in a crumpled heap on the floor. My mother and father, your grandparents – though fortunate for you you never met them - they used to come in to our room, turn on the light and wake him up. They didn't soothe him, didn't take him to their bed, they never were particularly warm people, but they would straighten his bed clothes and put him back in bed, at least when he was still a bairn.

When he turned six, so I would have been five, I distinctly remember father coming in to our room, in the middle of the night during one of Ian's nightmares. Our father stood in the doorway, backlit by a lamp on the landing. He didn't even bother turning on our light, didn't come into the room at all. He just stared down at

Ian, who was curled in a ball in the middle of the room, rocking backwards and forwards and crying, sobbing in this most peculiar way, more like a keening than a cry. And our father, he simply said, "enough Ian, that is enough." And then he turned around and went back to bed. I lay in my bed for a few moments, sure my father, or perhaps my mother, was going to come and put Ian back in bed. Then, when they didn't, I climbed out of bed, went to your father, and coaxed him, calmed him, until he stopped crying and got back into bed himself.

The next morning, at breakfast, neither of our parents mentioned what had happened in the night. But later, when we were getting ready for bed that evening, my father took us upstairs, our mother was already half soaked and sitting on the front porch smoking her foul-smelling cigarettes. Father took us upstairs and told us we would not be sharing a bedroom anymore. Instead I was to sleep in our spare bedroom, and Ian would sleep in our bedroom. We started to protest, but one look at our father, whose hands were already clenching and unclenching, silenced us. We dutifully went into our separate rooms, and, as I settled under my covers, I heard the turn of a key and the click of a lock coming from my old bedroom.'

Mac paused, opening his eyes, slowly focusing on Michael as if he was surfacing from sleep.

'They locked you in your rooms?'

'Just your father. This didn't stop the dreams of course, the nightmares continued to wake me on a regular basis, but nobody went to comfort your dad, I couldn't, and our parents wouldn't. Neither were we allowed to talk about the dreams. If we tried to, we would be silenced with a sharp word or a swift look. Occasionally Ian and I would talk about them when we were by ourselves, but mostly we pretended they didn't happen. Ian was embarrassed you see? Our father always said that only babies had nightmares, and Ian, particularly as he was the older one of us, he didn't want to be seen as a baby.'

Michael spoke, filling the silence left by his uncle. His mind was whirling, trying to process the news, imagining his father in a different, softer light than ever before. 'What did he dream about, do you know?'

'As I say, we didn't talk about it much, but, when we did, he always told me he didn't remember anything about the nightmares. He swore that he never dreamed at all. As we got older the dreams seemed to become less frequent, or at least they didn't end with Ian screaming, and then one night they forgot to lock his bedroom door.'

Michael started, sitting up straighter in his seat as he anticipated the end of the story while Mac continued.

'I was ten, your father eleven. And I remember, very distinctly, hearing him walking around the house in the middle of the night. I nearly went to him, to check he was alright and guide him back to bed, but I was scared of leaving my bed, scared of what our father would do to me if he caught me out of my room. And then I heard Ian going back into his bedroom and closing the door, heard through my wall the sounds of him settling back into bed. So, I just turned over and went back to sleep.

'The next morning, we were sat having breakfast, Ian and I cramming toast in our mouths because we were running late for school, when there was a knock at the door. Father went to answer it and we heard him having a conversation with someone, presumably the postman.

'When he came back into the room ten minutes later however, he was ashen faced, and visibly shaken. "Ian" he asked, his voice clipped "did you leave your room last night?" "No sir" your father replied in a deferential tone, the voice we both had to use when addressing our parents. "How could I, the room is locked." "It was not locked last night." Father continued with a slight tremor in his voice "Your idiot mother forgot to lock it." He glared at his wife at this point, though she missed the look of disgust as she was gazing absently out of the window. "Well I didn't know that, I swear it sir." Ian's voice was shaking now, fear of punishment etched onto his face.

"Steven, did you leave your room?" My father now turned his attention on me, his eyes cold, boring into my skull. I replied immediately "No sir". "Did you hear anything in the night?" I paused, just for a fraction of a second, but that was all that my father needed, a slight hesitation and he could tell I was not being truthful. "The truth Steven." Any tremor in his voice now gone, the customary steel back. I bowed my head, unable to lie but ashamed at this betrayal of my brother. "I heard Ian moving around. But he quickly went back to bed."

'Father turned his attention back to Ian, whose face was a study in confusion, mouth open, eyes wide "I swear sir, I did not wake in the night, do not remember any dreams, and I woke up in my bed this morning and waited for you to unlock my door". Our father glared at both of us for a moment before abruptly leaving the room. That was the end of the conservation.

'At school that day I remember the teachers kept having very animated conversations with each other, huddled together in corridors or classrooms during break time, always stopping abruptly when pupils were in earshot. The next day the local newspaper carried a story about a young girl, from our town but not from our school, who had gone missing.

'A few days later the girl was found, dead, in a wood less than a mile from our home. The authorities believed she had been taken from her home, attacked and then left for dead. The official cause of death was exposure.'

Mac, who Michael had never realised was actually named 'Steven' paused again, looking round the room, a look of profound sadness on his face. 'She was only seven years old'.

'Did the police ever find the murderer?' Michael sensed that he knew the answer, a sickening feeling growing in his stomach that threatened to bring his supper back up. He took a few breaths, trying to calm his churning mind and body.

'Point of fact, it would have been manslaughter, not murder. But no, the police never made an arrest. A local man, a loner who lived by himself, was unemployed and was considered by many people to be "crazy" was under suspicion for some time, but there was insufficient evidence linking him to the crime. So, eventually the case was declared to be closed.' Mac spoke in a weary voice, still feeling the impact of the events from his childhood.

Chapter 43

Michael found his voice, starting to ask the question to which he dreaded the answer. 'Did you, do you think it was....?'

Mac interrupted. 'Your father? No, he was a very young eleven, and I don't think he left the house. Certainly, he wasn't out of bed for long as far as I could tell. So no, I don't think it was him.

'But my parents did not feel the same way. No one ever forgot to lock his door at night after that, and when the next school year started, Ian was packed off to boarding school. I think our father wanted to wash his hands of him, and perhaps also wanted to get Ian away from town.

'I hardly saw your father after that, not until we were adults. He used to spend his holidays either at school, or with friends'

'Did the dreams continue?' Michael's voice was flat; he wished he could just end the conservation, run away from the house, but he was compelled to stay.

Mac gazed out of the window, gathering his thoughts. 'He never spoke about having them, and I never heard any reports of unusual incidents at his school. My guess is that if he had woken screaming in the night he would have quickly learned not to. Boarding school children can be very cruel and very unforgiving.'

Mac sighed. Leaning forward and taking Michael's hands, his skin was smooth, his hands surprisingly warm. 'And then, not long after school, your father met your mother. And his whole life changed.'

Michael smiled, believing his uncle was right about that. From the perspective of a child, his parents had always seemed to be very much in love, content to spend every hour together as they built their company as a partnership. They had certainly given both their children attention, but more to drive them on. It was clear to everyone in the family that they had had children out of a sense of obligation. Ben and Michael seemed to be a biological legacy, but always second best compared to Global Scotland.

'When you and your brother came along, I used to visit often, exercising my right as an uncle to spoil you. Your grandparents were already dead by the time you were born. Mother drank herself to death, and father had a catastrophic stroke, I believe due to a combination of stress and of being a bastard. So, I was your only relative on your father's side, beyond distant cousins.'

'I remember' Michael said, still smiling. 'You'd always turn up with pockets full of sweets and take us out to the park.'

246

'Aye. I also wanted to keep an eye on you, was worried that you'd have nightmares like your dad. And, you both did.'

Michael's smile died on his lips at this revelation, not remembering any sleep problems as a child.

'It worried your parents, especially your father. They told me that every few days one or the other of you, or sometimes both, would wake screaming. But always still in your beds. Fortunately, your parents were more enlightened, if not always more compassionate, than mine, and Ian and Joan sought medical assistance and advice. Through a combination of lots of fresh air and exercise, good sleep hygiene and infrequent and short-term medication you gradually started to sleep better or at least the nightmares seemed to occur less frequently.

'I never heard that you'd sleepwalked or acted out anything in your sleep.'

Michael shook his head, shocked by these revelations from his childhood. 'I don't remember having nightmares as a child.'

'I'm not surprised Michael, your parents probably told you that it was a normal part of childhood, something that you'd grow out of.

'But do you remember what happened when Ben was first at university?' Mac pressed his lips together, closing his eyes briefly.

Michael stiffened at this mention of his brother's name, about to launch into a rant about...... about what exactly he didn't know, but he always felt a need to defend his lost brother. With an effort he managed to bring his emotions back in check, gritting his teeth as he spoke. 'What are you talking about?'

'Ah, so your parents shielded you from that as well?

'Well, in Ben's first term at university, a girl - not one of the students, a local Glaswegian lass - went missing. It was reported in the national papers at the time, and Ben mentioned it to your mother and father because the girl lived close to, and worked at, the university. Her name was Charlotte, Lottie they called her. Ben was very upset because he liked the girl, had a crush on her. She was a cleaner in his digs.

Michael started to speak. 'Now look, that's ridiculous...'

Mac held his hand up to silence his nephew. 'There was no evidence that your brother was involved in the disappearance, but it worried your father, and it worried me. When it happened, Ian told me that *he* continued to sleepwalk at boarding school, and after, throughout his life. He said that it was more frequent and "active" the more pressure he was under, the more stressed he was. He told me, confessed to me, that when we were children, the night his door was unlocked and that girl got attacked, well that night when he woke up his hands were covered in small scratches, and there was blood under his fingernails.'

Mac swallowed, his face grave, 'he never told anyone else that. And thank God nothing like that ever happened again'

'Jesus Christ.' Michael stood up abruptly, knocking over his empty tea cup. He took a few steps towards the door, intending to open it to let in some fresh air, when a sudden wave of dizziness washed over him. He bent double, hands on his knees and took slow even breaths until the room stopped spinning.

In a shaky voice, one he didn't recognise as his own, he continued 'What happened to the girl, Lottie?'

'She was never found Michael.' Mac spoke simply, no sense of drama or emotion. Just a statement of fact.

Michael turned to his uncle, stumbling back to his chair but standing behind it, fingers curled tightly round the top of the chair back. 'I cannot believe that Ben would have done something to her, I would have known, he told me everything.'

'But Michael, he might not have known, or, like your da, he might have kept it from you. How was his mood when he came down from Glasgow after that first year?'

'Well, he was fine, the same as usual' each word was a lie that stuck in his throat as Michael spat out the sentence like shards of glass. Ben had been different. Tense, removed, agitated. Until the night of the crash, a week into the holidays, when he had suddenly seemed more like his old self.

Mac was studying his nephew closely 'I know what it's like Michael, to know someone so well, so closely, that it is like you share a mind.' He sighed, deeply, as if dredging his breath from the bottom of the ocean. 'Will you stay the night?'

Both men glanced at the clock above the fireplace, it was 3am.

'Of course you will, come on. The guest bed is already made up, and yes, there is a lock on the outside of the door in case you're worried you'll stroll around and murder me in your sleep. We can speak more in the morning.'

His uncle stood, shuffling from the room and Michael followed numbly, his body moving on autopilot, his world turned upside down.

Chapter 44

'How did you sleep?' Mac had unlocked the guestroom door when he had woken at 7am, then headed to the kitchen to brew some coffee and prepare breakfast. Michael joined him, rumpled but rested, an hour later.

'I slept really well, no dreams, or nightmares, just the most peaceful sleep I've had in weeks, other than when I've been knocked out by medication!'

Mac nodded, seemingly unsurprised. 'Do you have any questions, anything else you want to know about your dad?'

'Ben and I, we both had these dreams, but you, you never did? It was just Dad?' Michael spoke slowly, softly, a look of embarrassment on his face as he studied his uncle. In the bright light of day, in the airy and modern kitchen, the previous night's discussions felt like they had taken place a lifetime ago – or in a dream.

Mac paused, drew in a long breath, answer enough before he even spoke. 'Yes, I did dream, and I did sleepwalk, but less often, and less "actively". Somehow, I managed to keep it from our parents, though Ian of course knew. It seems that all the men in our family do.'

'So, your father too?'

'No, just the men on our mother's side of the family. The women, well they seem to have their own demons.' Mac lapsed into silence, thoughts turned towards his mother. 'I did wonder whether that trait, that tendency towards excess, was what attracted your father to your mother.'

Michael left his uncle's house an hour later, he'd eaten a large bowl of porridge - a cliché in which he was happy to indulge once he'd smelt the steaming dish - and an even larger mug of coffee. He was keen to get home, to see Dr Byfield, to see Russell and Rosie, and to resume the search for Jessica. He recognised a number of striking parallels between his sister's disappearance and the attack on the local girl who had died in his father's home town. Similarities seemed to exist too between the current circumstances, as DS West had called them, and the disappearance of Lottie when Ben was at university. Michael felt certain however that he had not been involved in Jessica's disappearance. How he could be so sure he didn't know, it was an instinct, a gut feeling, that she was OK.

His phone rang, cutting through his thoughts, vibrating across the tray table on the back of the seat in front of him. Michael snatched up the phone, glancing at the caller ID – unknown – before answering.

'Michael Manners.'

'Good morning Michael, I trust I didn't wake you?'

Michael recognised the man's voice straight away, 'Oh, Detective West, good morning.' Michael sat upright in his seat, pushing the phone more tightly to his ear as he struggled to hear over the sounds in the carriage.

'Is it Jess, have you found her?' As soon as the detective answered that no, his sister had not been found, disappointment drained Michael's body and he slumped back down in his seat. His face filled with confusion as the caller went on.

'There has been a sighting though Michael.'

'A sighting? Where?'

'Reading train station.'

'When?'

'Yesterday at 4pm.'

Michael's jaw dropped in shock. 'I was at the station then; Christ I might have walked right past her.'

West paused, momentarily confused on the other end of the call. 'Were you out searching for her?'

'No, I wasn't looking for her.

'I was heading off to visit a relative, in Scotland.' Michael shifted uncomfortably in his seat remembering again the conversation with his uncle, the disappearances of two women, one dead and the other still missing. 'And before you ask, yes, I can prove that. My Uncle can vouch for me, I have the bloody ticket.' Michael immediately regretted losing his cool.

West didn't speak.

'Look, sorry, I'm just worried about Jess.

'Who saw her? Was she alright?'

West spoke at last 'Another passenger recognised her from the description in the papers, the photo on the local news. And we reviewed the station CCTV afterwards.' West carried on speaking, but his voice began to cut out.

'Wait, what did you say?' Michael stood, almost banging his head into the luggage rack above his seat. The other passengers glanced round at him.

'Hang on, I'll move to the end of the carriage, I can't hear you very well.' Michael hurried to the vestibule between carriages. 'Say that again.'

'Michael, you were on the same CCTV as your sister.'

'That's impossible.' Michael's head was spinning at the revelation. 'I swear I didn't see her.'

'I thought you just said you *were* in the station.' West's voice rose in frustration and to make sure he was being heard

'Yes, I was there, I'm not denying that. I told you I got a train, to Scotland. But I didn't see my sister. 'Where did Jess go next, did she get on a train?'

'Well, unfortunately Michael we have not found out where she went next. But there is no evidence that she took a train.'

'You lost her?' Michael spat the words out, anger rising in his guts.

'I thought there were so many bloody cameras that you could track people from one to the next these days?'

West continued, ignoring the recrimination in Michael's voice. 'Miss Manners left the station concourse and went down into the car park.'

'She went into the car park? Why would she go there? She can't drive. She's 16 for fuck's sake.'

'Sir, I need to ask you again to try to calm down.'

'Sorry, but I can't calm down. Would you calm down if your sister was missing? If you were me? I'm going crazy with worry about her. You checked the car park I presume? She's not hiding down there?'

Michael stood in silence while he listened to the detective explaining that they had carried out a search of the car park.

'Look, I know you've only got so many resources, and I realise that she could have been in any of the cars seen leaving the parking lot. I understand that it will take time to follow up with all the vehicle owners. But Jesus, West, please, please prioritise that; don't waste time chasing me down.'

Michael ended the call, went into the toilet he had been standing beside and threw up his breakfast.

Chapter 45

The train ground to a halt on the outskirts of Reading, a delay at first unannounced, and then reported to be due to congestion. Michael sat anxiously in his seat, staring out at the steep banks that hemmed in the train, phone clutched tightly in his hand. 'Come on, come on already'. He'd called West's mobile phone every half hour after they'd spoken, demanding updates on the search for Jessica, sure that she had been abducted from the station car park. At first the detective had taken his calls, calmly answering his questions, but having nothing of note to report. The last couple of times however the call had been directed straight to voicemail.

Michael leaned his head against the cool glass of the window, shutting his eyes to the blur of rain drops smudging the world beyond the train. As soon as his eyelids closed, he pictured Jessica being bundled into a car, driven to a wood and unceremoniously thrown out at the end of a muddy track. His heart began to beat faster, his breath coming more quickly, shallowly, as his mind carried on with its horror movie. Jessica putting her hands up as she tried to see past the lit headlights of the car she'd been thrown out of. Hands grabbing her and dragging her deeper into the woods.

'No!' Michael's eyes shot open, he pushed back from the window and turned wide eyed, expecting to see trees, bushes and his sister's broken body. His breathing was still coming too fast, his heart racing, his body covered in sweat.

'Sir.' A firm, but kind voice broke through his reverie; a hand alighted on his shoulder. Michael swatted it away.

'Sir, wake up. You're having a nightmare. You're on the 3:47 from London, I'm the train guard. Please be calm'

Michael glared up at the man, 'I wasn't asleep. I need to get off the train and find Jess.'

The conductor took a step back, unnerved by the outburst, eyes darting around as he calculated his next move.

'Take slow, deep breathes through your nose Michael and try to focus to my voice.' A different voice, a woman, someone who knew him?

'You're on a train, we are about to pull into the station, Reading station. Then you'll be able to get off the train. That's right; just continue to breathe, slowly, regularly. Good'

Michael glanced up, looking past the guard to the woman behind him, Elizabeth.

'A panic attack?'

'Yes'

'I don't have panic attacks.'

'That's good to know.'

'So, what just happened to me? I was imagining what had happened to Jess. I started breathing faster, my heart was racing, and I felt like I was going to die.'

'Panic attack.'

'But I…'

Elizabeth interrupted Michael raising her hand, smiling and chuckling slightly. 'What you are describing are the textbook symptoms of a panic attack. Completely understandable given what you are going through right now.'

Michael frowned, his mouth set in a grim line, annoyed at this perceived weakness. He and Elizabeth were sat on a bench outside the station, making the most of a brief break in the rain.

Michael explained what had been happening over the last day, briefly summarising his uncle's revelations, but leaving out the visits by DS West. He wasn't sure why he didn't tell Elizabeth this, other than that the police involvement did not seem relevant to his history, from her point of view as a clinician. But there was definitely something else, another reason to hold back about the detective: embarrassment? Guilt?

'Ok, so it was a panic attack. That's better than me falling asleep and half killing people I guess.' He spoke bitterly, without mirth. He twisted his body on the bench, looking directly at Elizabeth. 'So, what were you doing on the train, touting for business? Spotting panic attacks?'

Elizabeth squirmed, shifting slightly away from Michael. It was not just his words that made her uncomfortable. She was also bothered by the fact that they were having a conversation on a park bench, rather than a scheduled session in a consulting room.

She had to admit that she found his case intriguing, exciting even, and the fact was that it had become all consuming – she'd already done more additional reading and had more supervision about this one case than she had about any other. This chance meeting however felt like it was drifting towards being unprofessional.

Michael touched her hand briefly 'I didn't mean to offend you.' The touch sent a spark through her body.

Bollocks she thought *that's the last thing I need*. She took a breath. 'Look, Michael, you didn't offend me, it's just that this conversation is turning into a chat, and, well, I would like to focus on you, on helping you. But I'm glad I was there on the train. I'd been in London on a training course.'

Michael nodded, muttering an apology as she went on.

'Are you still able to come in to the sleep lab tonight?' She was already standing, signalling the end of their session, or conversation, or chat, or whatever it was.

'Sure, I'll see you at nine?' He stood too, disappointed to be leaving Elizabeth's company, but keen to retrieve his car and head back home: Secretly hoping that Jessica might be waiting for him there.

As he took the stairs down to the car park, Michael's thoughts turned back to his sister, and as he pushed through the heavy door on his floor, he felt his heart beginning to race again. He studied the bright lit space for a moment, imagining he was Jess, being yanked by her arm into a waiting car, being bundled into the boot.

'I'm going to lose it again.' he spoke in a whisper, shocked by how fast his breath was coming, how rapidly he had moved from feeling fine to feeling like he was having a heart attack. With an immense strength of will he forced his breathing to slow, taking deep breathes though his nose as Elizabeth had told him, feeling his heartbeat returning to normal. He made himself walk at a normal pace, made himself open his car and get in, made himself drive out of the car park and home as calmly as possible.

Elizabeth had just sat down, book in hand, takeaway ordered, when her work mobile rang. She glanced at the display, intending to ignore it, but seeing the caller ID immediately pressed to accept the call.

'Michael, are you OK? Is it Jessica?' She yawned as she spoke.

'Yes, no; it's the police,' Michael's voice was shaky, almost unrecognisable. 'They're here, at my flat.'

'Has there been a break in, are you hurt? Elizabeth was instantly wide awake, surprised by how concerned she felt for someone she had known only a few days.

'No, I'm OK, but Jess...' Michael paused, his voice breaking.

Elizabeth's heart was full of dread as she imagined what had happened. 'What Michael, have they found her?'

Silence, an audible gulp, Elizabeth could vividly imagine Michael's throat working, trying to reply.

'They have found a body. I have to go and identify her. I can't come to the lab. Sorry.'

'Michael, my God. Do you want me to...?' Michael hung up before Elizabeth could offer to come with him to the mortuary to identify his sister.

Chapter 46

Michael sat hunched over in the back of a police car, head pressed against the window, eyes staring, unfocused, at the bright lights of shops and restaurants, houses and pubs, everywhere filled with people. Happy, sad, angry, jealous, depressed, content, he knew he couldn't tell what they were feeling, what was going on in their lives or what journeys they were on. Some would know each other, others, most, would be strangers, but what connected all those people was that they each had a pulse, a breath, they were alive; his sister was not.

Michael glanced towards the driver's seat, swallowing, trying to generate enough saliva to speak, to ask whether he was dreaming. The driver, Constable Johnson glanced in the rear-view mirror, 'We'll be there in a moment sir' he seemed to anticipate Michael's question, his eyes full of sympathy, pity.

Michael turned back towards the window, closing his eyes against the harsh colours of the world. But he found no solace in the dark behind his eyelids. Immediately he was transported to another night, the first time he had been in a police car, a night that had ended in the untimely death of his brother.

'So, Michael, I need you to come into the room with me, take a look at the body, take as long as you need, and then tell me whether it is your sister, Jessica Manners or not.' West, spoke slowly, making direct eye contact with Michael, making sure he understood. 'Of course, this is going to be an incredibly distressing thing to do, but so that you are aware of what you will see, the body is dressed, and there are no signs of injury, or of struggle.'

Michael, DS West and Constable Johnson, presumably there in case I 'kick off' Michael mused, were stood in a corridor on the second floor of the Royal Berkshire Hospital, opposite a door marked 'Mortuary'. Michael nodded his understanding, reaching for the door handle before West gently laid his hand on his arm, 'There's a separate viewing room, next door. I'll go in first.'

As West moved away to enter a room further up the corridor, the door to the mortuary was opened by a member of hospital staff and Michael glimpsed the space beyond. He took in details of the space with a detached interest, noting the wall of small doors, stacks of drawers for storing bodies, a tiled floor, gullies and drains within it, and an adjustable light above a table on which were laid an array of instruments. Above all he noticed how cold the room was, and a shiver passed through him.

Michael took a step back as the mortuary door closed again and quickly joined DS West at the entrance to the viewing room. A simple bed, of the type used for medical examinations, was positioned in the centre of the over bright room, a surprisingly small cloth covered form lying on top of it. It seemed to take a year to reach the table, where the member of hospital staff who had exited the mortuary stood waiting, a neutral expression on his face. Michael glanced at the name tag, 'George Khan' and then back at the man's face. George, a young man with a very beautiful, light brown face, smiled, very slightly, kindly, at Michael, and then he pulled back the cloth.

The young woman lying on the table was not Jessica. Michael saw that in an instant and almost fell against the table in relief, 'Oh thank God.' The prayer escaped his lips as if it was a breath being pushed out.

West nodded, signalling to the attendant to cover up the body. But Michael raised his hand, 'Stop. She looks so like her.'

The hair, the make-up, the style and colour of both were a perfect match for Jessica. He had known at once that it was not his sister, because Jessica had a scar on her chin, from a childhood brush with a fence, but beyond this the resemblance was uncanny. Michael turned his attention to the rest of the body. From what he could tell with her lying down this young girl, this terribly unfortunate victim was the same size as his sister. She was also wearing the same clothes, white and red sneakers, dark blue jeans, and a black SuperDry hoodie open to reveal a white t-shirt. 'She's wearing her clothes.'

'Yes' West spoke softly, that's why we thought it was Jessica, this girl's appearance matches the photos you gave us, and the clothes are similar to what we saw on the station CCTV. 'I guess they're popular for this generation.'

West started to turn from the bed; Michael grabbed his hand, commanding his attention. 'No, not similar clothes, these are *her* clothes. I recognise the mark on her left sneaker, I saw it the other day and she told me she'd got it trapped on an escalator. And the jeans, that patch, she sewed it on, it's from her school swimming club in the States.'

Michael leaned closer, looking again at the face, searching for the scar he didn't want to find. 'Christ, she smells of the same perfume, and I'd swear those are her ear rings.' Michael took a step back from the table 'what the fuck is going on?'

George, the attendant, jumped at the outburst, looking for all the world like he was about to reprimand Michael for his profanity. 'Are you saying this poor girl has been dressed in your sister's clothes sir?'

'Yes, that's exactly what I am saying. And, unless it's a coincidence she has had her hair styled and make-up put on to match Jess too. It's like some kind of sick joke.'

'It is no joke for this poor girl sir.' George whispered, eyes wide.

'No, of course.' West spoke calmly, with customary authority. 'Thank you, Mr Khan, you may cover her up now. We will however need to examine her clothing and see if any hair on them matches Jessica's hairs found at Mr Manners' flat.'

'Yes, of course' George cast another look of disapproval and bewilderment at Michael and then gently drew the cloth back over the corpse's face.

Michael turned to the detective, 'Was there no identification with the girl?' He swallowed, 'with the body?'

'Yes, there was, if you'll come with me it's in the office across the corridor.' West drew Michael forwards, a steadying hand on the man's back.

As they left the room Michael felt as though he was being plunged into darkness. The corridor, despite being well lit, felt dim and gloomy after the bright and sterile lighting in the viewing room, it also felt close, humid compared to the frigid temperature where the body was being kept. West directed Michael into a room across the corridor, shaking his head at the police officer still stood in the passageway as they passed.

Michael rushed to the desk as soon as he entered the room, reaching forwards to pick up the clear bag full of personal effects, recognising at once his sister's garish phone cover. 'Stop!' West called out, overloud in the confined space. Michael pulled his hands back, as if he had been burned. 'I'll show you the items. We can't contaminate the evidence.'

'God, no of course. Sorry.'

'It's fine; it's instinct to reach for them. Especially as they belong to your sister.'

Michael turned towards the detective confused.

'What do you mean?'

The detective opened the large plastic bag, removing smaller bags containing individual objects, listing them off as he did so:

'Mobile phone, which is still charged and once we turned it on and rung it, we confirmed it is your sister's; purse containing a credit card, identity card – both in your sister's name – and a mixture of English and American cash; some tissues, and a lip balm'.

'Where's her bag, were those things just in her, that girl's, pockets?'

'Yes. You said she took a handbag and her holdall with clothes when you went to Mr and Mrs McCloud's residence?'

'Yes, and you couldn't find them there, so Jess must have taken them. But where are they, where is she?' Michael's voice rose full of fear and frustration, begging the detective to magically provide answers, to conjure his sister out of thin air.

'We don't know sir, Michael. I am sorry.
'The first thing I want to do is confirm that the clothes are your sister's. So, can you stay here to help us to do that?'

Michael nodded, head spinning. He was relieved that the body was not that of his sister, but was harbouring a growing despair because she was still missing, and presumably being held somewhere against her will.

'I will also send an officer to your flat, to retrieve a sample of your sister's hair from your spare bed, for comparison with any hairs we find on the clothes and on the victim's body. Do you have a spare key I can give to the officer?'

'Yes, in my car, the glove box, I can give your officer my car key.' Michael reached into his pocket, then remembered something and shook his head, 'No wait,

Jess had it, it should be in her handbag' He paused 'Which is still missing, presumably with her.'

West went back into the corridor barking commands at his officer. 'Johnson. I need you to head back to Mr Manners' flat. Let yourself in with his keys. Retrieve a sample, and then wait there to be relieved by another officer. We need to have someone stationed at the flat until Mr Manners can change the locks. Then, head back here with the sample.'

The officer nodded, then strode up the corridor. West re-entered the office and found Michael standing at the desk, gazing in confusion at the phone and purse lying within their evidence bags. 'Coffee sir?'

Michael muttered something that West took to mean yes please, and then he spoke more loudly. 'What do you think has happened to my sister?' He didn't turn from the desk, barely moved his body as he spoke.

'I really don't know at this stage Michael.' The detective started to leave the room to get coffee from the vending machine nearby.

'What's your best guess detective?'

'I believe she is alive. But, honestly, I think she is being held somewhere, otherwise we would have heard from her.'

'But why?'

West glanced at Michael's back, wishing he could see his face, perhaps get a clue as to what was going on, and what involvement Michael had in it. He entered the room fully, walking round the desk to face the other man.

Michael looked up as West answered. 'I don't know why she may have been kidnapped, assuming that is what has happened. Perhaps that woman attacked Jessica, took her things, and then got attacked herself. But that doesn't feel right. What do you think?'

'I haven't a clue; I just want her found, alive.' Michael's voice was flat, a monotone; he felt completely defeated by the lack of progress and his face showed the same lack of emotion.

Michael returned to his flat at 1am. All the lights had been left on, but he was surprised by how tidy everywhere looked seeing as he had given his permission for the police to search for clues, samples, whatever they needed. He felt numb, slumping onto the sofa and closing his eyes against the light.

The clothes on the victim's body had been confirmed as being an almost certain match for his sister's, due to identifying marks. Hair samples found on the hoodie were being tested against the sample from the pillow that Jessica had been using at the flat. But he was sure they would be a match. The victim was wearing Jessica's watch, as well as earrings, and evidence suggested that the underwear on the body was also Jessica's – originating as it did from an American department store. Michael's stomach roiled as he remembered this, and he rushed to the bathroom.

The identity of the woman was as yet unknown and the cause of death had not been established, but there was no sign of a struggle. The only injury found by the pathologist conducting the initial autopsy was a puncture wound on the victim's left wrist, possibly caused by a hypodermic needle during an injection. Blood samples were being tested in the toxology lab, and results were due the next day. West had asked Michael casually if he knew the woman, if he recognised her, other than that she was not Jessica. Michael had almost missed the question, because he'd been so wrapped up in thoughts of his sister and had answered with a simple shake of the head. West had no evidence that this was a lie, and gut instinct told him that it was the truth, nevertheless the team that had searched the flat had looked for signs that someone else had been there recently, other than Michael and Jessica.

A police officer was stationed outside the flat, with a colleague outside monitoring the building from an unmarked car. Ostensibly this was to protect Michael because his spare keys were missing, but Michael thought that it was also in case he decided to leave. 'I'd suspect me in the circumstances,' he mused out loud.

'I'd suspect me of all of it; Jess's disappearance, Russell's attack, that poor girl's death…'

Chapter 47

'I really, really think you should contact the police about him.' James leaned on Elizabeth's desk, invading her space for what felt like the millionth time.

'And tell them what exactly?' Elizabeth glared at her colleague. 'That he is seeking therapy, trying to get treatment for a debilitating sleeping disorder? I don't know what your problem is with my client, except for some unfounded nonsense around drug use, but I think *you* should consider getting some therapy.' Elizabeth shoved her chair back, eyes sparking in anger as she stood.

'What's my problem?' James sputtered, narrowing his eyes as he returned Elizabeth's gaze. 'What's my problem? Look, this guy is violent; he takes drugs, and this.' He grabbed his newspaper off the desk and thrust it in Elizabeth's face, 'this is his sister, right?'

The front page of the *Reading Chronicle* contained a fuzzy image of Jessica Manners, above a headline reading *Missing teen spotted at railway station*.

Elizabeth rubbed her forehead, slumping back into her chair, all fight extinguished as she thought about the poor girl, lying cold in the mortuary only a few hundred metres from where she and James were arguing. She hadn't heard from Michael since he had phoned

Saturday evening to cancel the lab test, to tell her that Jessica's body had been found. She hadn't told James this because the news had not been confirmed, because she didn't want to discuss her client, but mostly because it was none of his bloody business.

James continued his rant. 'His sixteen-year-old sister is missing. His best friend is in hospital. Manners himself is injured. Christ, Lizzy, join the dots; there's a pattern here right? Bad things keep happening around him and he is clearly dangerous. I don't think you should be treating him. He either needs to be admitted to a psychiatric hospital or sent to prison.' James paused, glaring petulantly at his colleague.

'James, his sister just died. Now more than ever he needs psychological support.' Elizabeth stared up at him, battling her emotions. 'Surely even you can see that?'

James took a step back, momentarily lost for words. He stared at her, no hint of sympathy on his face, more a look of confusion at the news that Jessica was dead. 'He killed her?' James exclaimed, eyes wide, looking between the paper, which showed a very alive Jessica, and Elizabeth. His mouth kept opening and closing, an unflattering look that brought to mind a goldfish.

Elizabeth almost laughed hysterically at this thought, before registering his words. 'No, of course he didn't kill her. He was in Scotland and only found out that she'd died Saturday evening, that's why he cancelled his lab test.'

James scoffed 'But you don't know when she died do you? Could have been the night he nearly killed his best friend. Some kind of drug fuelled murder spree. You don't know he was in Scotland at all, you only have his word for that.'

'Don't be ridiculous. Murder spree? He was asleep when he attacked his friend, he didn't know Jessica had gone missing, he ……' She trailed off. James was right; she didn't know, not for certain, anything other than what Michael had told her about that night. He'd certainly withheld some information, there were the drugs for instance, and violent accidents certainly orbited her patient. And yet, and yet she felt that he was telling the truth when he said he didn't know where Jessica was. When he had called to let her know she had been found dead, he'd sounded so broken, so utterly destroyed to lose his sister and Elizabeth could not believe he had had anything to do with her death – at least not consciously. And that was the point she realised.

'OK, look Liz…. Elizabeth' James held up a hand in apology when he caught himself using the nickname. 'Let's say everything he has told you is true. OK? But isn't it possible that he could have hurt his sister, killed her even in his sleep? And hidden the body? He might genuinely have no memory of that, might have truly believed she was missing. Until her body turned up.' James moved round the desk and reached out a hand to touch her arm. 'You know there are cases like that.'

Elizabeth stood to increase the distance between them, walking round to the other side of her desk. 'Yes, of course that's possible. But, given the timeline, it seems highly unlikely. I would also presume that the police would have held him if there was any evidence of a struggle where Jessica had gone missing....' Elizabeth was interrupted by her phone. Glancing at the display she saw it was Michael, and hurriedly answered.

'Michael, how are you doing?' She moved away from James, to the corner of their office. 'I know, that's a stupid question.'

She paused, listening, a look of relief spreading across her features
'It wasn't your sister? Oh, thank God.'

James raised an eyebrow from across the room, a look of confusion on his face.

'But she's still missing? You want to meet, sure, of course. Hang on.' Elizabeth pulled her phone away from her ear to access her calendar.

'I've got a gap at 12. Could you come to the clinic then?

'Great, see you in a few hours.'

She smiled as she ended the call, glancing at James with a look of triumph, as if to say 'see, you're the crazy one.'

'OK, great; so, his sister is not dead, at least not that the police know. But please, Elizabeth, be careful with this guy. Ask him about his history of drug use. I am not sure he is as innocent as he makes out.'

Chapter 48

Michael stood in the hospital elevator, shifting his weight from side to side, anxiety growing in his chest. As he had parked in the hospital's car park and walked into the reception area his mind was on Jessica, replaying his last visit to the hospital, to the mortuary, to view her body. No, he reminded himself, some other unfortunate girl's body. Riding the lift his thoughts turned to his destination.

He had spent Sunday in his flat, falling asleep around 3am, a couple of hours after returning from the hospital. He had taken the rest of the painkillers prescribed for his head injury and had not surfaced for twelve hours. He'd then been unable to sleep Sunday night, his body clock well and truly screwed up. Instead he had spent the night prowling around his flat, unable to settle to anything, waiting for the dawn to come so that he could return to the hospital.

He glanced up and down the corridor when he exited the lift, turning right and right again before being buzzed through to the ward. He knocked on the first door he came to and then opened it, taking a breath, a big gulp of air as he entered the room. 'Hi.'

Russell, turned to face the door, surprised to have a visitor, shocked to see who it was.

'Michael?' Russell's voice was still little more than a whisper, he shifted up the bed. 'What are you doing here?'

Michael couldn't answer, could not even take a step towards the bed at first. The sight of his long-term friend, face puffy, one eye still swollen shut, neck immobilised by a brace, bandages tightly wrapped round his chest, froze him to the spot. The knowledge that he, Michael, had caused these injuries brought bile to his throat.

Michael swallowed down the acid, forced his body to take a step towards the bed. 'Russ, I'm so sorry.' His words a whisper themselves, did not begin to do justice to what he was feeling. 'I, you're……' He held his hands up. 'I thought I'd killed you'

'Aye, so did Rosie. But it's going to take more than a Yank to finish off this tough old Scot.' Russell smiled thinly, and then twisted his body to reach for the cup next to his bed.

Michael stepped forward quickly 'Let me' he held the cup near his friend's mouth; Russell took a few slow swallows through a straw.

'Thanks. What I don't understand is how you didn't even get a scratch on you.'

Michael rubbed the back of his head gingerly tracing the stitches, 'well, I didn't exactly escape unscathed'.

Russell nodded, as much as the brace would allow. 'True, that wee woman is tougher than us both.'

Michael laughed lightly as he took a seat. 'Did Rosie tell you about Jess?'

Another nod.

'She's still missing, but…. the police think that she was attacked, maybe even kidnapped.' Michael's words fell out like lumps of lead, settling on the floor between them. As he continued however, he seemed to take strength from his silent friend.

'I had to come here, to the morgue, identify a body' Russell started to speak, but Michael rushed on 'It wasn't Jess, but it – the corpse – was wearing her clothes and had her phone and purse. The police don't have a clue who she is, I mean who she was. They have no idea what's going on.

'Jess was spotted in the station, here in Reading, three days ago, but no sign or word since then. I just don't know what to think….'

'What the hell are you doing here? Get away from him!' Michael had not heard the door open he'd been so absorbed in telling Russell about Jessica.

Rosie grabbed Michael's shoulder, pulling him back, away from her husband. The action caught him off guard, he'd just been turning towards his friend's voice, slightly unbalanced on the chair, and as Rosie pulled on his shoulder his chair tipped and spilled him to the floor. He fell awkwardly, his right arm colliding with the metal side of the bed, his head smacking into the floor.

Rosie leaned over him, hands clenched as if to strike his prone body. 'How dare you come here?' The words, a yell, held such venom that Michael pushed himself backwards, half under Russell's bed.

'Rosie' Russell tried to speak, to get his wife's attention, but she ignored him, her eyes wet with tears, her attention concentrated on Michael as she drew back a foot to lash out at him.

'Rosie, that's enough'. Louder, almost a shout.

Rosie's head whipped round towards her husband. She took a step back so Michael could roll and crawl from where he'd retreated to, emerging on the other side of Russell's bed.

She darted forwards as soon as he had moved, leaning over to hug and kiss Russell. 'Did he hurt you my love? Again?'

'No' Russell's voice was a mere croak, having exerted it too much shouting at Rosie to stop.

Michael had managed to sit up, leaning against the wall, his chest heaving and his arm aching from the collision with the bed. 'I'm sorry Rosie, I' Michael paused and swallowed his mouth suddenly dry, the words lodged in his throat. 'I just needed to see Russell.'

'Well, now you've seen him, go.' Rosie looked up, her eyes cold, but her voice shaking, betraying the turmoil she was going through. 'Just go. Please.'

Michael nodded, rising unsteadily to his feet, rubbing the back of his head and discovering it was wet. He looked at his hand, a thin line of blood covered his fingers, presumably his stitches had burst. 'I'm sorry Rosie. I love you both.'

As he left the room, he heard Russell's whisper 'We love you too. And we hope, we pray that Jess is OK.'

Chapter 49

Michael stopped on his way to his appointment with Elizabeth, pausing in the hospital's café for a double espresso and a cheese and bacon turnover. He also grabbed a pile of napkins, blotting them against his stitches, relieved to see the bleeding had already stopped. The pain in his head had receded to a dull ache, but his right arm was throbbing. As he gulped down the coffee, he saw the local newspaper, the picture of his sister, and felt bile rising in his throat. He tossed the pastry in the nearest bin without taking a bite.

Michael began speaking as soon as he sat down in the consultation room, filling Elizabeth in about what he knew, or mostly didn't know, about his sister, describing the visit to the mortuary in detail, a cathartic experience that Elizabeth let run its course. 'So, this woman, practically a child in the morgue, no one knows who she was.' Michael's voice tailed off as he finished his account.

'My God that's awful. I'm so relieved it wasn't Jessica, obviously! You two are very close, aren't you?' Elizabeth leaned forward in her seat, sensing an opportunity to gain more insight into her complex client, hoping that he wouldn't just fob her off.

'Yes, I practically raised her. My, *our,* mother has a drinking problem.' Michael paused, embarrassed, but continued, after a glance at Elizabeth revealed sympathy rather than judgement.

'She hides her drinking from the world, but in private she's a mess, a complete disaster much of the time.

'Brett, that's Jess' dad, gives everything, his time, his attention and his money to just two things: his horses and his wife – in that order. He's never got anything left for Jess – and certainly not for me. That's why I didn't leave home until I was in my thirties, until Jess could look after herself. Some protector I turned out to be.' Michael slumped in his seat.

Elizabeth nodded in understanding. The fact that Michael was part parent certainly explained the bond between the siblings, the intensity of his response to her disappearance. 'You mustn't blame yourself.' she offered kindly.

'Really?' He shot back. 'Who should I blame then? There's no one else. And what if I did something to her in my sleep? I could literally be responsible for her disappearance, or worse, her death.' He shuddered as he crossed his arms.

Michael was about to say more about his sister when a sharp pain in his right arm reminded him that he'd not told Elizabeth where he'd just been.

'I just went to see Russell – my friend.' Elizabeth nodded that she knew who he meant. 'He is doing OK, thank God, but Rosie – you know, his wife - turned up, and attacked me. Understandably.'

Elizabeth did not feel it was understandable and *was* surprised, but she kept her emotions in check. She felt sympathy for Michael's friend but was also shocked that he was being abandoned by those closest to him, at a time of such obvious need. She waited for him to continue, when he didn't, she decided to change tact.

'Michael, when we last met, I meant to ask you some questions, standard in cases of disordered sleep.'

Michael nodded, 'OK, shoot.'

'Well, obviously I know that you are somewhat, in fact completely addicted, to caffeine, and we've discussed the impact that might have on your sleep, as well as other health implications.' Elizabeth paused, watching her client closely; Michael made a spinning motion with his still bandaged right hand, encouraging the doctor to continue.

'I need to ask though, are you under the influence of any other non-prescription medication?'

Michael tilted his head, momentarily confused before he realised what she was asking. 'Alcohol, no I'm a light weight, one beer a week max. And drugs? No, I never touch them. Other than over the counter medicine or prescription drugs of course.'

Elizabeth glanced at his arm, where James had been told that there was a puncture wound. Wondering how she could ask about it, to challenge her patient, she noticed a red stain on the bandage. 'What's wrong? Is your arm bleeding again?'

Michael looked down, surprised to see a fresh stain of blood on his right forearm. 'Damn, it must have happened when I fell, I banged my arm into the bed I think.'

Elizabeth leaned forwards. 'You should get that checked, to make sure it doesn't need stitches.

He shook his head, starting to unroll the bandage. 'It doesn't hurt enough; I guess I've just opened up an old cut. As he peeled back the dressing, she caught a glimpse of the words carved neatly into the fleshy underside of his arm, weeping slightly where some of the scabs had been knocked off.

'What's that?' She pointed at the inside elbow, where a separate wound was just visible, a very angry red. 'Is that a puncture wound?'

Michael bent over his own elbow, gently fingering the cut. He looked at her quizzically, 'another injury?'

'It looks more like an injection site.'

He shrugged, leaning back in his chair, as he put the dressing back in place and hurriedly wound the bandage back round it. 'I guess I was given a shot of something for the pain, or to numb me, or a tetanus jab to make sure I didn't get infected.'

'Perhaps, I'm sure you may have been given a tetanus shot at some point recently, more likely when you injured your arm the first time. Your medical records will show that.' Elizabeth pushed a strand of hair behind her ear.

'But that's not a normal spot for injections – not clinical ones at any rate. Normally they would go in the upper arm.' She touched the place on herself. 'Blood tests might leave a puncture wound in the lower arm, but not normally that close to the elbow – and again records will show if you've had any blood tests recently.

Michael's face clouded as he understood her meaning. 'You think I injected myself? That I'm a druggie?' He half rose from his seat, embarrassed and angry, the emotions flaring up and colouring his cheeks. 'I told you I don't do drugs. Why doesn't anyone believe me?' His voice had risen in pitch, whining.

Oh shit, I'm losing him, again. Elizabeth hurriedly held up her hands, in apology, 'Look, I believe that you don't remember taking anything, but the evidence suggests you injected something into your arm.'

'So, what, I'm sleep 'using' now as well as sleepwalking?' Michael slumped back in his seat, his anger draining away as quickly as it had appeared. 'Christ, Dr Byfield, Elizabeth, I don't know what the hell I'm doing to myself or to anyone anymore.' He curled his arms around his body defensively.

Elizabeth leaned towards him, again fighting an instinct to bolt from the room in the face of his explosive emotional responses. 'Then let's find out together. Look, we'll run blood tests, get a toxology report to see if there are any unusual substances in your bloodstream.'

Michael screwed his eyes tightly shut, speaking through gritted teeth. 'OK, OK. How soon can you run tests?'

Elizabeth glanced up at the clock. 'I'll have to have my colleague, Dr Booker request them; can you head down to the pathology department? There's normally a queue I'm afraid. But by the time you get there the order should have reached them.'

Michael grunted his assent, standing to leave.

Elizabeth continued, 'And I will see you back here for the sleep tests this evening?'

Another nod. Michael's whole demeanour had changed since she'd raised the question of drugs. He had shut down, a light going out in his eyes. It could be defeat, that's what it looks like, she considered, gathering her files once he had left the room. Defeat, betrayal, he accused me of not believing him, of no one believing him. But it could also be a defence, a wall put up to hide something else; to hide his guilt?

Chapter 50

'I am getting way too familiar with this place' Michael muttered to himself as he headed straight to the pathology department, not even checking signs. He had formed a map of the hospital in his mind, having been to several different locations within the sprawling site. Glancing at his watch he was surprised to see that it was still only early afternoon. Hours until he would be in the sleep lab. He knew that he was building his hopes up, desperate to find a solution, pinning his future on Elizabeth. It was probably unrealistic, wishful thinking, but he felt sure that she would present him with a clear explanation for what was happening to him. And a road map for how to solve the problem.

The next half hour was taken up with queuing for and then having blood tests. He received a dark look from the nurse managing the queue when she reviewed the order from Elizabeth, via James Booker. Whether because the tests were marked urgent, or because they were looking for illegal drugs in his system he didn't know.

Michael left the hospital late in the afternoon, due to return five hours later. He phoned Detective West on his way back to the car park. 'Any news detective?'

'No, sorry. However, I understand that you paid a visit to the McClouds this morning?' West's voice sounded weary, making Michael wonder whether the detective had slept himself since the pair had first met. 'I would strongly advise against doing that again without first arranging a visit with Mrs McCloud. It seems that you turning up unannounced caused a fair amount of....' West paused, considering his next word carefully 'distress.'

Michael chuckled in spite of his dark mood. 'You could say that I suppose.' He touched his head tentatively, his fingers skimming over the lump where he'd collided with the floor.

'Sir, it really is no laughing matter. Mrs McCloud is planning on issuing a restraining order.'

'What the fuck? Why? She attacked me, I was just checking on how Russell was doing.' Michael's voice rose in a shout that caused hospital staff and other visitors to glance round.

'Please sir, try to calm down. From your friend's perspective, she saw a man leaning over her husband's bed, a man who recently put him in that hospital bed.'

'Have you spoken to 'her husband'? He didn't seem to mind me being there.' Michael spat his words out not bothering to disguise his anger.

'Nevertheless sir, I would be grateful if you don't attempt to visit them until this all settles down.' West spoke in a measured tone, but Michael imagined he could hear frustration barely concealed.

'Fine, whatever. I'm going to keep looking for Jess. Somebody has to.' Michael jabbed at his phone, ending the call and shoving his mobile back into his pocket.

The phone vibrated and began to ring before he'd taken another step.

'What is it West?' Michael spat the words. 'I won't go and see them again, OK?'

'Michael, is that you?' The voice on the other end of the phone spoke in a tentative manner, cautiously, but the speaker was instantly recognisable.

'Oh my god, Jess, is that you? What happened? Where are you? Are you OK?'

The questions spilled out in one breath, and Michael leaned against his car suddenly unable to stand unaided.

'Yes, I'm OK big brother. I'm back home with mommy. I was so scared when you were fighting Russell. I just had to get out of the house.' Jess's voice, normally bubbly sounded subdued, her words clipped, devoid of the slang that coloured almost all her conversation.

'Christ, thank God you're OK. I am so sorry I scared you. Why didn't you answer my calls though?'

'I lost my phone. I was in the airport, getting changed out of the clothes I'd slept in - they have those big changing rooms y'know? And someone grabbed my stuff, my phone and purse too. Thank goodness I had my passport and more clothes. My plane boarded soon after, and I've only just arrived at mom and dad's, so I couldn't phone before.'

'Shit, have you reported the theft? Jess, I thought you'd been kidnapped, or worse. I had to identify a body; they had your clothes....'

She interrupted, cutting him off 'Sorry, I have to go Mickey. Mommy's calling me. I'll phone back when I can.'

'Wait, Jess, hand me over to Mum!' Michael stopped speaking as soon as he realised his sister had ended the call.

Chapter 51

'Can you remember exactly what your sister said?' West sat forwards, pen poised above his open notebook.

Michael was sitting across a bare desk from West, in a stuffy room with recording equipment off to one side on a wheeled table. One wall was taken up by a large mirror.

He had headed straight to the police station as soon as Jessica had hung up, demanding to speak to the detective.

'No, can you remember everything?' Michael responded angrily, his voice rising, he took a slow, deep breath.

'She said she'd gone home straight after the attack on Russell. But that on her way, at the airport, someone had stolen her clothes, phone and purse while she was getting changed.'

West raised an eyebrow at this. 'And how did Miss Manners seem to you?

'Well that's the weirdest thing. She was 'off'?'

'How do you mean 'off'?'

'You know, not herself? She referred to our mother as Mommy and Mom. I don't think I have ever heard her say that, she hates her parents 90% of the time.'

West nodded, making notes. 'Anything else?'

'Yes, she called me Mickey. Again, something she has never called me before, even when she's been winding me up. Michael, Mikey, once maybe Mike, but never Mickey. To her Mickey is Mouse, nothing else.

'And that story about her clothes? That sounds really odd, completely implausible to me. Plus, what about the person who saw her in the train station, and the CCTV?'

'Well, the eyewitness could have been mistaken, and the camera footage could have been a different woman, the woman who unfortunately later ended up in the mortuary. But the clothes, that is odd, as you say. And I am sure your sister would have reported that to the police at the airport.' West gazed up at the mirror, aware that Johnson was watching from the small room on the other side, observing the interview. Michael was also aware of this and had been completely nonplussed. This reaction was unlike other interviewees West had questioned in the same room and who had been outraged by the suggestion of being 'secretly watched', as if it was some kind of ploy by the police force – a trick to get them to admit to something they had not done. West normally found that this response was an indication of a guilty conscience, further evidence he mused that Michael – whilst being an angry and somewhat disagreeable person – was not responsible for the disappearance of his sister.

West returned his attention to the man in question. 'Can I see your phone please sir?'

'Yes, of course.' Michael unlocked his phone and passed it across the table.

'Thank you, Michael.' West swiped to recent calls, noting down the number from which Jessica had phoned. He passed the phone back across.
'Is that your mother's number?'

Michael shook his head, 'No, it could be Brett's, my stepfather's, though. 'Should I call it again?'

'Again?'

'Yes, I tried it straight away when Jess hung up, but I couldn't get through. I couldn't get through to my mother either.'

West took his own phone out of his jacket pocket, dialled the number he had just written down, and put the phone to his ear. He frowned as soon as he pressed dial, listening to the pre-recorded message "the number you have dialled has not been recognised. Please try again." He double checked what he had dialled, and that the number he had written down was the same as the one in Michael's phone memory.

'Can you try your mother again please, Michael?'

Michael nodded, started the call and straight away gazed at West, shaking his head in frustration. 'Voicemail, no ringing.'

West nodded slowly, sharing the man's frustration, but also unsurprised that the case was not about to be resolved in a neat and tidy fashion. 'Michael, I'd like you to head back to your flat, try to get some rest. I am going to contact the American authorities and ask them to dispatch a police officer to your parents' address. Can you give me the details? We are also following up with passport control to see if she actually left the country.'

Michael scribbled the address on the pad and slid it back across to West.

'In the meantime, stay home because it is possible that your sister will call again, either on your mobile or landline, please let me know straight away if she does.'

'Of course, but I'll only be home for a few hours. I'm due at the hospital tonight.' Michael replied, shrugging.

West stared, feeling confused and more than a little annoyed. 'I asked you to not visit your friends for now.'

'No, I'm not, I got the message loud and clear that I'm persona non grata right now. I'm going back in for a sleep test, with my therapist, Dr Byfield. I'll be under observation all night, so don't worry, I won't be attacking people.'

'Ok, but can you reschedule? It's really important you're there, at home, if your sister gets in touch again.'

'I had to cancel Saturday night, because of going to the morgue. Look, detective, tonight I can direct my landline to my mobile, and leave that with Dr Byfield, she can wake me if it rings. And you can post an officer at my flat in case someone turns up there.

'I have got to try to get to the bottom of these problems, sleepwalking, insanity, whatever it is. You can see that right?' Michael's voice shook, and the detective could see the desperation in his eyes.

West took a breath before replying, he was in two minds: part of him wanted Michael to do exactly as he'd been told, but mostly he wanted to know whether there was any truth to his sleeping disorder or if it was another psychological issue, or whether it was simply a distraction, an attempt by Michael to divert attention from his crimes. 'OK, go. But let me know if anything out of the ordinary happens.'

Michael stood, blowing air out in a sigh. 'Thank you West, I'll be in touch.'

'One other thing Michael.' West glanced up, standing. 'We received the results of the toxology exam on the dead woman.'

Michael turned at the door, curious but dreading the news in equal measure, fearing that the fate of the woman he'd seen in the mortuary would end up being the same fate as his sister's.

'She had a massive quantity of GHB, you might have heard of it as the "date rape drug" in her system. The amount present would have rendered her unconscious within minutes, and in all likelihood she would have never woken up.' West watched Michael's face closely as he spoke, seeing only horror and sadness in the man's expression. 'We've still not identified the victim; however, she was mostly likely a homeless person with the right face, but in the wrong place at the wrong time.'

Chapter 52

'Mr Manners, thank you for coming back in for observation and for going for those blood tests this afternoon. We don't have those results yet but should do so in a couple of days' time.' Elizabeth spoke in a formal tone of voice and with a disinterested affect that was unfamiliar to Michael. Her behaviour was completely at odds with how she'd been just a few hours earlier, and in all their previous meetings. She sat stiffly across the table from him in the small room adjoining the sleep lab.

'Who's this?' Michael shifted in his seat, confused by the change in Elizabeth. He raised a finger to point as he acknowledged the tall man standing behind her. He was clearly a doctor, a few years younger than Elizabeth, maybe mid-twenties, and was leaning against a wall with cocky assurance.

Elizabeth gave a thin smile. 'This is my colleague, Dr James Booker. I mentioned we were working on this study together? He will be observing tonight.'

Michael nodded his understanding, disappointed at having to share Elizabeth's company.

James had insisted on being present, at least for the first part of the evening, when Elizabeth had told him about Michael's denial regarding substance use and had then reluctantly admitted that her patient had lost his temper. At first, she had been glad of the company, more than a little frightened of Michael and happy to give in to the idea of James being present. Now, sat across from a calm and seemingly relaxed Michael she felt somewhat foolish.

'Observing you observing me?' Michael grinned, a brief moment of levity. Elizabeth shrugged as if to say, *I know, crazy right.*

Michael spoke again, a mixture of excitement and wariness in his voice. 'Before we begin, Jess called me this afternoon.'

Elizabeth gasped and covered her mouth in shock, relieved for her client. All her formal demeanour – which had been purely for James' benefit – was temporarily forgotten. 'That's fantastic news. Where is she? Is she OK?'

'She's gone back home, to the US. She says she is OK. But there are holes in her story. So, I'm hoping she will call again. Can you answer my phone if she does?' Michael slid his phone across the table, 'And wake me up?'

Elizabeth nodded at once, picking up the phone and placing it on top of her papers.

'Who is Jess?' James began, breaking his silence for the first time. Before either of the others could speak, he made the connection himself. 'Oh, you mean the missing sister - the dead, then not dead girl. Has anyone actually seen her, or are you the only one who has spoken to her?' His drawling voice made Michael think of Professor Snape, Potions Master from the Harry Potter novels. The content of his speech made him want to leap up and punch him in the face.

'What are you implying, Doctor?' Michael had gone very still, his eyes on the table rather than looking at James. 'Detective West – he's the senior police officer investigating my sister's disappearance – and I have spoken. And we have both been trying to re-establish contact with Jess, and with her parents, to confirm she is OK.' Now Michael looked up, meeting James' dull, grey eyes with his own navy blue. His face was alive with passion and he punctuated each word of his next sentence with a pause. 'Hence the phone.'

There's more to this story thought Elizabeth, even as she spoke to defuse the tension. 'OK Michael, that makes sense. Are you still happy to go ahead, do you need to be at home in case she calls?' She spoke calmly, moving in her seat to bring her patient's attention back to herself.

Michael shook his head. 'No, there's an officer at my place in case she turns up. Let's do this.' he started to rise to his feet.

'Sure.' Elizabeth was very happy to move the conversation back to the purpose of the night. 'Let's continue the briefing in the lab, get you comfortable.' She stood as well.

'Dr Booker, you stay here and make sure all the monitoring equipment is good to go. Thank you.' James opened his mouth, as if to argue with his colleague, but closed it again when he saw the look on her face, merely nodding instead.

As Michael and Elizabeth entered the bedroom, Michael turned to take in his surroundings for the night. He had been in the room before, a few days and a lifetime ago, but had not really paid attention to the space. The room was large, bigger than his spare room, and decorated with calming colours, far removed from the institutional tones of the rest of the hospital. Pictures hung in a few places, and two of the walls contained windows. One, running almost the length of the room, was the observation window, through which Michael could see James looking over some monitors. Seeming to sense Michael's stare the young doctor looked up, raised his hand in greeting and then pressed a button in front of him. The glass tinted, essentially becoming a large mirror. Michael quickly looked away, not wishing to look at his own haunted face. The other window, opposite the door through which he and Elizabeth had entered the room, was obscured by curtains. Michael strode across to the room, pulling back the curtains and then taking a step back in surprise. Elizabeth grinned, somewhat sheepishly, joining him where he stood. He was staring at a blank patch of wall.

'Yes,' she bit her lip as she spoke, to suppress a sudden urge to giggle 'It's fake. I think the idea is that it makes the room feel more like a real bedroom, but if there was a window here it would just look into a corridor.'

Michael started to turn away before he noticed an outline of a door, flush with the wall. 'Where does that go?' He asked in surprise.

'Oh, it's a service hatch. It leads to a maintenance room.' Elizabeth spoke quickly to reassure her client. 'Don't worry, its locked.'

He nodded and let the curtains fall back into place, looking instead at the rest of the room. The space was dominated by a double bed, flanked by a couple of bedside tables. It was a normal, domestic bed rather than a hospital bed, made up with a duvet and several pillows, as far removed from hospital linens as possible. The rest of the room contained a couple of chairs, where Elizabeth and Michael had sat while he had told her about his brother's death, and a coffee table.

'Remember, home from home, right?' Elizabeth smiled, 'I'll just leave you to get ready for bed.' She indicated a door Michael hadn't noticed, in the far corner of the room. 'You can get changed in the bathroom. And then I'll come back in and set up the monitors. OK?'

Half an hour later and Michael was lying in the soft, comfortable bed, gazing at the ceiling. The bedding was crisply laundered and cool against his skin. He turned on his side, feeling slightly uncomfortable where electrodes were attached to his skin in order to monitor his heart rate, temperature and brain waves. He was grateful that these were all working wirelessly, part of the experimental technology that Dr Booker was developing. He could move around in the bed as much as he wanted while he tried to get comfortable, without risking disconnecting the monitors or tying himself in knots.

He closed his eyes and tried to relax, attempting to shut down any thoughts of Jessica, Russell and Rosie. He found his thoughts wandering instead to Elizabeth, as they had the night that he had stayed at his friends' cottage. She was such a calming presence that he found himself relaxing further. Although he'd only known her a week, he felt like he could tell her anything and indeed had told her practically everything. He wished that he could get to know more about her. He relaxed further and felt his head sink deeper into the pillows 'dammit' he whispered, 'life is complicated enough'.

James and Elizabeth sat side by side in the connected observation room, watching the interior of the now dark bedroom. Elizabeth sighed and turned her attention to the monitors. Michael's heart rate, breathing and brain waves suggested that he was already falling asleep. 'That's fast' she mused 'He clearly needs it and must have taken my advice about not having any more coffee since I saw him earlier.'

She turned to James, 'I think you can go now. Thanks for staying to set the kit up.'

James shook his head, lifting his bag off the floor beside him. 'No fear, this guy does crazy ass stuff in his sleep – apparently – I'm not leaving when it could be about to get interesting. Besides, I brought snacks' He pulled out packets of crisps, chocolate bars and bottles of Coke. 'Or as I like to call it, dinner.'

Elizabeth rolled her eyes, and grabbed a bar of Galaxy from the pile, resigned to a long night of James' somewhat obnoxious company.

Chapter 53

Michael's vital signs indicated he went to sleep around 1030, half an hour after getting into bed, and Elizabeth and James spent the next hour and a half in awkward conversation, working their way through the pile of snacks James had brought with him. The cameras and microphones had picked up nothing out of the ordinary in the room, the monitors showing nothing exceptional.

'Well this is dull' James announced loudly, indicating the monitors. 'Not your company of course Lizzy, sorry, Elizabeth. What *is* that about?' He looked at Elizabeth, attempting his best 'I'm listening' expression. She ignored him.

'Why don't you just go home James, I don't think anything is going to happen tonight. If it was, I would have expected to see signs by now, probably within the first twenty minutes of him falling asleep'. Elizabeth felt disappointed that Michael was sleeping normally, hoping for more interesting observations to add to her research. She immediately chastised herself, aware that in Michael's case she should be pleased that he was finally getting some peaceful sleep. On the other hand, she thought, a normal pattern of sleep undermines his explanation for all the violence that has been surrounding him.

'No, I'll stay a while longer.' James yawned as he spoke, clearly bored. 'I will stretch my legs though. Want anything from the café?'

She nodded, 'Hot chocolate please and something a bit healthier than this junk. I'll have a....' she was interrupted by the piercing tones of Michael's phone. She hit answer, raising the phone to her ear.

'Michael? What is going on? I've missed a dozen calls from you while my phone was off earlier today, and a policeman just came to our house. They said they'd received word from a detective in England that Jessica was back here?' A shrill voice filled Elizabeth's ear.

'Hi, Mrs Manners. My name is Elizabeth' Elizabeth paused, unsure what to say or how to introduce herself 'Michael was phoned by Jessica earlier today. She said she was back home with you, but...'

Michaels' mother interrupted. 'Who is this? Where's Michael? I need to speak to him.'

Elizabeth was about to answer when the lights went off in the observation room, and all hell broke loose.

James had been standing by the door that led out into the hospital corridor when the phone had rung, turning to wait for the rest of Elizabeth's order before heading to the café. When the lights went off, followed by the cameras and monitors going dark, he was about to pull open the door, to see if the power cut was throughout the hospital, when something heavy slammed into his back.

He fell awkwardly, hitting his head on the edge of the desk on his way to the ground. Stars exploded, blurring his already compromised vision, and when he attempted to stand, a weight crushed his legs, pinning them to the floor. He brought up his arms to push off whatever was on his lower body, but before he could do so a fist collided with his nose, followed by a second to his jaw, and he dropped back to the floor unconscious.

Chapter 54

When James came to, he was temporarily blinded by the bright light flooding his vision. He blinked, and a face began to swim into focus, a woman, her mouth open in shock and concern. 'Elizabeth, what's going on?' As his vision cleared however he realised it was not Elizabeth.

'Doctor, what happened?' We heard shouts and banging.

'Is Elizabeth, Dr Byfield is she OK?' James attempted to stand, gingerly feeling his jaw.

'Don't stand. The nurse put a hand firmly on his chest. 'We need to get you checked out. You've had a nasty fall.'

He tried again to push up from the floor, 'I fell?' He was struggling to remember what had happened. 'No, the lights went out then something, or rather someone knocked me over'. He felt his face again, his nose was agony to touch, and when he brought his hand back down it was covered in blood.

'His nose looks broken Sister.' The nurse, Jenny, was speaking over her shoulder to someone out of James' view. He recognised her now, he'd dated her a couple of times a while back. They'd had a good time, but then he'd started working with Lizzy and ended it with Jenny. Lizzy; the memory brought him back to his senses.

'I think I was attacked. Where is Elizabeth, check the lab, maybe she went in there?' James sat up again, planning to stand as Jenny vanished to check the sleep lab. His head felt as if it had expanded like a balloon to twice its normal size, and his chest seemed to have been crushed by an elephant. As his vision blurred, he aborted his attempt to stand, shuffling back to lean against the wall instead.

This action brought the other person who'd entered the room into view, Sister Matthews. The sister ruled with an iron fist, her nurses practically running about their duties, her patients recovering quickly merely in order to be discharged from her draconian care. Matthews was looking down her nose at James now, she'd never been a fan of the young clinician and was constantly dismayed by his seeming lack of morality when it came to dating her nurses. 'What happened?' She barked, a harsh Irish lilt to her voice. 'There was no power cut.'

'Dr Byfield and I were conducting some tests, observation of one of her clients, Michael Manners.' he paused, he'd forgotten about Manners until he said his name. He raised his voice now 'Jenny, have you found them?'

As he spoke the young nurse came back into view, a puzzled look on her face. 'No James, there's no one in there'.

'Walk me through it doctor.' West was sitting beside James in the sleep observation room. Sister Matthews had contacted the police as soon as James realised that he'd been attacked, and mention of Michael Manners had meant West was roused from sleep, yet again, to head to the hospital.

The doctor, his head now a dull ache thanks to the wonders of codeine, spoke slowly, his voice thicker than usual due to the swelling around his mouth and the strapping across his broken nose. 'So, we were in here, Dr Byfield and I, and Manners was in the bed next door. Seemingly asleep according to the monitors', James indicated the bank of equipment in front of them.

'I was just going to grab a drink, then the lights went out and someone smashed me to the floor and started punching me. He knocked me out.'

'He?' West raised an eyebrow in question.

'Well yes of course "he", Manners. Clearly, he must have attacked me, had to have been faking sleep or something. Maybe the wireless sensors malfunctioned, so that's why we didn't get an indication that he was awake.

'He must have dragged Lizzy off somewhere. He's got form for that hasn't he?' James voice was a mixture of disgust and anger.

West leaned forwards 'How do you mean sir?'

'His sister, Jessie, or whatever her name is. You know? She went missing then Manners came up with some bollocks about her being back in the US, when actually he kidnapped her – or worse.'

West raised a hand for James to pause. 'Mr Manners *was* contacted by his sister this afternoon and she told him that she was back at her home.' This was something West already knew to be untrue however, having been caught up on the case by Johnson while he was en route to the hospital. Passport control had confirmed Jessica Manners had not flown since entering the country a few days ago, to the US or indeed anywhere. And the police force local to her home in California had paid a visit and been informed by her mother that she was neither there, nor had she been in contact.

'Yes, but her mum phoned here earlier, just before the lights went out, and she told Lizzy that the girl wasn't there.' James slammed his hand down on the table. 'I told her he was dangerous. You need to find her.'

West considered the doctor, he had clearly been attacked, the facial injuries alone would be impossible to self-inflict, or to sustain through falling.

'You told who he was dangerous? Dr Byfield?' He consulted his notebook, recalling that Michael had mentioned he was seeing the therapist. James nodded impatiently.

'Why did you think he was dangerous?'

James threw his hands up incredulously 'Why do you think? He came in last week, to A and E, bashed up and talking about a burglar that no one else saw; then he half kills his friend; then his sister goes missing. Isn't that enough of a pattern detective?'

'You're very well-informed sir, is Mr Manners your patient?' West looked again through his notes.

'Yes. No. Well, sort of. Lizzy told me about him. And one of the nurses who treated him shared some information too. You know he takes drugs too right?' James was smiling, a sickly grin, distorted by his swollen lips, taking pleasure from sharing the salacious fact with the detective.

'Drugs sir?' This *was* new information to West, but could explain a lot about the case, more easily than if Manners had been sleepwalking.

'Yes, he's a junkie.' James was warming to his topic.

'The nurse who treated him saw a puncture wound on his arm, right in the crook of his elbow. He denied it when Lizzy called him out about it. But of course, he would, and the blood tests will come back positive for some substance, or substances, I guarantee it.' James paused briefly, glancing out through the observation window, at the bed, 'Detective, you have to find him, find them, before it's too late.'

Chapter 55

Elizabeth surfaced from a nightmare. She'd dreamt that Michael had been chasing her through the endless corridors of the hospital. He had finally cornered her in an operating theatre, backing her up against the operating table. She'd stumbled and he'd loomed over her, hands reaching for her throat. She'd reached out a hand, blindly grabbing something, slashing out at his face with what turned out to be a scalpel. Hot blood had burst from his cheek, spattering Elizabeth's face, landing in her mouth and eyes. She'd woken up screaming.

She shifted her body, trying to ignore the aches from the uncomfortable position in which she had been laying. Her head felt thick, as if it was full of fog, and she was disoriented from the dream.

'Where the hell?' She murmured aloud sitting up and looking round. Her movements felt slower than usual, a feeling she associated with being dosed up on drugs during a heavy cold. The room was dimly lit, lighter and darker shadows revealing glimpses of her surroundings. She had a sense of volume, that the room was huge, and she could discern the grey outline of boxes or crates on all sides. The floor she was lying on was hard, cool but not freezing, concrete. For a moment she thought she was still dreaming, and then she remembered that she'd been in the hospital, was this the basement, the loading dock?

'Dr Byfield, you're awake? Good.'

The sudden noise made her jump, and she glanced around, trying to see the speaker. 'Michael?'

The speaker was hidden in shadow, and though it sounded like Michael there was a quality to his speech, a slur, making her wonder if he was asleep.

'Where are we?' Elizabeth shook her head, trying to clear the fog.

'I hope you're not hurt. Did you speak to Jess?' Michael was speaking slowly, almost like he was reading from a script.

'No, I am not hurt. I am a little confused, but I'm OK. I haven't spoken to Jessica. But your mother called.' Her eyes were starting to adjust to her surroundings, the edges of the packing crates were more defined, and she could see further into the gloom, she looked up and saw metal rafters vanishing into the murk. It was far too big to be the loading area of the hospital. A warehouse maybe?

She glanced at her wrist, to check how much time had passed since the lights had gone out in the lab. Her arm was bare, her watch had been removed, and her pockets had been emptied. She couldn't remember what had happened in the hospital after the power failure, it was as if her memory had been put on pause, a clean break. The next thing she remembered was the nightmare that had ended with her waking in this warehouse, or whatever it was.

She looked around slowly. Behind her were more wooden crates, piled two and three high, the nearest less than a metre from her back. She started to stand.

Michael's voice came again, this time she tried to get a fix on where he was, to triangulate his location. She was fairly certain he was standing in front of her, but all the boxes, combined with the large space made for some very strange acoustics, his voice reverberating off surfaces. 'Stay sitting please, I don't want you to trip over something in the dark.' So, he can see me then, she thought. So much for sneaking off.

'I'll go get Jess; I would love you to meet her.' His voice faded as he spoke. Elizabeth stayed rooted to the spot for a moment, listening, straining to hear any sounds from her captor.

She was shocked that Michael had kidnapped his sister, as James had theorised all along. She was finding it difficult to accept that this and her own abduction could be explained by sleepwalking, forced instead to consider it more likely that Michael was conscious when committing these crimes. That would mean he had been manipulating her, a disturbingly impressive demonstration of acting ability.

She shifted slightly, undecided as to her next move and not quite trusting that Michael had actually left to get his sister. Slowly, at first pausing between every movement, she shuffled backwards until she bumped into the box behind her. She listened, and hearing nothing was emboldened to move again. She turned over and crawled round the back of the nearest crate, then rose to a crouch and moved more quickly between the piles of containers, trying to head in one direction.

After a few moments she reached one of the walls. The perimeter was visible in the gloom as a darker surface, continuing left and right from her position. 'Which way is out' she whispered to herself. She'd just decided to head to the right when a voice came from that direction.

'Elizabeth, I thought I asked you not to move.' Michael was back and still speaking in a weird staccato. She started moving to the left, keeping low and hugging the wall. She had gone perhaps twenty metres when a loud cracking noise broke the silence. For a second she thought it was a gun shot, the noise echoing around the warehouse. Then the gloom was banished, and as bright overhead lights began to turn on she realised the sound she had heard was a large switch being pulled. She hurried forwards again, sure she was about to be discovered.

'Elizabeth, I just want to talk to you.
Jess is sleeping, and I don't want to wake her so you two will have to be introduced later. Sleep is so important you know?' The voice sounded closer, an edge of urgency beneath the sleepy, trancelike tone.

Ahead a door was propped open, leading to a corridor running at a right angle to the main room. She ducked into the opening and down the passageway, noticing a 'running man' fire exit symbol above the door. The corridor was in darkness, and after the recent brightness of the main space she was forced to move slowly, concerned that she would fall, or miss an exit in the gloom.

She had travelled about ten metres when she noticed a door to the left. It was marked as the manager's office, so she moved on past it, continuing to look for an exit. Before she'd gone another step however, she heard a sound behind her. A long, low sound, as if something was being dragged along the floor. She turned, taking a step back towards the closed door. The room was unlocked, and the handle turned easily and, as she pushed the door open, she heard Michael's voice in the corridor.

'Come on now Dr Byfield. There is no point in running, and nowhere to run to.'

Elizabeth moved into the room and closed the door as quietly as possible. She crouched, her back braced against the door, listening intently. Footsteps, unhurried, were coming closer. They didn't pause at the door, carrying on for a few metres. Then she heard the sound of a door being rattled, presumably an exit from the building. She let out a breath, slowly, quietly, but froze as the footsteps returned; Michael was coming back down the corridor.

She looked around the room, searching for anything that could be a weapon, and almost let out a scream when she spotted a body lying in a heap on the other side of the room.

Chapter 56

'What the hell?' James exclaimed loudly.

He and Detective West were watching the camera feed from the moments before the lights had gone off. They had already reviewed it twice. As the timestamp read 0000, midnight, they could see the bed, Michael's form visible as a lump under the covers, clearly still asleep. At 0001 the footage abruptly stopped, the image turning to a snowstorm of static. Rewinding slightly, they had spotted the curtains, just at the edge of the shot, opening and a dark shape emerging.

'Michael must have got out of bed, hidden behind the curtains without us realising. The lump in the bed must be pillows.

'Then he cut the power somehow – there's some kind of services corridor accessed through a door, behind the curtains. Then he attacked me and kidnapped Lizzy.' James spoke excitedly, all pain forgotten or numbed by medication.

West scratched his chin unconvinced. 'Yes, doctor, perhaps. But can you show me the monitors? They would show if he was out of bed, wouldn't they?'

James nodded, moving to action the detective's request.

'Yes, well that will show if he was awake, but the sensors are wireless, new tech invented by me.' James puffed out his chest as he spoke. 'So, he could have got out of bed but kept them on.' He pointed at an abrupt break in the feed. 'But look here. This looks like he pulled off the sensors.' The timestamp on the monitors also showed 0000.

'That's weird' James, confusion in his voice, looked more closely at the recordings in front of him.

'Presumably the recordings ended when he got out of bed?' West spoke calmly.

'Presumably.' James responded in a distracted tone. 'But look, if he got out of bed at midnight, the same time that the curtains opened, then that can't be him coming out of the service area.'

'Isn't it possible the clocks on the camera and monitors are out of sync?'

James nodded, 'Absolutely that's possible. But that's not what's bloody weird. Look at these recordings.'

West leaned in, the brain waves were a mystery to him, but he could see that they changed shape a little before they ended. 'Is that when he woke up?'

'No, they're the patterns we see when people are dreaming. He was still asleep when the sensors stopped recording.' James glanced round at the detective. 'I was convinced he was lying.'

West rose from his seat, keen to be away from the arrogant doctor, reassured that his gut instinct, that Michael was telling the truth, seemed to be correct. He turned in the doorway 'Thank you for your assistance doctor, I'll be in touch as soon as we have any more information.'

'Where are you going?'

'My team have been checking the hospital CCTV; I'm hoping they'll have a lead.'

'We've got them sir.' Johnson grinned as West entered the hospital's security suite. 'There's a camera directly outside the sleep lab, and just after midnight you can see a couple of people coming out and heading down the corridor, the angle of the camera is not ideal and the quality of the recording is not good enough for identification, but that must be Manners and Byfield. One of them, presumably Byfield, has been subdued and is being pushed in a wheelchair.'

West moved close to look at the few seconds of grainy footage. 'Where do they go next?'

'We see them again, a few minutes later, in a lift headed to the basement, that time we see them from the front, the person pushing the wheelchair has a hoodie on though, so their face is in shadow.'

'And the person in the wheelchair?'

'Look.' Johnson nodded to the hospital security guard who sat next to him, and the guard brought up another file, this time of a still image. The screen showed the interior of the lift and two figures in the centre of the image. Behind the chair, the person could have been Michael, from his height and posture, and West thought he could see an edge of a bandage on his right arm. The person in the wheelchair seemed to be unconscious, arms dangling over the arms of the chair, body slumped so much that they looked in danger of falling out. The head was lolling backwards, against the backrest of the chair, and the face was clearly visible. Next Johnson slid a print out across to West, an HR photo of Dr Elizabeth Byfield. West saw at once that it was the same person as in the wheelchair.

'OK, this is great. Where do they go next?'

'We don't have anything else useful from the hospital, but we do see Manners' car – you can hardly miss that – leaving the car park. We are now widening our search to try to trace that.'

'Excellent work, right, I'm heading to the station.'

'There is something else sir.'

'Go on Johnson.'

'Well, Charlie here.' Johnson indicated the security guard, 'He tells me there is another way in and out of the lab, a maintenance door, accessed behind the curtains. It's obviously staff only, and you need a key and an electronic pass for it. There's no camera covering it unfortunately, but every access is recorded, and earlier tonight it was accessed twice, once around 2350 – when it was opened from the corridor – and then again, fifteen minutes later it was opened from the other side. Could Manners have an accomplice sir?'

'OK, yes maybe.' West replied.

'That doctor, Booker, mentioned a door, but he thought it was just a hatch. Very good work Johnson; if you're done here, head back down to the sleep lab and make sure forensics check that door. See if the results of Mr Manners' blood tests are back as well.'

Chapter 57

Elizabeth moved towards the opposite end of the room, approaching the body with caution as soon as Michael's footsteps began to fade signalling that he was heading back into the main area of the warehouse. In the moonlight shining through a dusty window she had immediately seen that it was a body, curled around itself, half-covered with a blanket, but she couldn't see a face. She looked back at the door, torn between her desire to escape and her need to check who was under the blanket. Her first thought was that it must be Jessica, and as she lifted the edge of the cover she saw at once that it was a young woman. Although Elizabeth had not met the girl, she had seen Jessica's face on the news and in a newspaper earlier that day, and the blond hair, lying tangled and matted across the girl's face was certainly the right colour.

Elizabeth let out a soft moan, tears welling up as she let go of the edge of the blanket and hurried back to the door.

She turned the handle of the office door, opening it slightly to peer out into the corridor. It was empty in both directions. She was about to head out when she heard movement behind her. She turned abruptly scanning the room again. The body was shifting under the blanket, and a faint voice spoke in an American accent. 'Hello, is someone there?'

Elizabeth's heart leapt into her mouth and she backed into the door, causing it to fall closed. She moved quickly to the form, 'Shhhh!' She bent to help the girl sit up, noticing for the first time that she was handcuffed to the leg of the desk.

'Jessica?' she whispered, sinking to her knees in front of the girl.

'Yes, who are you?' Jessica coughed, rubbing her face with her free hand, clearly struggling to wake up. Before Elizabeth could answer, Jessica looked over the woman's shoulder, towards the closed door.

'Where is he?' Jessica's eyes widened, suddenly alert. 'We've got to get out of here.'

'Well yes' Elizabeth said exasperated, 'Michael is looking for me at the minute, but he's in that store room, warehouse, or whatever it is. He already checked down this way, so hopefully we've got some time.'

Jessica's eyes widened, 'Michael? Michael's here too?' She smiled with relief at the mention of her brother's name.

'Yes, of course he is. Wait, who did *you* mean when you said, 'where is he?'

'Well, I don't actually know who he is; but I heard one of his guys call him Ben and I remember that because that was Michael's brother's name. Anyway, whoever he is, he forced me to phone Michael, I think it was yesterday – I've lost track of time. He told me to say that I was back at home in California; I tried to give Michael some clues that something was up though, to warn him I wasn't safe.' Jessica shrank back into herself, pulling hopelessly on the handcuff.

'What? Someone else is here, right now?' Elizabeth's confusion deepened but as desperate as she was to ask Jessica to explain what had happened to her she was more anxious to escape from the warehouse. She looked at the desk, realising that the handcuff was looped around the leg. She stood, moved to the side of the desk and bent to lift it. It had built in drawers and was much heavier than she'd expected. Jessica could never have lifted it whilst restrained, but Elizabeth managed to get it a few centimetres off the ground. Jessica, watching, quickly pulled her hand free with the handcuff still attached. Elizabeth let the desk drop to the ground as quietly as possible, but the sound still seemed too loud for safety. Jessica stood, legs cramping from lying down for so long, and Elizabeth had to half-carry her to the door.

They took a few awkward steps towards the exit but before they reached the door it swung towards them, revealing a man, backlit by the bright corridor. 'Going somewhere ladies?'

Chapter 58

The low hum of an engine cut through the paralysis that had taken hold of Elizabeth since the door had burst open and she and Jessica had been discovered.

Michael was standing in the doorway, but as he took a faltering step forwards into the room, Elizabeth realised that it had not been his voice she had heard. It had been a deeper voice, more like a croak, and the tone had been full of malice – something that she had never detected in her encounters with Michael.

'Michael, what's going on?' She was battling to keep the fear out of her voice as she spoke. She moved her body to shield Jessica, but the younger woman pushed past her and ran to her brother.

'Michael, thank God you've found me.' Jessica's voice broke as she reached up to her brother, the handcuffs restricting her movement. Michael stood, staring into the room, oblivious to his sister. Elizabeth noticed that his gaze was unfocused, as if he wasn't seeing the office, but was looking somewhere else. His stance too was unusual, his body rigid, unresponsive when Jessica attempted to hold his hand.

Recalling the way Michael had been talking when she'd woken up in the warehouse, a strange tone, almost trancelike, Elizabeth made a connection and put her hand out to the younger woman. 'Jessica, step away from him.'

Jessica looked over her shoulder 'What? Why?'

Before Elizabeth could answer another voice spoke up. 'Michael, grab your sister.' This was the deeper voice that had spoken moments before when Jessica and Elizabeth had been about to leave the office.

Michael raised his arms as if to hug his sister, and then grabbed her, gripping her arms tightly at her sides.

Immediately Jessica began to struggle, to pull away, her face turned up towards her brother's 'Michael! What the hell?' Michael ignored her pleas, effortlessly holding her still.

'Jessica, he can't hear you, he's not awake.' Elizabeth could not stop the fear from entering her voice, from her clinical work she was well aware of the damage that people could do in their sleep, to themselves, and to others. She also recalled the injuries that Michael himself had inflicted on Russell. Her mind raced, considering what she knew about the man before her, searching for a clue, anything that she could use to connect with her client.

The hum of an engine came again, and now, behind Michael, Elizabeth saw a shape moving into the doorway, a motorized wheelchair. 'No, Jessica, he cannot hear you. But, as you can see, he can hear me' the occupant of the wheelchair spoke again, a mocking voice. 'And he will do exactly what I tell him to do.'

The man in the chair was still half obscured by Michael, but Elizabeth could see the left side of his body, a slumped form, small against the large chair. The body of an old man. The face, what Elizabeth could see of it at least, was young, maybe around 40, eyes shining with energy, mouth curled in a sneer. 'Ben?' Elizabeth suddenly remembered what Jessica had said she'd heard the man called and, recognising something in the facial features of the stranger, she drew in a sharp breath 'Ben, you're his brother!'

Benjamin smiled, manoeuvring slightly to the side to get a better look at Elizabeth. 'Very good doctor, most astute.' His smile was without humour, and as he advanced into the room Elizabeth's fear intensified.

'Michael, knock out Jessica, and then secure Dr. Byfield.'

Michael did not at first respond to the command, and Elizabeth thought she saw a flicker of something in his eyes, and in that she saw hope. 'Michael, you don't have to do what your brother says. Listen to me, it's Elizabeth.' She watched Michael's face as she spoke, and saw again a change in his eyes, a look of focus coming into them.

'Actually, he does have to do what I say.' Ben spoke with cold fury, 'Michael, subdue Jessica.' In the split second that it took Elizabeth to process his words, Michael had acted upon the order, twisting Jessica's body so that one of his arms was tightly round her neck, squeezing her throat. Jessica tried to scream but her airway was already obstructed and a minute later Michael released her body and it fell, lifeless at his feet.

'Good.' Ben spoke as if to a pet that had performed a trick correctly. 'Although, honestly that looked like a little too much pressure to simply knock her out.... No matter. Now, grab Elizabeth, we can't let her leave.' Michael took a step forward, almost tripping over Jessica's body.

'Michael, listen to me. Remember who I am, Elizabeth, your doctor, your friend. Rosie called me earlier.' Michael paused, and again a movement in his eyes suggested he had heard her even in his sleep-wake state.

He muttered something, something that sounded like 'Rosie?'

'Yes, Rosie. She wanted to tell you she forgives you. Russell's going to be OK. And Rosie forgives you.' Now Michael definitely responded to Elizabeth's words, his face turned towards her, actually looking at the doctor.

Ben sighed in exasperation, moving his wheelchair further into the room, and Elizabeth noticed that he could hardly move his body, that he was controlling the chair with one finger of his right hand. 'Michael, listen to me, hear my voice.' He was speaking in a rhythmic tone now, attempting to regain control over his brother. 'The doctor is lying. I told you, Russell is dead. He could not recover from the injuries you gave him. Rosie is broken, she will never forgive you. And now it looks like you have killed your sister as well.'

Elizabeth watched in horror as the light went out in Michael's eyes, his gaze becoming unfocused again.

'Yes. Rosie is lost to you. She is gone. And it is Dr Byfield's fault. She told Rosie that you had meant to kill Russell, that you had confided in her that you had not been sleepwalking, that you had been fully aware of what you were doing.' Ben paused, drawing a deep rattling breath 'So now, you know what you must do. You must kill Elizabeth'.

Michael's eyes were wet, silent tears running down his face. He advanced on Elizabeth, reaching out his arms to grab her. Elizabeth looked to her left and right. Past Michael, to the right, her way was blocked by Ben's chair but to the left she could see a gap. She dashed forward, pushing out at Michael and feinting right before moving to the left. Michael, even in his trance-like state anticipated the move, casually reaching out an arm and knocking her to the floor. As she fell, Elizabeth's back collided with the desk, her breath knocked out of her by the force of Michael's attack.

She fought hard to control the pain as it exploded through her body and as Michael closed in she knew that she was running out of options and out of time to save herself.

Chapter 59

West listened intently to his team as they filled him in on the progress that had been made over the past hour. 'There was definitely someone else in that lab tonight boss.' PC Johnson, still at the hospital, was on speaker phone to the briefing room, 'there are finger prints all over that maintenance door. Still no CCTV footage of who it was though. But one thing we do know is that the fingerprints are not those of Michael Manners.'

'Good work Johnson.

'What else have we got?' West addressed his question to the whole room.

A young WPC was the first to speak. 'We've been able to track his car. It left the hospital and headed west on the A4, towards the motorway. It turned off in Calcot heading towards the industrial estates in that area. Then we lost it.' She frowned apologetically as West scowled. 'We're still searching through cameras, meantime a unit has been dispatched to go street by street through that area, a flash car like that, middle of the night, they may spot it first.'

West nodded, 'Good work Samira.' The young officer blushed.

'Anything else? Any more sightings of Jessica Manners, anything at Manners' flat?'

His questions were met with shaking heads and answers in the negative. 'Well keep looking. Johnson, any news on the blood tests that other doctor, Booker, mentioned?'

'I'll chase that up sir.' Johnson answered and then hung up.

Chapter 60

Elizabeth moved her body to back away from Michael's advance, but the desk behind her blocked her movement. Something rolled off the desk, a pen, and she quickly grabbed it, concealing it half up her sleeve. She spoke in desperation. 'Michael, Michael, wake up!'

Behind his brother, Ben chuckled, a sound filled with loathing. 'You of all people should know that's not going to work. Not when someone is so very deeply asleep. As I make sure that my brother is.'

Michael's hands reached for Elizabeth's neck as she tried to bat him away with her fists and feet. From her position on the floor it was difficult to get much range and power to her attacks, and he brushed them aside with ease. Kneeling on her legs he grabbed both her arms in one hand and closed his other on her throat.

'Ben, it's your brother. He's alive.' The pressure on her throat eased, but just a fraction. Elizabeth spoke again, before Ben could interrupt, speaking more loudly, insistently. 'That's right Michael; Benjamin, he didn't die in the car crash. He's alive, and he's here. Don't you want to speak to him?'

Michael mouthed his brother's name. 'Yes, Ben, that's right. Michael, look, you can speak to him.' The pressure on her wrists reduced slightly and she broke free, striking out at Michael.

He immediately released her and fell back exclaiming in pain, the pen still sticking in his chest.

'What have you done you bitch? What was that?' Ben demanded, his voice full of confusion.

'An Epi pen.' Elizabeth replied, 'I gave Michael a shot of epinephrine and it looks like it's woken him up.' She had recognised the pen when it fell from the desk because her grandfather had a severe nut allergy and always carried one with him in case he had a reaction and went into anaphylactic shock.

Michael was still lying on the floor. He shook his head, as if trying to shake off sleep, and when he saw Elizabeth his face filled with agony.
'Christ, Elizabeth, what have I done?'

He stood slowly and took a step backwards, stumbling over Jessica's body. He looked down in shock, 'What, oh God no.' He sank to his knees. 'Jess.'

'It wasn't you.' Michael turned in confusion to look at Elizabeth. 'It was Ben.'

'Ben?'

'Yes, dear brother, 'Ben'.'

Michael spun round at the voice. 'Ben.' He rushed forwards to embrace his brother, mirroring the actions of his sister moments earlier. He stopped, recoiling in shock at the sight of his brother, slumped in his wheelchair.

'Yes, quite a surprise to wake up to I suppose.' Ben moved his chair closer, pushing Jessica's legs out of the way with his front wheel.

'Not as much of a shock as I felt, when you abandoned me so very many years ago. Leaving me to die alone.'

'Abandoned you? No. I looked in the car, you…. I couldn't see you. I thought you'd been flung out. Or that you jumped.' Michael shut his eyes, picturing the crash, when he opened them fresh tears streamed down his face. 'I reached for you, when I saw you were somehow in the back of the car. I reached for you. And then the car slid down the mountain. How did you survive? God, it's a miracle.' He took a step towards his brother again, reaching forwards to touch his face.

Ben stared at his brother for a moment. 'You call this survival?' He looked down at his own body, twisting his right hand to awkwardly indicate himself. 'You call this a miracle?' He raised his voice now, a raspy shout issuing from his throat.

'This is not a miracle brother. This is hell. A curse.' He edged closer.

Michael's instinct was to back away, but with Elizabeth behind him he had nowhere to go.

'I'm sorry.' Michael whispered, lowering his head, looking away from his brother's broken body.

Elizabeth put a comforting hand on the back of his shirt, warm against his suddenly cold skin.

'You're sorry?' Ben's voice rose as he spoke, but this time with hope, rather than with anger. Michael looked up. His brother was smiling now, a grotesque expression as one half of his mouth remained slack.

'You are sorry? Oh, how I've longed to hear you say that. All the years that I have been apart from you. Rebuilding my strength. And now you say you're sorry.' The smile did not reach Ben's eyes.

'That. Makes. Everything. OK. Then.' He spat the words.

Michael and Elizabeth froze, Ben's words washing over them like ice.

Ben nudged his armrest controls, pressing a button. 'Come to the warehouse. I need your assistance.' He spoke quickly, staring at Michael and Elizabeth as he did so.

Ben's words made no sense to Michael at first, they were in the warehouse. Did he mean they needed to go back to the main room? Then he realised. Ben had been speaking to someone by some kind of phone or radio communication, controlled via his chair. Looking again at his brother he noticed something in his ear, a micro speaker of some kind.

'Who are you speaking to?' Elizabeth spoke, having come to the same conclusion as Michael.

Ben smiled, though to Elizabeth it looked more like a sneer. 'Some friends of mine. You'll meet them soon.'

Michael clapped his hand to his head. Of course, Ben must be having help. He clearly had very limited movement, could certainly not have brought Jessica, Elizabeth and himself to the warehouse.

Jessica. Michael's throat closed like a fist at the thought of his sister, glancing at her body. I can't let Elizabeth die too; his thoughts hardened his resolve to act. He strode forwards, hand held out behind him for Elizabeth, moving to go past his brother. 'You can't stop us from leaving.'

Ben nodded, not even turning his chair to try to stop them. 'No, not in this thing, you're right. I'm sure there must be windows in this place you can break, climb out of – all normal activities that I can no longer do. You will be able to escape before my men arrive. I'm sure.

'But I will catch up with you eventually, with Russell, with Rosie, with delightful baby Donny. And with Dr Byfield as well of course.

'So, yes, you can escape for now. But I will haunt you, every waking hour, every moment you sleep and of course your dreams dear brother, for the rest of your pitiful life.'

Michael turned in the doorway, ignoring Elizabeth's tug on his arm. 'You do something to me don't you? Somehow. In my dreams?'

Ben nodded, a small movement that cost him a lot of energy.

'You want to destroy me? Have me. But spare Elizabeth, spare the others.'

Michael broke contact with Elizabeth now, moving back to his brother's chair. The room seemed to grow darker, shadows claiming its features as he focused his attention on Ben.

The engine whirred as the chair turned. Ben appeared to be considering the proposal. 'OK, fine; but not here. I know a place where we can continue this conversation in private, and without interruptions.'

Michael nodded.

'Michael don't go with him. You can't trust him.' Elizabeth reached out to him.

'Ben, call off your men. Call the police to come and get Elizabeth.' Michael spoke firmly, with a strength he did not feel in his heart, gazing again at Jess's lifeless form.

'Stand down Alpha team. I repeat Alpha team, stand down.' Ben touched the controls on his chair again before issuing commands to his team. 'And, once we are out of the building, I will call the police and tell them where to find the delectable Dr Byfield, and our poor dead sister.

'You killed her Michael, you do realise that?' Ben spoke in a conversational voice, as if discussing the weather, as he drove his chair from the room. 'Just like you killed Russell.'

'Michael, don't go with him, don't...'

Michael interrupted, 'Don't trust him? No, I won't. But I have to try to protect you. Hide as soon as we are gone. The police are bound to have tracked you here by now.' He looked past Elizabeth, to his sister's body. 'Stay with Jess. Please?'

Chapter 61

Standing outside the warehouse, Michael shivered even though the night was warm. His body was coated with sweat, his shirt plastered to his back. He looked down at his legs, realising with surprise that he was wearing jogging bottoms, with no socks or shoes. Suddenly he became aware that his feet were hurting, stinging from contact with the rough surface of the ground. 'Of course I'm not dressed,' he muttered under his breath 'I was in bed, at the lab.'

'Come along brother.' Ben's chair was moving slowly across the building's car park. He stopped alongside Michael's Ferrari. 'Beautiful. Quite an upgrade from *my* last car. That was an Audi. Do you remember?'

'Of course I remember. I've dreamed about that night so many times.'

Ben spun his chair round, causing Michael to jump back or have his toes crushed. 'Oh, poor Michael. Has it been awful for you?'

Michael scowled. 'Yes, but of course not as awful as for you.' He stopped, taking slow, even breathes, trying to bring his emotions back in check.

'That temper, so quick to flare up.' Ben grinned, delighting in his brother's discomfort.

Michael ignored the barb, indicating the sports car as he spoke. 'We can't take this though. I wouldn't be able to fit your chair in.' he shrugged, apologetically.

'Of course we can't. I have my own ride. I just wanted to see yours.' Ben began to move off in his chair, heading round the front of the car. As he moved off there was a screech of metal against metal, like nails on a blackboard.

The source of the sound was revealed as soon as Michael turned back towards Ben. A deep gash had appeared in the side of the Ferrari, and as Michael watched it grew, Ben's chair tight up against the car, was gouging through the paintwork and into the car's body beneath. Passing the side mirror, the hard back of the chair crushed against it. The mirror fell in pieces to the ground.

'I know,' Ben spoke as he continued moving across the car park. 'Petty. But I do have to get my kicks where I can.'

Ben's 'ride' turned out to be a modified van, the back adapted so that the chair could be secured. A ramp was already lying in place behind the vehicle, the doors open so that Ben just drove his chair confidently up into its shadowy depths.

'Push the ramp in and close the doors Mikey, there's a good chap. Then come around, you'll have to drive.'

Michael began to follow the instructions, numbly. 'How did you get here?'

'My associates drove me here and then they left to collect you and Dr Byfield. Once they'd delivered you both I sent them back to monitor the police at the hospital.

'Now, get a move on and don't try anything clever, unless you want Elizabeth to get hurt. I am not sure your conscience could take the weight of another death,'

Michael hurriedly slammed the back doors, then went around to the driver's side and got in the van clenching and unclenching his fists with each step.

Ben's voice came from the back of the van. 'Now, drive. I'll direct you. It'll be fun, like a little road trip.'

Elizabeth had started to follow Ben and Michael as soon as they left the office, reluctantly leaving Jessica's body lying on the floor. She'd stayed out of sight, always half a dozen paces behind them, moving quietly, hugging the shadowy walls of the poorly lit passageway. When she reached the exit the two men had already left, and the door was tightly sealed behind them. She swore under her breath and then made her way back to the office.

'Hide' She spoke, remembering Michael's words. 'But where, how, and why?' She was exhausted, her body sagging as the adrenaline surge she'd felt when Ben had made his appearance was spent. She moved towards the desk, dragging it across the room to barricade the door. The furniture was heavy, but thankfully the floor was lino and she was able to move it by herself. She had to pause in the middle of the room, to move Jessica's body. She bent down, gently lifting the girl under her arms, surprised at how light she was, but also how warm she felt. She laid her back down, tenderly, fanning her hair out across her face, covering the angry bruising on her neck so that it looked like she was sleeping.

Elizabeth jumped back in shock. She felt the girl's neck again, pressing two fingers against it. A pulse. Very weak. But there none the less. She smiled for the first time since Michael had gone to sleep earlier that evening back at the hospital. Then she hurried to finish barricading the door.

Chapter 62

West, Johnson and two other officers in a second car arrived at the warehouse ten minutes after Michael and Ben had left. They parked on a side street nearby, and walked through bushes, crouched low, to join their colleagues at the edge of the car park. PC Andrews and WPC Leslie had called in that they had spotted Michael's car heading into the Pincents Kiln Industrial Park, and then followed instructions to hide their car and to proceed on foot to observe the scene.

'Sir.' Andrews acknowledged his superior officer before continuing to speak rapidly. 'Two people left the warehouse ten minutes ago, headed off in a van, we got the registration though' He waved a piece of paper at West.

'Why the hell didn't you radio it in, or follow them?' West grabbed the paper and thrust it at Johnson, who immediately radioed in the details.

Andrews winced. 'I said we should.' The WPC, a rookie that West barely recognised, spoke with a pout.

'And you don't have a radio yourself WPC Leslie?' Leslie scowled at West's rebuke and turned away. 'Anyway, could you identify the figures?'

'No sir. One tall, IC1 male, could have been Michael Manners. The other was in a wheelchair, large motorised thing. Could have been male or female. They stopped at the car, and then proceeded to the van.'

'So probably Elizabeth Byfield in the wheelchair again. So probably the warehouse is now empty. Dammit!' West's frustration was in danger of boiling over; he needed to move, to act.

'Let's go and have a look anyway. Johnson, call in forensics if you please.'

'Sir,' WPC Leslie spoke up in an urgent tone. 'We've got company.'

Everyone turned as two cars streaked into the car park, driving directly up to the side entrance of the building. Four figures leapt out, and after a moment's hesitation proceeded to the door. At least one figure was brandishing a gun.

'Dammit.' West swore again. '*They* obviously think someone is still here.'

'Andrews, radio for armed response.'

Elizabeth heard someone unlock the door through which Michael and his brother had left; then there were voices in the corridor.

'Nah, the van's gone. Hawking's off somewhere else. Can't reach him.' A deep, guttural voice rose above the others.

Several voices laughed at the crude joke.

'But he wanted us here; you know Alpha is his stupid-arse code.' A higher pitched, whiny voice replied.

'And we're here, aren't we? Go and search the office Jimmy, he had that fresh bit of tail in there.'

Elizabeth shrunk back into the shadows, arm protectively across Jessica's body. The girl had still not regained consciousness, but Elizabeth could feel her chest rising and falling within their awkward embrace.

Footsteps stopped outside the door, the handle rattled. Elizabeth had locked the door from the inside before pushing the desk against it.

'Angel?' Jimmy, the whiny one, spoke again 'It's locked.'

'Fuck sake Jim. Of course it's locked. The kid's his prisoner you twat.'

'What if Stephen's been captured by zombie-man.' Jimmy laughed.

'Who the hell is Stephen?'

'Um, y'know......Hawking, Stephen Hawking?'

'Idiot. Blow the lock. Grab the girl. Alpha means clear out and meet up at the res.'

Elizabeth looked hopelessly around the room, searching for an escape. She'd tried the window as soon as the brothers had left. Unsurprisingly it was locked, but also a line of bars protected it from the outside. Once she'd realised that Jessica was alive but unconscious,

Elizabeth had realised that the window was also too high up for her to drag the girl out of. Other than the desk and an aged swivel chair, the room contained a filing cabinet, too heavy to move, and a small wall mounted cupboard full of emergency first aid supplies. She had forced this open and dragged the contents out onto the floor, quickly scanning the supplies and shoving the long-handled scissors into one of her pockets. She pulled these out now, gripping the handles tightly, knowing they would be woefully inadequate against a gun.

A shot rang out, echoing in the corridor, reducing the wood around the lock to kindling.

Chapter 63

Whiteknights reservoir, part of the University of Reading's land, was deserted when Ben instructed Michael to pull the van to a halt deep in shadows. Traffic had been almost non-existent as they had driven from the warehouse, providing Michael with no opportunity to alert any other drivers that he was being held hostage. Ben had sat in silence for most of the short journey, merely issuing directions from time to time.

Michael stared out of the windscreen now. In front of him a huge weeping willow blocked out most of the moonlight, an indication that a large body of water was nearby. Looking left Michael saw the emergency access road that they had driven in on vanish into the gloom. To the right a set of concrete steps provided access up the steep embankment. Beside this a narrow gravel path curved away, cut into the slope on a shallow gradient, presumably to allow machinery to be transported with relative ease.

'Come on brother let's do a spot of sightseeing, it's a good place for bird watching I believe.' Ben's voice was cheery, almost manic as he broke the silence.

Michael exited the van reluctantly, leaving the keys in the ignition, but taking a screwdriver from the door pocket as he stepped out into the warm night. He held the tool behind his back as he went to the rear of the van and opened the doors. His brother's chair was facing away from him, and Michael considered jumping into the van and pressing the screwdriver to his brother's throat.

'I have to say Michael; the drive here was rather erratic. Not to my standard, or that of the Highway Code. It really is a good job that we didn't pass anyone, especially the police. It was almost as if you wanted to draw attention to us.' Ben paused.
'But that would be rather foolish. You see, my men will be at the warehouse now.'

'You stood them down. I heard you.' Michael sensed a trap, standing his ground until he understood what Ben was talking about.

'Did I? No, I'm afraid not. I referred to them as 'Alpha Team', a redundant term as they are my only team, here in England at least. So, in fact the word Alpha is a code to clear out the warehouse, and to rendezvous here.

'If I want to, I can contact my men at any point, and abort that current mission, and instead have them initialise the 'Beta' protocol.'

Michael stood, stock-still and numb, any hope of subduing his brother gone. 'What's Beta?' he asked with a sinking feeling that he already knew the answer.

'I'm glad you asked. Beta would result in them immediately killing Dr Byfield. Then returning to me and killing you.' Ben spoke in a jovial voice, but with an edge that implied that he was far from joking.

Michael shuddered, his mind showing a sudden vision of a gun being placed against Elizabeth's temple, a trigger being pulled.

'So, Alpha at least means that Elizabeth is taken from the warehouse alive and brought to join us here. It also sadly means that the warehouse is burned down, which will mean an impromptu cremation for our dear sister.' Ben paused, letting his words hang in the air before continuing matter-of-factly 'Can you get the ramp please Michael, we are on the clock here.'

Michael retched into the bushes at the mention of Jessica. He imagined, all too vividly, her lifeless body lying on the hard ground, while flames erupted and consumed it.

'Something you ate Mikey?' Ben remarked casually, hearing his brother heaving up the contents of his stomach. 'The ramp, please?'

Chapter 64

West set off towards the warehouse, sprinting across the car park as soon as he heard the gunshot. He shouted over his shoulder for the rest of his officers to secure the gang's vehicles, and then to wait for armed response. As he ran West realised that Johnson was doing the same, a couple of metres to his left, a move calculated to present the gunmen with multiple targets, and a flagrant disregard for West's command that was nevertheless welcome – and unsurprising. Johnson and West had been working together for over a decade and were used to covering each other's backs without needing to telegraph their intentions. The two men arrived beside the warehouse wall without the alarm being raised, and cautiously moved towards the open door. 'Stay low, and follow my lead' West whispered to Johnson, turning off his radio as he spoke, and then proceeding into the building. Johnson silenced his radio, and then raised his baton as he followed the DI.

The office door opened less than an inch after the lock was shattered. Elizabeth heard the shooter, Jimmy, grunt as he pushed against it. 'Door's jammed.' He called in frustration.

The leader, the unexpectedly named Angel, called out from further away, towards the main body of the warehouse. 'Put your back into it Jimmy.'

The desk shuddered, but didn't move, as Jimmy threw his weight against the door.

'Better be quick lad, we're setting the timers.' Angel continued.

'Wait' Jimmy's whine was beginning to irritate Elizabeth. 'Or shall we just leave her in here to fry?'

Shit, thought Elizabeth, could this situation get any worse?

'No Jimmy' Angel spoke as if to a child. 'I'll send Tiny to help you with the door and the 'ickle girl inside.'

A few seconds later and a huge bang was accompanied by the door shuddering, the desk scooting back several inches on the lino.

'Tiny' hurled himself against the door a couple more times, each time opening the gap in the door a few more inches.

'Stop you oaf, I think I can get in there now.' Jimmy's voice was full of fear as he spoke to the other man, trying to assert some kind of authority through the insult, but earning an ironic deep throated chuckle from the other.

A scuffle, sounds of something colliding with something, or someone, else erupted outside the door. Followed by silence. For a second Elizabeth thought the two men had attacked each other, and then a black man in a rumpled suit squeezed cautiously into the room.

'Dr Byfield? I'm Detective Sergeant West.' He glanced at the body Elizabeth was half crouched over. 'Is that Jessica Manners?'

Elizabeth nodded, not trusting herself to speak.

'Is she alive? Can she be moved?' West pushed the rest of the way into the room.

Elizabeth found her voice. 'Yes, she is alive, but listen, there are others, at least two more.' Her voice was wheezy, panicked. 'They mentioned setting timers?'

West grimaced, speaking over his shoulder. 'Johnson, watch the corridor, we need to get these two out of here.' He turned back to Elizabeth, moving forwards to lift Jessica. 'Where is Manners?'

'Michael? He left, with his brother' Elizabeth saw the confusion on the detective's face. 'I don't know what you know. But his brother, Benjamin is alive, though God knows how. But I don't know where they went.'

Chapter 65

Michael and Ben faced each other across a wide concrete platform. A metre behind Michael and a short distance below him the surface of the reservoir was still, an oily blackness. Ben grinned, an expression that came close to transforming his face to the one Michael remembered from their childhood.

'So, what shall we talk about?' Ben moved his chair closer to his brother.

Michael, throat burning from the remnants of vomit, spat onto the ground, then took a step backwards, towards the water's edge. 'How did you escape; your body was identified? What happened? Where have you been for twenty years?'

'That's a lot of questions. Where to start, where to start......?' Ben hummed, a comical expression on his face as he feigned deep thought.

'Well, the body that was identified wasn't mine. Obviously. The experts really cocked that one up.

'How I escaped, well that was quite an adventure. When the car hit the water, my body got sucked out of the shattered back window. I would shrug at this point to let you know how surprised I was that that happened. But, as you'll have gathered, shrugging, along with pretty much any other movement is a luxury that I no longer have.'

Michael stared in wonder, his heart full of guilt that his brother's condition was somehow his fault, his mind still full of questions.

'So, then, I surfaced. And then I passed out.

'I can't tell you what happened next. On account of being unconscious. But I didn't die.' Ben paused, a distant look in his eyes.

'Though, honestly over the years I have wished fervently that I had died that night. I did dream. That I remember vividly. I dreamt that I swam away from the car, to the shore. I walked up the bank and waved down a vehicle. But Michael,' Ben was almost shouting at this point, 'Dear brother, look at me, how could I have walked away from that crash?'

Michael took a step back, shocked by the ferocity emanating from his brother.

'And yet, the man who found me. My saviour, he told me that he came upon my body, crumpled where I had passed out beside the road.'

Michael's mind whirled, could it be that Ben's unconscious mind had moved his body? 'Who was it, your 'saviour'?'

Ben smiled, ruefully, 'I dropped lucky there you could say. My saviour was an influential multibillionaire from the US. He took me to his private jet. Flew me back to his home in New York and paid for the best and most discreet health care money could buy. And if you're wondering why he did not alert the authorities, well,' Ben paused, 'He wanted to keep me to himself, almost as a pet, a plaything.'

Michael grimaced, turning away.

Ben continued, 'Whatever you are imagining, it was much, much worse. As I recovered, bones setting, muscles knitting back together, it was quickly apparent that I would never walk again, that my body was no longer under my control.

'My "saviour"' Ben spat the words 'he could control my body. It reacted to his touch and he enjoyed making me watch how it responded to his depravities.'

A shudder passed through Michael, and Ben continued. 'Quite. But even though I could not move my body, my mind was whole. At first, I wished that it was not, that I could be brain dead, so I did not have to endure the humiliation, the shame of what was being done to my body.

'However, it became apparent that certain, let us say "abilities" were very much alive. Abilities that had laid dormant other than in extreme circumstances, were now completely within my control.'

'What do you ……?' Michael's words broke off abruptly as he felt his throat being compressed, his breathing and speech suddenly interrupted.

Chapter 66

Michael grabbed his neck with his right hand, horrified to discover that his throat was being squeezed by his other hand, the fingers tightly wrapped around his Adam's apple. He was completely unaware that he had gripped himself in this way, and for a moment was too shocked to act, merely staring at his brother in bewilderment as his vision started to turn grey. With an immense effort of will, focusing on feeling his left hand, Michael was able to extend his fingers, one at a time, until his hand fell back to his side. Panting both with effort and lack of breath, Michael doubled over.

'*That's* what I mean. As a child I had vivid dreams, you know, our father did too? And on occasion I sleepwalked, acting out the mundane, and sometimes more salacious contents of my dreams. This was particularly the case when my dreams were fuelled by strong emotions, or desires.'

Michael felt sickened, his thoughts immediately turning to the story his Uncle had told him, about the missing cleaner from Ben's university. He continued to draw in deep breaths, regarding his brother in stunned silence.

'Ah, you're thinking of the delectable Lottie, aren't you?

'That was truly a crime of passion. But how did *you* find out about that? Our parents? No, 'Mac' told you, didn't he? He's a boring bastard, isn't he? But Lottie, ah yes, she was far from boring.'

Ben's face took on a faraway look and Michael edged closer to the water's edge while his brother was distracted.

'What happened to Lottie?'

'Who knows? Perhaps I killed her and buried her in the university grounds.' Ben chuckled as he enjoyed the look of disgust on his brother's face.

'But that's ancient history, a pleasant digression. But, back to the night you abandoned me. It is quite possible that I managed to rescue myself from drowning; my unconscious mind is clearly a thing of beauty and a thing of strength. But the real kicker was when I realised I could link my mind to others with similar abilities. Not weak or susceptible minds, like our mother's, but strong, more developed brains. Like yours, dear brother, and like father's.

'Do you know brother, that Daddy's power and his success in business was at least in part due to his ability to manipulate people?'

'Did you do something to Dad?' Michael's voice was thick with loathing.

'Yes. Of I course I did. He was under my control for quite a while, subtly at first. I was working towards taking over Global Scotland, changing his will to disinherit you and gain control of his assets through a shell company. Then, well then, I pushed too hard, too far. Essentially, I caused his heart to explode, like a blown fuse.'

Michael recoiled in shock, taking another step closer to the water.

Ben continued, seemingly oblivious 'it was the first time I'd done that, quite exciting, if not the result I was looking for.

'Did you know that you too have this tendency to dream, to sleep 'act' given the right circumstances? The correct, how shall I put this, motivation.'

Michael nodded, horrified yet too curious to not hear more.

'Of course, how could you not know? Well, I discovered a couple of things about my gifts. First, I learned I had a real talent for chemistry, well, more specifically pharmacology, a use at last for my curtailed education. Given the right physical assistance, a surrogate body to do my wishes, I can create all sorts of cocktails of drugs that can do things like shorten a wealthy, but deviant, benefactor's life, without leaving a trace.

'Or, you'll recognise this recipe, how to combine ingredients to induce a deeper than natural sleep, providing a wider window of opportunity to take a body for a joy ride.'

Michael automatically touched his right arm at the inner elbow. 'You've been drugging me? How? You're...'

'A cripple? Yes, I had noticed.' Ben's voice dripped with sarcasm. 'Well, luckily my ill-gotten wealth means I can get *pretty much* anyone to do *actually* anything for the right price.
'But the other thing I discovered I could do was make people – people like you – do things. Even when they are wide awake.'

Ben cocked his head slightly at Michael, who instantly felt his hands rising towards his neck on their own accord.

Chapter 67

As his hands began to move Michael quickly reasserted control over his limbs, Ben having lost the element of surprise.

'Oh, what a pity, well maybe next time.' Ben looked slightly disappointed that his party trick had not worked a second time.

'Speaking of time, what time is it?' Ben asked casually.

'Two o'clock.' Michael again glanced over his shoulder at the reservoir.

'Hmmm, surprised Angelo and his band of merry men aren't here yet, maybe they are taking their time handling Dr Byfield....' Ben lingered over the word 'handling', clearly imagining the sordid activities the word implied.

'So, you did what to me? Were you in the US when dad died?' Michael spoke quickly, desperate for answers while there was time to get them.

'No, why, what happened to you?' Ben was curious, but only for a second. 'Never mind. I was in Scotland......with our father.

'But I was with you after that, closer than you'd guess at times.'

Ben moved his chair nearer, the motor loud in the silent night.

'When you thought you were being burgled? It turns out you were, or at least one of my associates broke in and left the door ajar – depositing some listening devices in our father's cosy little flat too.

'Then when you woke, wrote on the mirror, and on your own flesh, that was most definitely an assist'

Michael shifted his weight, glancing again at the water behind him.

'Wait, how?'

Ben sighed, theatrically, 'Mikey, Mikey, Mikey, so slow on the uptake. No wonder I can get into your head so easily. You were alone in the flat that time, right? So, I waited until you were asleep. Got close enough to connect to your mind and to induce deeper sleep. One of my men then entered, administered a shot of my own recipe 'sleepy bye bye', erased your hippy affirmation on the mirror, carved up your arm, then left.

'I had to have my team assist with Russell as well. One of them knocked him half out and then I 'encouraged' you to keep attacking him. You're weak; you'd have never been able to beat him by yourself. They also kidnapped Jessica during all the excitement, made it look like she had run away, and took her to the warehouse.

'I must say it was a lot of fun messing with your mind and incriminating you in her disappearance while she was in my "care". Of course, it was not so much fun for blond body double Jessica. She was just some poor homeless girl nobody would miss in a hurry. A good likeness though eh?'

'You absolute monster, why the fuck don't you just kill me?' Michael cried out, he had almost forgotten the unknown teen in the morgue.

'I guess I'm just a psycho.' Ben considered his brother, the shock on his face.

'So, cliché that it is, everything that happened was 'all a dream'. Ben paused, his face twisted into a sneer.

'Except it also all happened.

'Now that Russell is conscious, how is he, do you think he'll forgive you? And what about his gorgeous wife? Remind me, did you ever bone her?'

Michael took a couple of steps closer, anger flowing through him, bending to seize his brother's jacket.

'What do you want?' Michael's voice came as a growl, spittle spraying his brother's face.

'I want you to suffer, again a cliché. But yes, you suffer, I control the suffering, I take all your money, your friends, and so on. You get nothing.' Ben grinned again, enjoying himself.

Michael slowly shook his head. 'I will give you my money, just leave me alone.'

'You're right, you *will* give me your money; you'll happily sign everything over to me so that I – or rather my enterprises, because I still have to play dead – will get everything once you die.

'So, terribly sorry to say, but I hold absolutely all the cards.'

Michael released his grip on Ben's jacket. Stepping back, he felt the low barrier running beside the water pressing against the back of his legs.

'And if I kill you?'

'Well, gosh you went right to the point there didn't you brother? No softly, softly. I like that, it reminds me of me. But, kill me, and my friends on the shadowy side of life would ensure that you, and the small collection of people you care about, would all meet slow and painful ends. And those unfortunate demises would be engineered to make it look like you were behind them all.

'Careful by the way, don't want you to fall in that water, I don't think swimming away from me would get you far, metaphorically – or physically for that matter.'

Michael closed his eyes and sighed. He was attempting to focus on the sensation he had felt when Ben had tried to control his hands moments earlier. If there was a door Ben could open into his mind, perhaps it worked both ways.

Opening his eyes, he watched his brother carefully, there was a flicker of confusion on Ben's face.

'Saying your prayers Michael?' Ben tilted his head as he considered his brother.

'Why don't you just let me make you drown yourself? The same fate you left me to? It would be....' Ben paused. '..... poetic.'

'I did not leave you to drown. I was thirteen years old and I'd just escaped a crashed car. I tried to find you. I would have stayed in the car to rescue you if I had known you were there. The crash was an accident. This is not my fault' Michael gestured at the wheelchair as he finished speaking. Ben nudged his controls, bringing himself closer to his brother, to the barrier. He looked confused again.

'Of course it's your fault, I was trapped. You got out. I died – to all intents and purposes – you survived.' Ben's finger nudged the joy stick again, the chair moved forwards, to within a foot of Michael. 'Dammit, what's wrong with this fucking chair?'

'Call your men off. You don't want to die. Tell them to abort all missions.' Michael's voice was low, calm and with an edge Ben had not heard before.

'Stand down, Alpha master command.' Ben spoke in a shaky voice. A look of panic crossing his face.

'No. What?' His eyes found Michael's. 'Are you doing this? How are you doing this?'

'You've exhausted yourself Ben. So, *I* took *your* body for a joyride this time.' Michael took a quick step forwards and ripped the communicator from his brother's ear, tossing it aside. 'It's over. You've lost.'

As Michael stepped back again the roar of car engines filled the night, and headlights appeared to the left, approaching the car park. Momentarily distracted, Michael's concentration broke, and Ben drove his chair forwards, taking them both backwards and into the water.

Chapter 68

Two police cars sped into the maintenance parking area, one stopping close behind the van. West and Johnson leapt from the first vehicle. Having rescued Elizabeth and Jessica, moving them to a safe distance from the warehouse, they had planned to re-enter, to bring out the two members of the gang they had subdued. Before they could do anything however, they had come under fire from the rest of the gang and were forced to retreat to the edge of the car park, sheltering behind Michael's Ferrari. Armed response arrived minutes later and returned fire, killing the lead gunman, Angel, without friendly casualties. The other gunman had immediately surrendered.

West had rapidly interrogated the three captives, learning from the most communicative one, Jimmy, that Ben had likely headed to the reservoir. Elizabeth had overheard this, and confirmed that she had heard them mention 'the res.'

Arriving at the reservoir Johnson and West cautiously headed up the stairs from the car park, keeping low to the ground, flanked by members of the armed response unit. Drawing nearer West heard a loud splash as something heavy fell into the water.

Michael plunged beneath the water again, diving through the darkness, groping blindly for his brother's wheelchair. He had been trapped beneath the heavy chair when they had first crashed into the water, sinking like a stone. His head had cracked against the hard surface lining the reservoir, and Michael had almost lost consciousness. Something, almost like an external force, had given him renewed strength however, and he'd pushed the chair off his legs, stroking powerfully for the surface. He'd taken a deep breath before diving down to free his brother from the chair, determined that he would not abandon him a second time. Disorientation and the darkness of the water however prevented him from finding either the chair, or his brother. He'd stayed beneath the water until his lungs started to burn, and as he surfaced, he had a sudden vision, a single word emblazed across his mind: survive.

'Let go of me. He's still down there!' Michael attempted to pull away from Johnson, but the younger man was too strong, wrapping his arms around Michael, holding him on the bank of the water. West and the other officers were shining lights into the depths but couldn't illuminate the bottom.

'Michael, I'm sorry. He's been under too long. He couldn't possibly have survived that.' West's voice was for once full of emotion, his customary control having temporarily deserted him. He was stunned at the direction the case had taken in so short an amount of time.

'That's what everyone thought last time. My brother has…. special abilities.' Michael begged the officers to keep searching the water.

'Well I've radioed for support; divers will be here to conduct a search as soon as possible.' West turned to face Michael. 'What happened?'

'That's a long story.' He paused to gather his thoughts, suddenly remembering something. 'Elizabeth, did you find her? Is she OK?'

'Yes, they're fine, a bit battered but I'll take you to them now.'

'They? What do you mean?'

'Dr Byfield and your sister.'

Michael slumped, dropping to his knees as Johnson was forced to release the suddenly dead weight of his body. 'Jess is alive?' Michael gazed in wonder at the detective, 'I thought I'd killed her.'

'No, according to Elizabeth you must have rendered her unconscious, an impressive skill or blind luck, rather than doing permanent damage. Come on, let's get you checked over and warmed up.'

Michael allowed himself to be led away from the water, glancing back a final time at the broken barrier.

Chapter 69

Two weeks later

'So, mind control?' Russell slowly shook his head, now free from the neck brace. 'Ben? Shit, aliens would have been easier to believe.' Russell was sat in a chair, back home. Weak, but recovering steadily and already bored with playing the patient.

Rosie hovered behind him, cradling Donny like a shield in front of her chest. 'Michael, I, I don't know what to say. I am so sorry that I didn't believe you.' The woman looked away, shame written all over her face.

'Hey, Rosie. Please. I wouldn't have believed me either. I thought I was a crazed homicidal maniac. So, if that's what you thought too, then fair enough.' He reached out to her. Rosie took a step back, and Michael let his arm fall, disappointed at the rejection. He quickly understood however as Rosie went around Russell, handed Donny to his father, and then stepped to Michael, holding him in a crushing embrace.

Poppy answered her door, dressed in black jogging bottoms and an oversized University of Reading t-shirt, comfortable study wear for a day without lectures or court. Her face fell when she saw Michael stood there.

'What?' Her voice was ice as she surveyed him, a man she had felt sure could be the one before he went crazy, standing back outside her flat.

'Can I explain?'

Michael spoke for an awkward five minutes, acutely aware that his tale was fantastical, but hoping Poppy would believe him.

'That actually makes sense. Do you want to come in for a coffee?' Poppy's ability to just believe anything, dangerous for a law student, was a breath of fresh air and Michael almost took up the offer. He knew they could resume their relationship with ease. But he had places to go.

'No, sorry. I'm not right for you.' He looked at her, feeling deep affection. 'I truly wish I was though.'

Poppy took the rejection in her stride. 'A friendly coffee though? I've just brewed some?'

'No, thank you. I'm trying to give caffeine a break. I think I already had my lifetime quota.' Michael smiled, as he turned away from the door.

Jessica bounced up and down on the guest bed. 'I cannot believe it.'

'What?' Michael smiled, exhausted just by watching his sister's energy, but sure he would never tire of it having seen her body, lifeless at his feet. He shuddered at the memory.

'I cannot believe I get to live here, like forever!' She squealed and jumped into her brother's arms. 'You have to, I mean *have to* let me do some grocery shopping though!'

'So, how are you doing?' Elizabeth sat across from her former client, in the hospital coffee shop.

Michael lifted his glass of iced water, taking a sip. 'Not your problem anymore Doc.' He smiled. Elizabeth returned the grin.

'At your suggestion I'll be continuing my therapy with Dr Rosenthal, and I think we are going to be firm friends. Professionally of course.'

He slipped his hand across the table Elizabeth placed hers on top without hesitation. 'Of course.'

'And sleep?' She indicated the water, the absence of coffee.

Michael met her eyes, 'You know what, I think I dare to dream'.

The End

Printed in Great Britain
by Amazon

13171984R00222